THE FLOATING BODY

A 1930s MURDER MYSTERY

Also by Kel Richards

The Corpse in the Cellar
The Country House Murders

THE FLOATING BODY

A 1930s MURDER MYSTERY

Kel Richards

Marylebone House

Originally published in Australia in 2015
as *The Floating Corpse*
by Strand Publishing

First published in Great Britain in 2016

Marylebone House
36 Causton Street
London SW1P 4ST
www.marylebonehousebooks.co.uk

British Library Cataloguing-in-Publication Data
A catalogue record for this book is available from the British Library

ISBN 978–1–910674–30–7
eBook ISBN 978–1–910674–31–4

Manufacture managed by Jellyfish
First printed in Great Britain by CPI
Subsequently digitally printed in Great Britain

eBook by Midland Typesetters, Australia

Produced on paper from sustainable forests

THE TIME: The start of summer in 1935 (the end of Trinity term at Oxford).

THE PLACE: Nesfield Cathedral—and the Cathedral Choir School that adjoins it in the cathedral close—in the Cotswolds town of Nesfield.

ONE

~

'Yarooooh! Oh crikey! Ow! Wow! Beast! Oh crumbs! Ow! Oooooooooh!'

The voice that uttered these sounds—they could hardly be called words—was a schoolboy's voice, and it came from around the corner of the archway in which I stood. I had just finished pinning a paper to the noticeboard inviting interested boys to submit their names to try out for the school cricket team when the cry came.

'Beast! Oh crumbs! Oh crikey!'

I hurried in the direction of the sound to see young Stanhope of the Fourth being held in a headlock by a larger, older boy.

'Let him go at once!' I demanded with all the authority that the Acting English Master at Nesfield Cathedral School could muster. To my great relief the bigger boy released Stanhope from his grip. The younger boy straightened up and ran a finger around the inside of his shirt collar, presumably checking to see if his neck had been broken. He appeared to decide that it had not.

'Come here and explain yourself,' I said to the larger boy. As he approached I managed to put a name to this solidly built youngster with the rather bland, round face.

'It's Fox, isn't it, boy?' I said. I was still uncertain of many of the names, having been at the school for less than a term. It was a smallish cathedral choir school, but one grubby schoolboy looks pretty much like any other grubby schoolboy to an Acting English Master trying his hand at teaching for the first time.

'Yes, sir,' he replied.

'Explain yourself,' I demanded again. 'Why were you trying to prise young Stanhope's head from his shoulders in that way?'

'How should I have been doing it, sir?'

The blank look on the young fathead's face told me this was not a feeble attempt at schoolboy humour.

'Explain yourself!' I repeated with a sense of exasperation.

Fox's face flushed pink with anger. 'He asked me to steal next week's exam paper for him, sir,' he spluttered with indignation. 'In fact, he said I probably already had it and would I sell him a copy? I was very offended, sir.'

Not knowing exactly how I should react to this extraordinary announcement, I stroked my chin thoughtfully and looked at both boys.

Provoked by my silence, Fox continued, 'I'm not the School Cheat, sir—I'm the School Bully.' Something like pride swelled his fat face as he said, 'I never steal exam papers, sir.'

'No, you just hurt boys who are younger and smaller than you,' I growled accusingly.

Fox looked puzzled by this charge. Surely, his fat face seemed to say, if he was the School Bully it was his job to go around hurting younger, smaller boys.

Then I turned to the smaller boy whose name I knew was Stanhope. 'And where exactly do you fit in?' I asked. 'Are you the School Bounder, or the Swot, or the Pride of the School, or the Boy Who Is Led Astray and Takes to Drink in Chapter Sixteen?'

Stanhope looked hurt that I should ask such a question, that his fame and reputation had not already reached my ears. 'I'm the School Toff, sir,' he replied. He was a skinny boy, short for his age, with a head of tousled fair hair and an ingrained look of vast superiority to the world around him.

'My father is Lord Saltire, sir,' Stanhope continued, blinking at me through large, round glasses.

'But why on earth,' I asked, 'were you trying to buy next week's exam paper?'

My question seemed to surprise him.

Stanhope explained patiently, as if speaking to the slow boy at the back of the room, 'My pocket money has just arrived from home in the form of a generous postal order. So I thought I might as well purchase next week's exam paper to save the trouble of studying. I thought Fox might have beaten up one of the School Cheats and taken a copy of the exam paper off him, sir.'

I found it difficult to respond to this refreshingly different approach to education, but no immediate response was required of me since Fox reacted to this explanation from Stanhope by punching the smaller boy in the arm.

'You wotter!' cried Stanhope, rubbing his sore limb. 'You absolute wotter! You beast! You utter bounder you!'

'That's enough, both of you,' I said firmly. 'Now, what shall I do with you?'

Fox looked at me blankly. I had the impression that a good deal of his young life had been spent standing in front of schoolmasters who were trying to decide what to do with him. Stanhope blinked at me furiously through the round lenses of his spectacles.

'Fox,' I said, 'you will write out a hundred lines of Virgil and bring them to me in my study by this time tomorrow. Now, be off with you.'

'Yes, sir. Thank you, sir,' he mumbled and shot away as quickly as he could.

'As for you, young Stanhope—all I'm going to give you is advice. There's no point in your being at this fine school if you purchase exam papers and cheat. You are here to learn, boy. So stop wasting our time and your father's money. Take out your books and do the work, boy—do the work.'

Stanhope gurgled a reply that I chose to take as agreement, and I dismissed him.

His departure left the quadrangle deserted. This cobbled square was the cathedral close, and was surrounded by buildings on all four sides. Directly in front of me was the Nesfield Cathedral itself, or 'The Cathedral Church of St Peter and St Paul' to give it its full and official title.

Behind me was the stolid stonework of the Old School, built some centuries ago by a noble benefactor for the education of the boys of the cathedral choir. To my right these two buildings were connected by a row of terrace houses that accommodated the staff members of both the school and the cathedral, and their families.

The square was linked up and made complete by the two-storey grey stone building on my left that held the dormitory rooms for the boys who were boarders and the common rooms, along with the flat occupied by the House Master who had charge of the boarders.

TWO

~

At that moment the House Master himself made an appearance in the wide gateway that led from the quad to the town road.

His name was Gareth McKell, and as I looked towards the gateway, I saw him get out of the Nesfield town taxi (Geo. Weekes, prop.), pay his fare and turn and walk towards me. McKell was dressed in hiking clothes and had a rucksack slung over one shoulder and a pair of spiked rock-climbing boots, still caked with clay and mud, over the other.

As Geo. Weekes rattled away in the town taxi, I walked over to McKell—I had half an hour to kill until it was time for the Head's afternoon tea for the staff, and killing time in conversation with McKell was as effective an execution as any other.

'Back again, I see,' I remarked cheerfully.

'Ah, it's you,' responded McKell unwelcomingly, 'and still pointing out the obvious.'

Somehow this man had the ability to make me feel awkward and uncomfortable—as if I had suddenly appeared in a public place in my pyjamas.

'Just being friendly,' I spluttered apologetically.

McKell said nothing. He stared at me for a moment, his face as blank as those vertical granite slopes he spent his spare time climbing. Then he turned his attention to counting his change. McKell was an unfriendly and untrusting soul—and he clearly did not even trust the town taxi driver to give him the right change.

'How long were you away for?' I asked, still making an effort at friendly conversation. 'Three days?'

'Four.'

McKell started to walk along the side of the dormitory building and I fell into step beside him.

'You were very lucky to get four days off in the middle of term,' I remarked.

He stopped and scowled at me as if I were a caterpillar in the salad of life. As the Deputy Head and House Master of Nesfield Cathedral Choir School, he clearly regarded young and inexperienced acting masters as one of the lowest forms of animal life.

Finally he turned his scowl into words: 'Seniority does bring certain privileges.' Then he resumed his slow perambulation towards his flat. 'Besides which, it was little more than a long weekend.'

'Still, you missed the rugger match against Greyfriars,' I said.

This, apparently, did not deserve a reply, so once again I fell into step beside him and offered another remark in my increasingly pointless efforts at friendliness.

'This trip was about your rock climbing, I take it?'

'Take it any way you like, Morris,' grumbled McKell. 'But, yes, since you seem to be so interested in my affairs—my flying visit to Austria was for a meeting of the European Rock Climbing Association.'

Silence followed this grudging concession that since I was one of the masters, not one of the boys, I had some right to engage in conversation with him.

Perhaps following this train of thought, McKell then added, 'I am, after all, the British representative on the council of the association, and so the Head thought it right and proper for me to take a few days off—even, as you so rightly said, in the midst of term time—to attend the meeting.'

'And did you manage to squeeze any climbing in during your brief visit?' I asked, more out of politeness than genuine curiosity.

'As it happens, I did,' McKell replied with something like a hint of friendliness finally creeping in his voice, and the merest suggestion of a smile flickering over his face. 'I, and two of the other representatives, took a couple of hours on the Saturday afternoon to do a rock face in the Innsbruck National Park not far from our hotel.'

I glanced at my watch and then said, 'Only ten minutes until the Head's tea.'

'I'd better clean up then,' said McKell, glancing over his shoulder. 'Dr Rogers doesn't like his guests to be late.'

He turned towards the front door of the House Master's flat, then stopped and turned back to face me.

'By the way—how did the rugger match go?'

'Splendidly! A close fought game the whole way, and we snatched a win in the closing moments with a field goal. Victory by one point!'

'Good, good,' he muttered. 'Mustn't let those Greyfriars chaps get above themselves. I'll remind Quelch of our rugby superiority next time I see him.'

With those words he entered the House Master's flat and the door swung closed behind him.

I turned to make my way across the quad to the Head Master's house for afternoon tea. I moved slowly, not wanting to be the first to arrive and thus be cornered into awkward small talk with the Head Master, Dr Adrian Rogers.

Although he had hired me a month earlier to fill in for two terms as Acting English Master (while the permanent occupant of that post was visiting relatives in America), he barely knew me, and often seemed surprised when he encountered me in a school corridor. There were moments when I think he had trouble remembering who I was. Under those circumstances, filling in time with small talk was not an attractive option.

At that point in my slow amble over the quad the north door of the cathedral opened and Ryan Carleton emerged. He was carrying his academic gown over one arm. When he saw me he stopped to put on the black, broadcloth gown that Dr Rogers insisted all the staff wear and waited for me to catch up.

'Afternoon, Morris,' he said cheerfully, 'time for tea and scones.'

Carleton was one of the younger, and friendlier, members of the academic staff. He combined two roles at Nesfield: the cathedral's Choir Master and the school's Music Master.

'Was that McKell I saw you talking to?' he asked.

'Yes, he's just back from this quick visit of his to some European confab of rock climbers.'

'Lucky blighter,' said Carleton with a grin, 'getting a few days off in the middle of term. Dr Rogers wouldn't do that for anyone except McKell, I suspect.'

'He's a favourite?' I asked.

'Not so much that,' Carleton explained, 'just that he's been here such a long time that Rogers has come rather to rely on him. Come along, step lively or we'll be late for tea.'

THREE

~

As we approached the Head Master's house on the far side of the quad, a distant movement caught my eye. I turned my head and saw it was young Stanhope again, acting furtively and scuttling towards the far archway that led into the school building.

This was the boy I believed to have gone to his study in obedience to my instructions. What was he doing about the quad now? His furtive movements reminded me of a garden spider creeping tentatively back out onto its web once the gardener has departed, taking his garden spray with him.

Clearly he could be up to no good, and I was determined to investigate.

'Carleton, would you do me a favour?' I asked, speaking in a low voice.

'Anything within reason, old chap,' chortled the cheerful Music Master.

'Would you make my excuses to the Head and say I'll be a few minutes late?'

'Certainly. Is there a problem?'

'There's a boy I'm concerned about,' I explained, 'and I've just spotted him on the far side of the quad—when he should be in his room studying hard. I'd like a quick word with him.'

'Cheerio then,' said Carleton. 'I'll make your excuses for you.'

With those words he hurried on towards the front door of the Head Master's house. I turned around to see young Stanhope disappearing into the shadows of the archway leading to the main school building. Moving as quietly as I could over the cobblestones of the quad, I stepped briskly in the same direction.

I was puzzled. Stanhope had given every impression of acknowledging that he should be spending this time with his books preparing for next week's exam. And yet, here he was, mere minutes later, on the prowl again.

As I approached the archway I heard the sound of voices and slowed down. Stepping closer to the wall of the school building, I approached the opening to the archway cautiously, keeping myself out of sight, and came to a halt just around the corner from the source of those voices. I would find out more, I thought, if I stopped and listened in silence for a few minutes.

Feeling like a character in a John Buchan spy novel, I stood very still, listening carefully.

Drifting around the ancient sandstone blocks of the Old School came several young voices. One of them I recognised as Stanhope's—the other two I couldn't immediately place.

'I say, you two chaps—you wouldn't do a chap a favour, would you?' The voice asking this question was that of Stanhope.

'Well, young Toffee Nose—what is it you want?' came the reply in a sneering tone.

'Are you really asking a favour of us?' said the third voice. 'I thought you spent all your time looking down your nose at the school "roughs"—and now you want a favour from us? Well, let me tell you—you can whistle for it. What do you think of that, Toffee Nose?'

'Don't you take that tone with me,' responded Stanhope in his haughtiest voice.

'Just listen to him!' said the sneering voice.

'Clear off, youngster, or you'll get a thumping,' added the third voice, now growling threateningly. 'Your rich father isn't here to look after you, and you can't ring for the butler to protect you now, snotty nose. So clear off or you'll get a belt around the ears.'

I wondered if it was time for me to step in and prevent an act of violence. But I decided to wait a moment more. It was clear to me that Stanhope was talking to two of the older boys, although what he could possibly want from them I couldn't imagine.

'Now don't be like that,' Stanhope whined. 'I have a jolly good proposition to offer you.'

'Why should we be interested in your propositions . . . ?' The threat in the voice was now obvious.

'. . . you crawling little snob,' added the other voice, the two of them speaking almost as one.

I thought Stanhope might back down in the face of this opposition, but he stood his ground.

'Because there's money in it for you, that's why,' he said.

This must have caused the other two to stop and think, as there was a noticeable pause before one of the voices said, 'How much money?'

'There's ten shillings in it for each of you,' said Stanhope, sounding, I imagine, rather like his father giving orders to the butler. There was a longish pause. Clearly young Stanhope had given these two older boys, obviously two of the school 'roughs', something to think about.

'What do we have to do for this ten shillings?'

'There's an exam next week,' Stanhope explained, 'and it would be rather easier for me to pass that exam if I had a copy of the paper in advance. If you two steal that paper for me, I'll give each of you ten shillings.'

I couldn't believe my ears. This lad had been caught less than half an hour ago trying to cheat on next week's exam—but because I'd let him off with a warning and some good advice, now he was trying it on again! The sheer cheek of the boy was simply amazing.

'Ten shillings, you reckon,' challenged one of the unseen older boys. 'How do we know you're good for it?'

'My pocket money has just arrived from my Pater—a rather generous postal order. You can rest assured I have the money,' replied Stanhope in his best lord-of-the-manor voice.

'Payment in advance,' said one of the older voices, but he was interrupted by the other voice, which said, 'Why don't you do it yourself? Why ask us?'

Stanhope cleared his throat, and, speaking in a lower, more confidential voice, said, 'This is a delicate task that requires certain skills. You two are well known as the School Bounders, and you have skills in burglary that I lack. Therefore I propose to employ your services rather than attempt the theft of the exam paper myself.'

'Why, you insulting little squirt! You nasty, puffed up, pompous little pimple!'

'Do you want the ten shillings or don't you?' Stanhope demanded.

'Do you really think we're your hired staff?' was the sneering reply. 'Do you think we're just here to do your bidding whenever you wave a ten shilling note in our faces?'

'Don't adopt that tone of voice with me,' snapped Stanhope. 'Remember who you're talking to!'

'Get him!' growled one of the older boys, now starting to sound angry. 'He's a bit too big for his britches, don't you think?'

'Far too big for his britches! Someone needs to teach him a lesson. Cut him down to size!'

'Now listen, you two,' hooted Stanhope, rather in the manner of his father addressing the House of Lords, 'you should have some respect for the nobility of this land.'

That was when I realised that Stanhope had gone too far and was now really in trouble.

FOUR

~

'We'll show you what we think of your stuck-up ways,' growled one of the voices threateningly. A heavy silence descended, signalling, I thought, an approaching storm.

Then there was the sound of feet scuffling on the stone pavement of the archway and suddenly Stanhope shot around the corner and collided with me. He looked up at me, puffing and trying to catch his breath. When he saw my face, and realised who he had collided with, he was not best pleased.

Stanhope was closely followed by two squat, solidly built boys. They were both older and larger than the lad trembling before me. Their faces were red with anger and their fists were raised. But they came to an abrupt halt when they saw me. They had not expected to find a master waiting for them around the corner of the archway.

Stanhope stepped, in a scuttling sideways movement, behind me, to a place of safety, while the two boys who'd been pursuing him came to a skidding halt, dropped their raised fists, shuffled their feet and looked embarrassed.

'What are your names?' I demanded.

They were slow in answering, so the reply came in Stanhope's voice from behind my back.

'Conway and Wynyard, sir,' he said.

I made them identify themselves. Once I was satisfied as to which one was Conway and which was Wynyard, I said, 'I take it that the plans you had for Stanhope here were plans he would have found painful in the extreme.'

They didn't reply, but they looked awkward, so I chose to take their silence as an admission.

'Stanhope is both younger and smaller than you, and you outnumber him two to one. Quite frankly, you should be ashamed of your attack upon him.'

One of the plug-uglies in front of me then stammered a reply. 'But, but, but . . . we didn't actually attack him, sir.'

'Only because you didn't get a chance,' I pointed out. 'But since you did not, in actual fact, succeed in laying your fists on this boy, I will not impose a punishment on you—this time.'

Those last two words were uttered in the most menacing tone I could manage. Then I sent them on their way, and turned around to face Stanhope.

'I warned you about this less than half an hour ago,' I said in exasperation. 'What is the point of being at school if, instead of learning, you steal exam papers? Or, in this case, offer to pay other boys to steal an exam paper for you. What's the point?'

Stanhope's jaw gaped open.

'How did you know, sir?' he asked incredulously.

'I heard everything, Stanhope,' I explained. 'Just a short time ago, right here in this quad, I had to reprimand you for exactly this same activity. I thought you had accepted my reprimand and agreed to knuckle down to some serious study. Instead of which I find you once again resorting to this astonishing behaviour.'

I shook my head in frank disbelief at the boy's cheek.

'Why on earth,' I asked, 'do you imagine that it's appropriate for you to pay someone else to do your schoolwork for you?

Or, in this case, to obtain an advance copy of next week's exam for you?'

'But at the Hall, sir, we have servants to do everything for a chap!' Stanhope complained. 'So why shouldn't I employ servants to assist me here at school?'

'You know why, Stanhope,' I replied. 'I've already told you why. It doesn't matter who your father is, what his title is, how much money he has, how important his role is in the House of Lords, or how many servants he has. There are some things in life each of us must do for ourselves. And one of them is learning how to stuff our heads with knowledge.'

I glanced upwards and breathed a great sigh. None of what I was saying seemed to be making an impression on young Stanhope.

'Let me ask you a question, young man,' I said, still struggling to get through to the boy. 'When you're at home, do you ride to hounds?'

'Yes, sir,' Stanhope replied, clearly puzzled by my question. 'I was blooded last year, sir. Now I have my own horse.'

'Would you pay one of the servants at the Hall to mount your horse and ride to hounds for you? While you rested back in your room? Would you?'

'Of course not, sir. That's the sort of thing that one does for oneself. Besides which, none of the servants knows how to ride in a hunt.'

'And so it is in studying for exams. If learning to ride and jump is a skill that can only be learned by the doing of it, then filling your head with knowledge of the civilisation to which you are an heir is the same. It is something you must do for yourself. Do you understand me, Stanhope?'

He stood in front of me trying, and failing, to look properly meek under my ticking off.

'First there was your encounter with Fox,' I reminded him, 'and now this incident with Conway and Wynyard. What have you learned from these events this afternoon, young Stanhope?'

'I have learned, sir, if you don't mind my saying so, sir, that there are some people in this world who have no wespect for nobility—no wespect for noble blood!'

I must have looked stunned at this remark, for he hurried to add, 'Oh, I don't mean you, sir. I mean those two wotters, Conway and Wynyard. They are complete wotters, sir. They are beasts who have no wespect at all!'

At those words I shook my head and then stared up at the grey clouds rolling across the sky above Nesfield Cathedral School. I was desperately trying to find the right words that would penetrate the skull of this dim-witted, pompous and foolish lad. But before I could find them he spoke again.

'People have to know their station in life, sir. And those two bounders, those beasts, those absolute wotters, Conway and Wynyard, don't seem to understand that their place in life is to serve their betters. And, of course, to be pwoperly paid for their services, sir.'

At this reply I threw up my hands in despair and sent the boy scuttling back to his study, with a firm and strict command that he was to start doing his own prep for next week's exam.

FIVE

~

'Sorry I'm late, Head Master,' I said as I stepped into the
drawing room in the Head Master's house. 'I had to deal with
some boys in the quad.'

'I quite understand, dear boy, I quite understand,' muttered
Dr Rogers, all the while, I was convinced, trying to remember
who I was.

Dr Adrian Rogers was an impressive looking man: tall,
with a distinguished face and high forehead surrounded
by waves of white hair. He was like the Head Master from
Central Casting. And his manner matched his appearance.
A good deal of the success of Nesfield Cathedral School—and
it was successful—came, I was certain, from the impression
that Dr Rogers made on parents, benefactors and the board
of governors.

I glanced around the room and saw that I was the last to
arrive—all my fellow masters were already assembled and were
scattered around the tastefully furnished drawing room, each
one balancing a cup and saucer in his hand.

The Deputy Head and House Master, Gareth McKell, had
not bothered to change out of his hiking clothes, but he had, at
least, left his haversack and mud-caked climbing boots behind
in his flat. Wearing such casual attire to the Head Master's

afternoon tea was something no one but McKell would dream of doing.

Next to him was our Classics Master, Henry Beard, with his grizzled, grey hair and his permanently bitter and unhappy expression. Beside him was the much younger Mathematics Master, Dave Fowler. Like me he was also a recent addition to the staff. He had red hair plastered with too much Brylcream, a rather smug expression, and what I always thought of as furtive, scheming eyes.

Sprawled in an armchair was History Master Geoffrey Douglas, the most totally relaxed and easy-going schoolmaster I had ever encountered. He sipped on his cup of tea with his lazy eyelids half closed.

And leaning against the back of that same armchair was our young Music Master and Choir Master, Ryan Carleton. He smiled at me and nodded as a signal to let me know he had passed on my excuses for my delayed arrival.

Our school nurse, Mary Flavell, had retired to a distant corner of the room, keeping in the background as she always did.

Dr Rogers' wife, Brenda, was also in the room, supervising the maid and ensuring that everyone had a cup of tea and a scone with jam and cream.

'How do you take your tea, Mr Morris?' she asked me. 'I know I've asked you before, but I'm afraid I've forgotten.'

'Black please, Mrs Rogers,' I replied. 'Black and very sweet. With a slice of lemon if you have one.'

Hearing his wife utter my name reminded our venerable Head Master of who I was and he turned to me with a gleam of recognition and an anxious look on his face.

'I was just telling the others, Mr Morris,' he said, 'before you arrived, about the difficulty we find ourselves in with respect to our Speech Night. Which I need not remind you is only two weeks away.'

He seemed to think this was sufficient explanation and that I had now been brought fully up to date and was as completely informed as everyone else in the room.

'What Dr Rogers means,' volunteered Geoffrey Douglas, picking up the slack, 'is that at the moment we seem to have a Speech Night without a guest speaker.'

'What's happened?' I asked, sounding as puzzled as I looked. 'I thought that chap, the geologist chappie—I've forgotten his name—was coming as guest speaker. You organised him, didn't you, McKell?'

McKell nodded and took a sip of his tea.

'What's put a spanner in the works?' I asked, turning back to Dr Rogers.

'Mumps,' growled the Head unhappily. 'The wretched man has come down with mumps. His sense of timing is most unfortunate. We were just discussing,' he said, waving his hand vaguely in my direction, 'before your somewhat late arrival, whom we could get as a substitute at this very late notice.'

He looked around the room as if accusing every staff member of being part of a conspiracy to ruin this year's School Speech Night.

'So far,' resumed Dr Rogers, 'without success.' Then his eyes lit up as he said, 'You wouldn't have an idea, would you, Mr Morris? For a substitute guest speaker, I mean?'

'Well . . .' I began cautiously as I took a sip of my tea. 'There is one man.'

'Go on, dear boy, go on,' urged the Head.

'I'm thinking of my old university tutor, C. S. Lewis. He's very highly regarded at Oxford. His lectures on Mediaeval and Renaissance Literature are extremely popular and well attended. He's certainly a good speaker—and he's thought rather a lot about educational trends. I know that from my correspondence with him. So perhaps he would be suitable—if he is available.'

'An Oxford man,' said Dr Rogers, more to himself than the rest of room. He closed his eyes and rocked back on his heels deep in thought. 'Yes, an Oxford man always goes down well with the parents, and with the governors. Yes, an Oxford don would be most acceptable. Which college is the fellow of?'

'Magdalen,' I replied.

'Magdalen, Magdalen,' muttered the Head approvingly. 'Yes, a thoroughly sound college. A Magdalen man would be most acceptable. Might he come, do you think?'

'I've always found him most agreeable,' I said. 'He's helped me out of an awkward spot on previous occasions. I'm happy to write to him, if you wish.'

'Oh, I do wish, I do indeed,' urged Dr Rogers. 'In fact, you must write to him this very afternoon. Do it quickly. Ensure it gets into the afternoon post. Indeed, when you've written your letter you must walk down to the post office in the town to get it into the mail at once.'

I wasn't at all sure that Jack, as Lewis was known to all his friends, would be able to come—but I was happy to write the letter, and I was hoping he would accept. It would be a pleasure to see him again—and to engage in another of our 'great wars', our on-going debates about deep and serious matters.

As I was thinking these thoughts, the maid began clearing up the afternoon tea things, always the signal that it was time for us to leave. The masters straggled out of the room like a herd of cows following their well-worn tracks at milking time.

I was the last the leave because the Head tugged at my coat sleeve as I approached the door and said, 'Be sure to write immediately, my dear boy. We need an answer as soon as possible.'

I agreed.

'And in this afternoon's post please,' he added as he ushered me out of his drawing room, and out of his house.

SIX

~

My flat was on the ground floor of the terrace house in the cathedral close shared by the single men on the staff. I sat at a window looking out at the grassy slopes beyond the school grounds—slopes that fell gently down towards the River Ness, which strolled, rather than ran, in its slow, meandering way around the town.

Then I picked up my pen and began.

'Dear Jack,' I wrote, 'thank you for your letter, and I apologise for not replying sooner. In fact, I feel guilty even now because I am pressed into writing at this moment to ask if a favour might be possible. You see, the school has a problem . . .'

In a page or so I spelled out the difficulty of the missing guest speaker for Speech Night. I gave him the date in question, knowing that it fell during the last week of Trinity term at Oxford, and expressed the hope that he might find a way to help us out.

I folded the page, sealed it into an envelope that I addressed and stamped, and left my flat. I had promised the Head I would walk into the town and post the letter immediately, and that was my plan.

As I descended the stairs, came out of the terrace house—the last one in the row—and started across the quad, I saw a few boys around the noticeboard in the archway leading to the Old School.

Two of them were writing on one of the notices. This I took to be a good sign—boys signing up for the trials for the cricket team, I hoped. So I walked across to see what fish I had caught with my notice.

As I approached I saw that two older boys—broad-shouldered, solid looking boys from the Upper Sixth, I assumed—were writing on the noticeboard and laughing unpleasantly as they did so. Drawing nearer I saw it was Conway and Wynyard, the two toughs I had intercepted in the company of young Stanhope earlier in the afternoon.

They completed their notations on the board and withdrew, still chuckling to each other in that same unpleasant manner.

Stepping up to the board I ran my eye down the list of the names of boys entered for the cricket trials. I saw Hamilton, Clifford, Redway and Cardew—and that pleased me very much. There were several other names of more marginal candidates and of some complete duffers whose hopes rose above their abilities. Then at the end of the list was the name 'Stanhope'.

For a moment that puzzled me since Stanhope was no athlete and had little interest in games. In fact, all he could do in trying out for the cricket team would be to embarrass himself.

Then the penny dropped. It was not Stanhope who had entered his name—it was Conway and Wynyard. That was what they were up to when I saw them at the noticeboard. This was their revenge for their run-in with Stanhope. Their aim was to encourage him to make a fool of himself in the nets in front of the rest of the school.

I dismissed this as grubby schoolboys with limited imaginations pursuing pointless feuds, and went on my way.

Crossing the cobblestoned quad towards the gate leading out of the close and onto the town high street, I passed the windows of the House Master's flat. The electric lamps were lit within, spreading a warm yellow glow in the cool evening light and making the front room of McKell's flat look like a stage set.

As I looked in I saw McKell open a large cupboard and place inside his hiking boots—the same hiking boots I had seen slung over his shoulder upon his return earlier in the afternoon. What was surprising was that the boots were still filthy. The spikes on the boots could be seen quite clearly, even from where I stood in the quad, to be thickly caked with clay and dried mud.

'How lazy,' I muttered to myself. I would not have put McKell down as the type who would pack his boots away without cleaning them first.

I must have been staring because at that moment Muriel McKell, the Deputy's sister who kept house for him—McKell being a single man—entered the room. She looked out of the window straight at me. An indescribable look flashed across her already sour face—she was even less friendly than her brother—and she strode purposefully across the room and pulled the curtains closed over the windows.

I felt a little uncomfortable. I had been seen apparently spying into another master's flat. But it was hardly my fault, was it? If he left the curtains open and the room was lit, then he was almost painting a picture in the purple shadows of the twilight that had begun to fall.

Shrugging my shoulders I told myself I had nothing to feel guilty about, walked out of the gate and down the high street.

The post office was in the middle of the town, at the bottom of the gentle slope of the high street, in between Jarrett Brothers' Jewellery and a pub called *The Pelican*.

It was *The Pelican* that I visited having slipped the letter into the red post box. In the pub I had a pint and a friendly game of darts with a couple of locals, then headed back up the high street towards Nesfield Cathedral and the cathedral close and school that lay behind it.

I was back in time to take my place, with the other masters, at the head table in the school dining hall. It was Thursday night, and Thursday meant ham, potato and peas. The menu was entirely predictable and never varied.

When dinner was over and the boys had been dismissed to go back to their study cubicles for their evening prep, I did my rounds of the school before returning to my own flat.

Under the archway leading into the Old School I paused once again at the noticeboard to see if any new names had been added to the list for the cricket trials. There were no new names, but there had been a change—Stanhope's name had been crossed out, and then had been written in again on a fresh line.

What had happened was obvious: on his way to the dining hall Stanhope saw that his name had been put on the list as a joke. He crossed it out. But then, I assumed, Conway and Wynyard had returned and written it up again.

Completely unamused by these schoolboy japes, I retired for the night.

SEVEN

~

Jack's answer to my letter arrived quickly: yes, he could manage a visit, and he would be happy to come as guest speaker for the School Speech Night. 'My current course of lectures has now been completed,' he wrote. 'Bennett has agreed to take my pupils for that last week in term, and I have a few ideas about education that I'd be happy to air. So I look forward to seeing you again, and joining battle once more over a worthy subject. Is it permissible to bring Warnie along to keep me company?'

I hurried, clutching Jack's letter in my hand, to the Head Master's study.

'Good news, Head Master,' I said. 'My old Oxford tutor has agreed, despite the short notice, to be our guest speaker at the School Speech Night.'

'Splendid, simply splendid!' cried the Head at hearing this news. 'Well done, young . . .'

And at that point he ran out of steam, having forgotten my name once more.

'Morris,' I said, filling the blank, 'Tom Morris.'

'Of course, of course! You don't imagine I'd forgotten your name, do you? Certainly not. I was just breathless at the good news. Now tell me some more about this Oxford man who is coming to be our guest speaker.'

'Lewis is his name, sir—C. S. Lewis, a fellow of Magdalen College and a university lecturer in the School of English Language and Literature.'

'Splendid,' said Dr Rogers once more, rubbing his hands together in delight. 'That will look fine upon our printed programs for the night.'

'He did ask me if he might bring his brother with him,' I added, 'for company. His brother is Major Warren Lewis, ex-British Army, retired.'

'Most certainly. They will both be welcome. The dean has two spare rooms in his house, and I'm sure Cowper and his good wife will be happy to accommodate them there.'

'I'll write and tell Jack so at once.'

'Jack?'

'Lewis's friends all call him Jack.'

'But you said his initials are . . .'

'C. S.—for Clive Staples. But it seems as a boy he decided he disliked the name Clive and insisted on being Jack instead. So he's been Jack to his friends ever since.'

'I see, I see. Well, you've done very well, young Morris, very well indeed.'

Leaving the Head's study I made my way towards the Senior Common Room for morning tea. This entailed walking down one of the dorm corridors, where I encountered a small group clustered outside one of the rooms. Standing in the doorway of study number five was young Stanhope, blinking furiously through his large spectacles at the crowd facing him.

This unpleasantly noisy and sneering group appeared to be led by Conway and Wynyard.

'Here you are, young Toffee Nose,' bawled Conway. 'We have a complete cricket kit for you—so you have no excuse for squibbing out of the cricket trials.'

'But I say, you fellows—' Stanhope began to complain. He didn't get to complete his objection as he was quickly howled down.

'I thought you were supposed to be descended from some great Norman knight,' sneered Wynyard. 'I thought you were supposed to have battling blood running through your noble veins.'

'Perhaps we should open a vein and see just how blue his blood is!' bellowed a voice from the back of the group.

At this point I intervened.

'All right, what's going on here then?' I demanded, striding up to the group. As I approached the uproar ceased and an uncomfortable silence descended upon the dorm corridor. 'Come along,' I said, 'one of you tell me what's happening here. You, Conway—you can explain what's afoot.'

'Well, sir,' he said, looking a little uneasy—a little, but not much. 'Since Stanhope's name is on the board to try out for the cricket team, and since Stanhope is a squib who says he's no good at games, Wynyard and I have put together a cricket kit for him, sir'—with these words he held up a canvas cricket bag—'so that he'd have no excuse, sir.'

'There's more to it than that, isn't there?' I asked suspiciously. 'Stanhope, if your name was added to the list for the cricket trials by other hands, and not by yourself, you are not obliged to go to the nets and try out.'

To my surprise young Stanhope said, 'It's all right, sir—if these wotters want to have a chance to bowl at me in the nets I'll give it to them. I'll turn up on the day of the trial, sir, and let them do their worst.'

The response to this announcement was a cheer from the small group assembled in the corridor.

'See you on the day, squirt,' sneered Conway.

'We'll keep this cricket kit for you in our room,' added Wynyard, 'so that you don't accidentally "lose" it before the trials.'

With those words the older boys departed, chuckling among themselves.

I was left facing Stanhope, to whom I said, 'Why did you agree? If you'd said no I would have backed you up.'

'Very kind of you, sir,' replied Stanhope rather glumly, 'but it was a case of noblesse oblige. Sometimes the squire simply has to keep the peasants happy.'

With those words he stuck his nose in the air, turned back into study number five and closed the door.

Now it's true I had only been a schoolmaster for a month—and I was already determined to keep the schoolmastering part of my life as short as possible—but this latest incident drove home to me how little I understood the mentality of the school-boy. Which was puzzling, since it wasn't all that many years since I'd been a schoolboy myself.

I descended the stairs towards the Senior Common Room.

At the foot of the stairs I saw the Deputy Head, Gareth McKell, speaking to his sister Muriel. Well, 'speaking' isn't quite the right word. It would be more accurate to say that their heads were very close together and they were whispering in hushed tones.

At the sound of my boots clumping on the stone stairs they pulled apart hastily and stopped talking. They both glanced at me and gave each other a significant look—although signifying exactly what it was impossible to guess—then turned and walked in opposite directions.

For all the world it looked like the behaviour of people who shared a guilty secret. Although what guilty secret a middle-aged schoolmaster and his spinster sister could possible share had me puzzled.

EIGHT

~

A week later Jack and Warnie arrived. They were carried up from the Nesfield railway station by the town taxi (Geo. Weekes, prop.), and I was there to greet them at the school gate.

'This is very good of you, Jack,' I said, shaking him warmly by the hand. 'And it's delightful to see you again too, Warnie.'

Jack was dressed in the same baggy grey flannel trousers and battered old tweed jacket as always. Warnie, as befitted an ex-military man, looked rather neater in his blue serge suit.

Following Jack's example, Warnie seized my hand and pumped it energetically.

'I must say you're looking well, young Morris. School-mastering must agree with you,' he said, his moustache flapping enthusiastically with each word.

'What you can see, Warnie,' I replied, 'is a level of fitness induced by trying to keep up with a wild mob of schoolboys, especially on the playing field.'

'So you're a games master as well as English Master?' Jack asked.

'Acting,' I stressed, 'only acting. I'm here for two terms—after which I look around in other directions.'

'Oh, I see,' puffed Warnie, 'like that is it? I take it that means you're not one of nature's schoolmasters?'

I laughed and agreed that you could put it that way if you wished. Then Jack asked for the guided tour, so I began by picking up their bags and leading them across the cobblestones of the quad to the Dean's house.

My knock on the door was answered by a maid, who showed us into the front sitting room, where we were joined a moment later by the Dean of the cathedral, Richard Cowper—who always insisted that his name be pronounced 'Cooper' ('I am not the least bovine,' he was fond of saying. 'There is nothing of the "cow" about me.')

'Ah, these are our guests, I take it,' said Cowper as he bustled into the room followed by his wife, Ellen. 'We have two spare bedrooms. Not very big, I'm afraid, but comfortable and both with a view of the river.'

Perhaps oddly for a churchman, the Dean was a shy man. Crisp and clear in the pulpit, he could be awkward and hesitant with strangers.

I made the introductions and handed over the suitcases to the maid to take upstairs.

Ellen Cowper ushered us all into armchairs and insisted on ordering tea.

'I've read your book, Mr Lewis,' said Cowper as we settled into our chairs and waited for the tea tray to appear. '*The Pilgrim's Regress*—most interesting, most interesting indeed.'

Jack chuckled and said, 'Since it first appeared I have discovered what a swampland I entered when I attempted allegory. It's always a balancing act. If the symbols of the allegory—the symbolic places, people and actions—are transparently simple then why write allegory at all? Why not a simple, straightforward exposition? But if, on the other hand, the symbols are rich and complex, one runs the risk of obscurity. And my readers tell me it's that latter difficulty I've given them.'

'I quite see the problem,' said Cowper, nodding thoughtfully. 'And it makes one appreciate Bunyan's genius even more.'

'Precisely,' said Jack with a loud guffaw, seizing the point with pleasure. 'I can now see that the tinker of Bedford had an imaginative gift of exactly the right sort. And a very rare gift it is too.'

'Mind you,' said the Dean, 'I could make out the shape of the journey you wanted the reader to follow—from atheism, to a kind of pantheism, through theism, to Christianity.'

At this Jack laughed out loud—a laugh of sheer delight.

'Then you've done better than most of my readers,' he said. 'I'm afraid my mistake was describing my spiritual pathway, and the scenes along the way, while making the assumption that my readers would find the journey as familiar as the railway line from Oxford to London.'

After we had all indulged in cups of tea and slices of Madeira cake, I took Jack and Warnie up on their request for a guided tour.

It being a Saturday, and hence a half day, we found most of the masters in their studies. We began in the adjoining terrace houses where we found History Master Geoffrey Douglas also in the midst of his afternoon tea, surrounded by books and open atlases. But he was welcoming and friendly. He offered us a sherry, which Warnie accepted but Jack and I declined.

Much less friendly was Henry Beard next door. He did his duty out of politeness but made it quite clear that it was a duty reluctantly embraced. His study, where we spoke to him, was cluttered by his fishing gear, his golf bag and all kinds of odd pieces of sporting equipment.

Noting the absence of a feminine hand, I said, 'Your wife not around at the moment, Beard?'

'Visiting her family,' he growled in his closed-mouth, unfriendly fashion.

'They live on the coast somewhere, I think you told me? Up north, I think you said?'

'Not far from Whitby they are. That's where she is. Well, I hope you gentlemen enjoy your stay among us.' As he uttered these words he rose and walked to the door. Clearly we were being ushered out.

We went upstairs to the flat occupied by Ryan Carleton, Choir Master and Music Master, and his wife, Julia. They were both out, so we went next door to the terrace house divided into three smaller flats for the single men: myself, Mathematics Master Dave Fowler, and David Evans, the cathedral organist.

Evans was out and Dave Fowler was just leaving as we arrived. He had a folded deckchair under one arm and a book and a straw hat in the other hand.

'Just off to sun myself,' he snapped, 'seeing the weather has turned so warm for spring.'

I asked him where he could possibly find a quiet spot in the sun, and he replied, 'Up on the leads—on the roof of the Old School—well away from all noisy schoolboys. There I shall read a book, and, in all probability, fall asleep.'

With those words he left us and walked across the quad in the direction of the narrow old servants' staircase that opened out onto the flat roof of the Old School.

'Hmmf—not all that friendly, is he?' snorted Warnie.

'He's always that way,' I said. 'Dave Fowler seems to be preoccupied with Dave Fowler and no one else gets a look in.'

I explained that there was just one more staff member to meet, Deputy Head and House Master Gareth McKell, and we'd find him out where the school's playing fields were, at the nets supervising the cricket trials.

'In fact, I'm supposed to be there helping pick the A-grade team for the coming summer season,' I added.

'Well, we'll come with you,' said Warnie with real enthusiasm. 'I might even be able to help a little. I have a good eye for cricketing talent.'

We walked through the archway under the Old School and let ourselves out onto the playing fields. And there to our right were the cricket nets.

NINE

~

As we arrived at the nets Clifford was bowling his medium pace swing balls at Hamilton—who was looking like a first-class batsman at the crease. Despite Clifford's ingenuity, which was considerable, Hamilton was getting hold of each delivery and putting it away. Ball after ball swung through the air and skidded off the crease, only to be picked up neatly by the willow wielded by Hamilton and slogged firmly into the netting.

'Ah, there you are at last, Morris,' growled McKell without taking his eyes off the action in the nets. 'It's about time. I expected you here an hour ago.'

'Sorry I'm late,' I said, 'but I had to look after our guests.'

McKell looked briefly over his shoulder, and then turned back to the cricket action.

'So I take it one of these gentlemen is our last-minute, short-notice guest speaker for the School Speech Night?'

McKell, I could see, was bent on being his usual charming, engaging self.

But Jack was not the least put off by the House Master's abrupt manner.

'I'm your man,' he said heartily. 'And I hope I won't let you down on the night.'

A grunt was the only reply he got from McKell, so he continued, 'And this is my brother, Major Lewis.'

McKell continued to watch the action in the nets as Warnie said, 'Any promising players here today?'

'Quite a few,' said McKell over his shoulder without turning around. 'Hamilton, Clifford, Redway and Cardew are all first class. We just need to find seven players strong enough to support them.'

At that point Wynyard sidled up to the House Master and said, 'Time to give Stanhope a go, sir?'

McKell grumbled, but said, 'All right—let's get him out of the way, and then we can look at some real players.'

Wynyard called over to the group of assembled schoolboys on the sidelines, 'Come on, Stanhope, it's your turn.'

Conway then appeared at Wynyard's side carrying a canvas cricket bag, which he opened. A sly look passed between them as the latter pulled a cricket bat out of the kit bag.

Stanhope approached wearing cricket creams and looking paler than ever, his flaxen hair tousled and his eyes wide with dread. From the kit bag he selected and put on pads and batting gloves, then Wynyard handed him the bat.

'To the crease, Stanhope,' ordered McKell. 'Clifford, send him down a few easy ones—let's see if he can even connect with the ball.'

Clifford did as he was ordered, sending down medium pace deliveries, straight as an arrow, on a line and length, with no swing, turn or deviation.

For the first ball Stanhope swung and missed—the leather missile, whistling through the air, missed the blade by an inch. This brought loud catcalls from the crowd of Conway and Wynyard's friends who were watching the action. Stanhope just shrugged his shoulders and took his stance again.

Knowing how uncomfortable he was, I admired the boy's spirit in taking on this unpleasant challenge which he saw as his duty to tackle.

As Stanhope took his stance again, and Clifford paced back to his mark, I told Jack in a few hurried, whispered words about the schoolboy drama that had led up to this moment.

'I'm not one for games, as you know, Morris,' Jack said, 'and I know how badly that can be received by the rest of the school. So that boy has my sympathies.'

The second ball was also a wild swing and a miss by Stanhope.

'Hey, Clifford—chuck it underarm,' called Conway derisively. 'See if he can hit that.'

The third ball went whizzing from Clifford's hand, and once again Stanhope was slow raising his bat and the ball flew past him into the back of the net.

Wynyard cupped his hands to his mouth and yelled, 'Send him down a grand piano—see if he can play that!' This was followed by hoots of laughter from the sidelines.

Clifford glanced at McKell to see if there was any point in continuing.

'Finish the over,' McKell commanded, so Clifford went back to his mark and commenced his run up once again.

This time the ball was so close to the top of the stumps it was unmissable, and Stanhope, who already had his bat in a backswing as the ball left Clifford's hand, managed to hit it in the centre of the bat and send it slamming into the side net.

Or would have done—if the bat had not snapped in two.

The moment the bat hit the ball, with a solid 'thwack' of willow on leather, the blade of the bat snapped backwards, almost breaking clean off just under the handle.

Stanhope looked confused and uncertain what had just

happened, while Conway, Wynyard and Co. were rolling on the grass howling with laughter.

'That's enough, Stanhope,' said McKell, bringing the ordeal to an end. 'Next boy!'

Stanhope walked miserably from the nets, dragging the broken bat behind him.

When he reached me, he said, 'I never expected to make the team, sir, but I didn't expect that to happen.'

'Here,' said Warnie, 'let me take a look at that bat.'

Stanhope handed it over. Warnie examined it for a moment and then passed it to me.

'Take a look at that, Morris,' he muttered. 'The shaft of the handle has been cut halfway through. There are clearly saw marks there. Someone has been playing a nasty trick on this boy.'

And, of course, I immediately knew who that was.

McKell, who had heard none of this, called out, 'We'll have a break from medium pace, Clifford. Is there anyone here who can spin the ball at all?'

There was a long silence, so at length Warnie spoke.

'If you'd like your batsmen to face some spin, I'd be happy to send them down a few of my leg spinners and off breaks.'

McKell scowled, so Warnie continued, 'In my army cricket team my leg spinners in particular were well regarded.'

'Very well then, Major,' said the House Master. 'You can give our boys a test. Let's see how they go with spin. Here you are, sir, take the ball. And Redway, you pad up and go into the nets—let's see how you go facing spin. I've heard the Greyfriars team includes a demon spinner, so this will be good practice for you.'

Warnie took off his coat, rolled up his shirt sleeves and tossed the ball from hand to hand while Redway pulled on pads and gloves. Then the boy took his mark and Warnie let fly with a ball that came out of a twisting wrist. It hit the pitch and spun several bat widths to the leg side.

'Well bowled!' called out Hamilton from the sidelines. 'Could you teach me to do that, sir?'

'Oh, ah, well, I can't see why not,' grunted Warnie. 'If it's all right with your Master, that is.'

McKell thoroughly approved of his key players being taught how to spin the ball, so Jack and I left Warnie happily giving lessons in the devious art of spin bowling while we went off to continue our tour.

TEN

~

'Come and have a look inside the cathedral, Jack,' I said. 'Quite a fine example of neo-gothic.'

We found the north door unlocked and walked inside the vast, vaulted space of the church. It was a sunny day, and warm sunlight streamed into the building through the tall stained-glass windows, casting a patchwork quilt of rainbow colours over all, and splashing amber light over the towering sandstone columns that supported the arched roof.

Jack politely admired the oldest window in the building—the rose window at the eastern end—and the delicate carving on the choir stalls.

As we strolled the length of the building I pointed out the series of windows portraying the life of Christ along the southern side. Then turning to look at the northern side, I pointed out the tall, multi-panelled window that depicted the martyrdom of Cranmer, Ridley and Latimer.

This particularly interested Jack as they were, famously, the 'Oxford Martyrs'. As an undergraduate I had frequently cycled over the spot in the Broad where they had been burned at the stake—Latimer and Ridley first, then Cranmer some months later.

We were halfway down the nave when we heard the north door click open behind us. We turned and saw the organist, young David Evans, striding down the aisle in our direction. Seeing us, his face broke into a sunny smile.

'Jack,' I said, making the introductions, 'this grinning Welshman is David Evans—a very fine organist. And David, this is C. S. Lewis, my old Oxford tutor.'

'You can drop "old" as an adjectival qualifier, young Morris,' chortled Jack as he and Evans shook hands.

'Doing the tour?' Evans asked.

I said we were, and asked if he had arrived for organ practice.

'Just a quick run through on the Tallis anthem for Evensong,' he said. 'You're welcome to stay and listen if you wish.' He gestured at the pipes on the north wall as he added, 'It's a Hill organ. Quite a fine instrument. Come on up to the organ loft and I'll show you.'

Jack was quite the music enthusiast and happily accepted the invitation. So we climbed up the steep, narrow stairs to the loft.

Jack chatted to Evans about the organ for a while. Having no particular interest, I stepped to the end of the loft and slid open the narrow window there to let in a little fresh air. From where I was standing, high up in the cathedral, I was almost exactly opposite the roof of the Old School.

I could see Dave Fowler lying back in his deckchair, book in hand, straw hat shading his eyes.

'What words will the boys be singing to the Tallis?' Jack asked.

'It'll be the Winchester hymn "Glory to Thee, My God, This Night",' Evans replied.

As they were speaking, I watched Fowler rise from his deckchair and try to rearrange it at a lower angle. For a minute or two he struggled with the recalcitrant chair. Its awkward hinges flopped in all the wrong directions as the Mathematics Master wrestled with it. Eventually he got it unfolded and refolded, and set up at a more comfortable angle. Then he flopped back into the chair and dropped the straw hat onto his face and the book onto his chest. He appeared to have little intention of doing much more in the way of actual reading.

Meanwhile, David Evans settled himself at the console of the organ, made a few tentative stabs at the pedals with his feet, raised his hands and began to play.

He had only opened a few of the stops and was playing the melody softly and sweetly.

Jack strolled over to join me at the window, commenting on the quality of the music as he did so.

'It's the words of the hymns I object to,' I said. Jack raised a questioning eyebrow, so I continued, 'Well, some hymns anyway.'

'You never miss an opportunity to have a sly dig, do you, young Morris?' Jack responded with a broad grin on his face. He was clearly relishing the prospect of a lively debate. 'Give me an example.'

I wasn't quite ready for that, so I hastily groped around for one. 'Well, we had a thing by Watts at Morning Prayer recently, "When I Survey the Wondrous Cross". The words of that hymn—quite frankly, Jack—are very demeaning of human nature. All that stuff about pouring contempt on all my pride. That may be all right for convicted murderers, but for ordinary, decent, upright citizens it is definitely demeaning.'

Jack then engaged in what I call his 'rhetorical guffawing'. Throwing back his head he came out with, 'Ho, ho, ho! You have a remarkably sanguine view of human nature, young Morris.'

I would have responded to his words but my attention was drawn at that moment to movement on the rooftop opposite.

Fowler had risen from his deckchair and seemed to be waving his arms at someone I couldn't see from where we stood.

'Something seems to have upset him,' I remarked. Jack joined me and we stood side by side at the tall, narrow window. Which is how we came to be eyewitnesses to the inexplicable, and fatal, melodrama that followed.

Fowler's mouth was opening and closing vigorously. Of course, no sound carried to us, but at a guess I would have said he was shouting.

'Something has definitely annoyed your friend,' boomed Jack by my elbow without taking his eyes off the roof opposite.

It was impossible to make out the exact expression on Fowler's face—he was too far away for that—but it appeared to be contorted with emotion. However, whether that emotion was anger or fear I couldn't have said.

'What's puzzling is who he's talking to,' I remarked. 'There doesn't seem to be anyone on the roof except Fowler.'

Behind us Evans was oblivious to what was going on. He was lost in the world of music, and the lovely sounds that filled the vast, cavernous interior of the cathedral were totally at odds with the inexplicable but highly emotional scene being acted out on the rooftop on the opposite side of the quad.

'Is he drunk?' I asked.

'He was perfectly sober when we spoke to him in the quad,' said Jack.

'Is he hallucinating then?' I puzzled aloud. 'I can't see anyone but Fowler on that roof, but he is clearly violently upset about something.'

I was about to suggest he had been stung by an insect, perhaps a wasp, but his movements were clearly not those of a man suffering from a wasp sting.

At that moment he suddenly doubled up, as if he had been punched in the stomach. He staggered several steps sideways, then turned around in our direction. He tried to straighten up and was looking down at his stomach.

I took a sharp breath: even from where we were, on the other side of the quad, it was clear that blood was streaming down from some sort of wound.

Jack, who has sharper eyes than mine, said, 'I can see a knife handle protruding from his stomach.'

Fowler staggered unsteadily across the roof, then seemed to lose his balance—and disappeared from view as he plunged over the far side of the roof.

ELEVEN

~

'Come along,' said Jack urgently, 'we must go to his aid.'

'What's up?' cried a startled David Evans, abruptly taking his hands off the organ console as Jack and I half stumbled, half sprinted down the steep stairs from the organ loft.

'Something's happened to Dave Fowler,' I called up from halfway down the stairs as my feet rattled on the wooden steps. Reaching the bottom I added, 'It looks as if he needs help.'

Jack and I ran down the nave and out through the north door. I sprinted across the old cobblestones of the quad, with Jack close behind me. It took us only a moment to hurry through the archway under the Old School, push open the heavy wooden door on the far side and step out onto the gravel road that ran behind the school building.

That was where we came to a sudden halt.

Here, lying on the gravel road, we had expected to find the body of Dave Fowler, severely injured and in need of urgent assistance. But it wasn't there. The road was empty—both immediately under the rear wall of the school building and in every direction.

It was just a bare, gravel road.

'I . . . I don't understand,' I gasped. 'We clearly saw him go over the edge of the roof. He should be here.'

Jack paced out into the middle of the road. He stood with his hands on his hips and a deep frown on his face. He looked up at the roof and then to the left and right.

'There don't appear to be any projecting cornices that might have snagged the body on the way down,' he said.

'There aren't,' I said. 'This part of the building is Georgian—no gothic decorations or gargoyles. Nothing, in fact, for the body to catch on.'

I joined Jack in the middle of road. 'And there hasn't been time for anyone to remove it,' I continued. 'He must have fallen no more than a minute ago at the most.'

Jack said nothing but continued to survey the scene.

'Besides which,' I resumed, 'there's no conceivable reason why anyone would want to remove the body.'

'Up to the roof,' Jack snapped decisively. 'The answer must be up there.'

We hurried back into the school, and I led the way past the classrooms and down the long corridor to the entrance to the narrow back stairs—normally used only by the servants—that led up to the roof.

Beyond the topmost occupied floor of the building, these stairs kept going. They ended at a landing, with a door leading on one side to the box room and on the other to a ladder-like set of wooden steps bolted to the wall that went up to a trapdoor in the roof.

I had never before been up to the roof myself, but the trap-door above our heads was clearly the way, so I climbed the steps. Reaching the top, I pushed up the trapdoor and saw sky above me. I clambered out onto the roof with Jack following close behind.

'Well, this is where he was,' I said, pointing out the obvious. On the flat leads of the roof was Dave Fowler's deckchair.

Beside it lay a book and a straw hat. But apart from those objects the roof was empty.

Jack stuffed his hands into his pockets and began prowling around.

'What are you looking for?' I asked.

'Some sort of gutter or channel your friend might have fallen into when he appeared—to us at least—to fall off the roof.'

But there was nothing of the sort. Together we patrolled the whole of that flat roof area, and there was no body, and nowhere a body might have fallen into. Standing side by side at the stone parapet, Jack and I peered over, looking down onto the gravel road we had been standing on moments before.

The road was still deserted and there was no body on the roof.

'Well, did we imagine it then?' I said, throwing my hands in the air.

Jack pulled his pipe out of the pocket of his old tweed jacket, filled it, lit it and began to puff great clouds of blue smoke.

'Two separate minds having the same hallucination at the same moment,' he said through the clouds, 'is, I think you'll find, a phenomenon unknown to modern science.'

'Then—' I began, but I found myself unable to finish the sentence, so I raised my hands and shrugged my shoulders in a sign of helpless bewilderment.

Jack continued to puff in deep thought as he walked across to the opposite stone balustrade and looked down into the quadrangle of the cathedral close.

As he did this I went over to the deckchair and picked up the book. It was a yellow-jacketed Gollancz thriller, *The Nine Tailors* by Dorothy L. Sayers.

Jack rejoined me, nodding at the book and saying, 'Quite a well-written book—for a detective novel.'

'Bother the book! What do we do?' I demanded irritably.

'Go to Mr Fowler's rooms,' Jack replied decisively. 'See if he's returned there, or has attempted to.'

'But he looked far too badly wounded to . . .' My voice trailed away. Clearly Fowler was not here on the roof, and clearly he was not where he should have fallen, so his rooms were as good a place as any to begin our search.

Fowler's rooms were in the single men's quarters—the end terrace house of the row. I was occupying the rooms of the (temporarily) absent English Master so I was on the ground floor. Fowler was above me on the first floor, and David Evans had the attic rooms, with their low ceilings and dormer windows.

I, of course, had a key to the house. I led the charge up the staircase to the first floor. Here we found, fortunately, that Fowler had left his door unlocked. His quarters consisted of a large L-shaped sitting room-cum-study, a large bedroom and a small bathroom. It took only moments to discover that all three rooms were empty, and there was no sign of Fowler.

Jack lingered in the bathroom, coming out relighting his pipe and saying, 'No signs of blood. If a seriously injured man had returned here he would have presumably gone to the bathroom to staunch the flow of blood and clean the wound.'

'But he hasn't done so,' I said with my usual gift for pointing out the extremely obvious.

'Where else might he have gone if he was hurt?' Jack asked.

'The matron?' I suggested tentatively, explaining that the school nurse was a quiet, middle-aged lady named Mary Flavell. She spent her days caring for the grazed knees, cut fingers and upset tummies of schoolboys. The masters would normally take their medical problems to the GP in the town, Dr Marcus Green, but in an emergency . . . Well, it was possible, I said.

Jack asked where she might be found, I said in the dorm building, and we set of again—not running now but walking at a brisk pace.

We found the matron in the infirmary making herself a pot of tea. She asked us to join her, but after introducing Jack, I explained that we had no time—and had she seen the Mathematics Master?

'Mr Fowler? No, I've seen neither hide nor hair of him. Are you sure you won't have a cup?'

'Where next?' I asked Jack after we had made our apologies and returned to the quad.

'We'll have to inform the Head Master,' growled Jack in his rumbling voice. 'He has to know both what we've seen and the inexplicable aftermath.'

TWELVE

~

'No, no, no, no—this makes no sense at all, dear boy. None at all,' moaned Dr Rogers. We were sitting in the Head Master's drawing room. His distinguished and expressive face had gone white as we told our tale, and then had wrinkled up in worry lines until it resembled a relief map of Switzerland.

'We saw what we saw,' I insisted firmly.

'What you *think* you saw,' corrected Dr Rogers, desperately trying to hang on to a thin thread of sanity. 'But in the light of your subsequent observations you can't possibly have seen what you imagine you did. That would be utter nonsense, and the world would be turned on its head.'

'You're perfectly correct,' responded Jack with considerable energy. 'It makes no sense at all. At the moment. But young Morris and I certainly saw something that appeared to involve serious injury for Mr Fowler. And now he can't be found. I think we should inform the police.'

Dr Roger's pale face flushed pink as he yammered, 'The police? Whatever for? No, no, no—we can't have the police invading school premises. No, no, not the right step at all, my dear chap.'

'Surely,' I pressed, 'if Fowler has been injured in any way, or even abducted, we need . . .'

'Abducted! You're allowing your vivid imagination to run away with you, Mr Morris. It must be all those dreadful thrillers you young men read these days.'

He glanced down at my hand, where I was still carrying Dorothy Sayers' *The Nine Tailors* with its vivid yellow jacket.

'No, no, no, no.' Dr Rogers was shaking his head to emphasise the negative. 'Schoolmasters being stabbed, bodies disappearing, vanishing into thin air—these things are the stuff of those crime shockers. And they are certainly not the sort of presumptions and gossip we want to take to the police.' The Head Master shuddered at the very prospect, and then he continued, 'Can you imagine those police officers tramping all over our school in their hobnailed boots? Horrible thought—horrible.'

With a final, decisive shudder, he lapsed into silence.

'Then what do you propose we do?' said Jack in his brook-no-nonsense lecturer's voice.

'Do? Do?' stuttered Dr Rogers. 'I'm sure I have no idea. In fact, I can't see why there is any need to do anything at all. Just go about your business and try to forget about this.'

'My friend Morris and I,' Jack replied, speaking in the firm, but gently persuasive, tone he employed with an undergraduate who had just read him a very poor essay, 'are neither schoolboys playing a prank nor fools. We both clearly saw the same thing. And what we saw involved a man—a member of your staff—apparently being seriously injured. If the police are not to be called, then we must find a way to pursue this matter.'

Dr Rogers nodded his head sadly as he said, 'Of course, you are quite right, Mr Lewis. Always look to an Oxford man for sound common sense, that's what I say. So we do need, as you so rightly point out, to take decisive steps.'

He gave himself to silent thought, and then said, 'What I propose is this: that we gather a group of the senior boys, the most trusted boys, and give them the task of searching the entire school property—and the cathedral too, if it comes to that.'

'What will we tell them to look for?' Jack asked.

'Why, for Mr Fowler, of course. And we may possibly tell them that he may have had an accident, and is perhaps injured. That would be quite sufficient.'

So that is what happened.

I went looking for some of the senior, and more reliable, boys.

I found Hamilton, Clifford, Redway and Cardew walking slowly up from the cricket nets—still deep in conversation with Warnie, who had his jacket draped over one arm and was demonstrating the various wrist movements that impart spin to a cricket ball.

These four boys liked to call themselves 'The Famous Four'—because they'd been reading too many Frank Richards school stories in *The Magnet* story paper. But despite this one conceit they were solid and dependable young chaps.

I explained that the Head Master had a task for them: namely, to search every room, every cupboard and every space in the school buildings and the cathedral looking for Mr Fowler, who may be injured. They were clearly puzzled by this instruction, but seeing my stern face they asked no questions.

Instead Hamilton, their natural leader, assigned each of the four different quadrants of the cathedral close and its surrounding buildings, and the four of them set off on their task.

'What was that all about?' asked Warnie as he rolled down his sleeves and pulled his coat back on.

In a few swift, clear sentences Jack explained what we had seen and what had happened.

A look of complete puzzlement came over Warnie's rather jolly face, and he puffed out his moustache as he said, 'Oh, ah,

I see. At least I don't see. I don't see at all. Seems all topsy-turvy to me.'

'And to me, old chap,' said Jack, patting him on the shoulder. 'So while the boys are conducting their search, why don't the three of us stroll down to the village and ask the local doctor if he's had an emergency case this afternoon?'

Once again Jack's plain common sense had pointed us in the right direction, so we set off at a good pace, through the front gates and down the high street of the town of Nesfield.

Halfway down the street, before we reached the cluster of shops, we encountered Dr Marcus Green coming out of his front gate, carrying his black Gladstone bag and about to set off on a round of house calls.

No, he assured us, he had seen nothing of Fowler, nor had he seen any emergency cases that afternoon, and he was afraid he couldn't help us. With those words he bustled off up the street.

Warnie had spotted the town pub, *The Pelican*, just ahead of us, and he licked his lips as he suggested we had time to drop in for a print. There was clearly no more constructive action we could take for the time being, so we agreed.

In the bar parlour some of the locals invited me to join them for a game of darts. I offered them Warnie as my substitute—a proposal that Warnie himself endorsed enthusiastically. That left Jack and me sitting in a quiet corner with our pints, chewing over the events of a puzzling day.

'Was he stabbed?' I asked as I sipped on *The Pelican*'s excellent local brew. 'Was Dave Fowler really stabbed?'

'I have no doubt of it,' Jack replied, his baritone voice rumbling with sombre concern. 'We both saw him double up with pain. Only I could make out the knife handle, but we both saw the blood streaming down. Yes, I have no doubt in my own mind that he was stabbed.'

I mulled this over in silence for some minutes, and then I said, 'Supposing it wasn't an accident . . .'

'Whatever we saw, young Morris, it wasn't an accident,' Jack assured me.

'Supposing that's right—and, like you, I'm sure it is—how could anyone do that? Just try for a moment to imagine thrusting a knife into a man's stomach. That's a vicious and violent attack. I could never do that. I don't believe any normal person could. It goes against the very grain of normal human nature.'

Jack's eyes sparkled as he lowered his glass onto the table, but his voice was heavy as he said, 'The grim truth, Morris my friend, is that we are all capable of murder. Within every normal human heart and mind there lurks a murderer—who, given the right circumstances and the right provocation, will escape and create mayhem.'

'I can't believe what I'm hearing,' I said with astonishment. 'You seem to have a very low view of human nature.'

'A very realistic view. The first crime, if you remember your Bible, was a murder, and every page of human history has been splashed with blood ever since. Darkness, anger, even violence are a normal part of every human personality.'

'But human nature is fundamentally *good*,' I stressed. 'Surely you, as a Christian, would agree with that.'

'Precisely the opposite is the case,' said Jack with a rather grim chuckle. 'It's because I am a Christian that I know human nature to be fundamentally defective.'

THIRTEEN

~

The next morning the air was still cool and the dew was still on the grass when I walked down the front steps of my residence and turned towards the Dean's house to rouse out Jack and Warnie.

The previous night had ended with 'The Famous Four' failing to find any trace of the missing Dave Fowler, despite, they told us, a most thorough search. They were responsible boys and I trusted their diligence. If they couldn't find Fowler, or his body, then he was nowhere to be found.

When the Mathematics Master was missing from the evening meal in the dining hall, and then when it was clear that his rooms were still unoccupied, even Dr Rogers began to show signs of agitation.

'It's most unlike Mr Fowler to simply disappear like this,' the Head Master complained to me as we walked across the moonlit cathedral close later that evening. 'Like yourself, Mr . . . ah . . . ah . . . Morris, he hasn't been with us very long. But in his short time here Mr Fowler has shown himself to be entirely dependable. And now this! Who will take his classes in the morning? I must speak to McKell about that.'

With those words he ambled back to his house and left me standing in the purple moonlight wondering what development we might expect to come with the morning.

And it was my concern over what should happen next that sent me in search of Jack and Warnie even before breakfast.

The maid who answered Dean Cowper's front doorbell told me that Warnie had not yet risen, but that Jack was in the morning room with an early cup of coffee. She showed me in, and I found Jack draining the last of his drink.

'Delighted to see you so bright and early, Morris,' he declared heartily. 'Come on,' he said, grabbing his hat and walking stick, 'let's go for a walk around the school grounds before breakfast. You know my brain always works best when my legs are moving.'

'Do we have time?'

'The maid told me that breakfast is not served here for another half an hour. When do you have to be in the hall for the school breakfast?'

'Not until after chapel.'

'Come along then,' boomed Jack as he rose and strode to the door, looking more than ever like a ruddy-faced, prosperous farmer about to stroll around his farm.

As we walked down the front steps of Dean Cowper's house, Jack asked, 'There's no more news on Fowler, I take it?' And then he added before I could reply, 'Of course not—you would have told me at once if there was.'

As we began to stroll across the quad, a movement on the far side of the close caught my eye. The sun was still low in the sky and the shadows were long, but there, in the grey shadows, were two figures close together in conversation. And their body language somehow conveyed the impression that their meeting was a clandestine one.

One of the figures was a schoolboy—the other was Muriel McKell. But who was the schoolboy she was talking to at this early hour of the morning? Their heads were close together and their conversation never rose above a whisper. Then it ended and Muriel McKell turned to go back inside the flat she shared with her brother.

As she did so the schoolboy turned in my direction. By shading my eyes against the rising sun and squinting I made out who it was. And it was none other than Freeman Fox, the School Bully—the same boy I had seen grappling with young Stanhope a week and a half ago. Now, what on earth was Muriel McKell doing in clandestine conversation with the School Bully?

That puzzle, however, was small beer compared to the astonishing and inexplicable disappearance of Dave Fowler.

'Have you any theories, Jack, about what happened to Fowler's body?'

'It is a capital mistake to theorise ahead of the facts. And in saying those words I am quoting, as you will have recognised, young Morris, from no less an authority than Sherlock himself,' said Jack, smiling as he paused to light his pipe. 'There is,' he added, turning his back against the morning breeze and shielding his pipe as he struggled to get it to light, 'a second puzzle just as substantial as the vanishing corpse.'

'Which is . . . ?' I prompted.

'His invisible attacker.'

'What do you mean?'

'Well, Morris, we both saw the same thing,' Jack explained. 'We saw Fowler alone on that roof. We saw him apparently arguing with someone we couldn't see. Gesticulating in the direction of an empty, flat roof. Then he doubled over as if struck. But there was no one in front of him to strike a blow. Then we saw that he had been stabbed—but there was no one on the roof to thrust a knife into him.'

I stopped in my tracks as if hit over the back of the head by a sock full of wet sand. 'You're right!' I exclaimed. 'I've been so obsessed with Fowler's corpse having gone missing that I hadn't stopped to think about how the man became a corpse.'

'Well, think on it now, old chap.' Jack gave me a sly grin, then continued, 'It's a pretty puzzle, isn't it?'

Having much to think about, we walked on in silence for a bit.

Then I asked, 'Did you really mean what you said last night? About human nature being fundamentally defective?'

'Most certainly. And there is nothing unusual or eccentric about such a view—it's simply the common or garden view of bog-standard, classical Christianity.'

'I had no idea Christianity was so bleak.'

'Not bleak at all, old chap,' said Jack. 'Just uncommonly honest. And it is, in the end, good news—because as well as offering an accurate diagnosis it also offers a cure.'

'But really, Jack! Human nature is "fundamentally defective"? That's a grim assessment.'

'Human nature, young Morris, is as broken as an electrical appliance with a blown fuse.'

I was about to say more but at that point we had reached the old timber door that led out from the cathedral close to the road behind the school building. It was a heavy door and required a mighty tug on my part to get it moving.

But move it did. And once it had swung open, Jack and I stepped out onto the gravel road—and in doing so stepped into the biggest mystery we had ever encountered.

For lying there, in the middle of the road, right where it should have been the day before, was the body of Dave Fowler.

I think my mouth must have opened and closed a number of times, like a goldfish in a bowl—perhaps a goldfish of uncommonly low IQ. My gaping and heavy breathing continued for some moments before any words came out. And even then the words didn't make any sense: 'But . . . but . . . but . . .'

Jack didn't waste his energy on words but hurried over to where the body lay face down on the road and felt for a pulse.

'Not only dead but cold,' Jack said. 'In fact, I think we'll find that he died yesterday—at just the time we saw him die.'

'Then where has he been in the meantime?' I managed to ask. 'Where?' I gestured at the space above our heads—the empty air between us the roof of the school building.

'Has he been floating up there somewhere?' I demanded. 'Floating invisibly? Waiting until this morning to finally come crashing down?'

FOURTEEN

~

My questions were good ones, and they were the same questions that very shortly everyone else was asking. In the course of that morning I heard those questions over and over again.

However, at the moment of our first discovery of that impossible corpse, what I went on to say to Jack was, 'One of us had better stay here with the body . . .'

'I'll do that,' Jack offered.

'. . . and in that case I'll go and tell the Head Master and then call the police.'

My knock at Dr Rogers' door was greeted by a maid who showed me inside. The Head was still in his dressing gown, seated at the breakfast table spreading Olde English Breakfast Marmalade thickly over a slice of toast.

'Do you realise what time it is?' he demanded when I appeared at the breakfast room door.

I said I did and apologised for disturbing him at this hour, but a serious matter had arisen.

'Very well,' he said with a deep sigh, leaning back in his chair and taking a bite from the toast. 'Go on, dear boy, go on.'

'Fowler has been found.'

'Well, that's good news!'

'Or, rather, his dead body has been found.'

This announcement caused Dr Rogers to drop his slice of toast, sending a cascade of butter and marmalade down the front of his dressing gown.

While he wiped this away with a serviette and retrieved the toast from the floor, I explained, 'Mr Lewis and I found Fowler's body on the gravel road behind the school—in exactly the same spot where we had expected to find it yesterday, after what we saw on the roof . . .'

I trailed away because the Head was glaring at me, blinking furiously. 'Dead?' he said in a voice hushed by disbelief.

'Cold and stiff. He's been dead for some hours. Probably since Jack and I saw him die yesterday. Would you like me to make the phone call to the police, sir?'

Dr Rogers nodded, and then told me to use the phone in the hallway, just inside the front door.

As I walked to the hall and picked up the phone, he brushed past me, muttering about needing to get changed before the police arrived and 'the whole horrible business begins'.

With one foot on the stairs he turned back and said, 'The boys will have to be told, of course. Perhaps I shall get the Dean to make an announcement at chapel this morning. Yes, that would be best—he would be tactful.'

Dr Rogers mounted the stairs, and I heard a click on the phone as the operator at the village exchange came on the line. I asked for the police, and a moment later there was another click and then the sound of a phone ringing.

'Police cottage—Butler speaking,' growled the voice on the end of the line.

I knew that the local police cottage did not employ a butler, but rather that I was speaking to the village bobby, Constable Bernard Butler.

'There's been a death at the school' was all I said.

'What? A death? One of the boys?' he asked.

'One of the masters,' I replied.

'Right then, I'm on my way.'

As soon as he was off the line I rang the exchange again and asked for Dr Marcus Green. His wife answered the phone and handed it over her husband, saying, 'It's the school calling, dear.'

I explained that there had been a violent death and that he would be needed in his capacity as the local police surgeon. Like Constable Butler, the doctor promised to come at once.

As I was hanging up, Dr Adrian Rogers was coming back downstairs, clad now in his usual dark grey suit and academic gown.

I told him the police and the doctor were on their way, and then explained that I should get back to where Jack was standing guard over the body. He nodded and waved me away.

From the Head's house I hurried next door to Dean Cowper's. Warnie was up and breakfasting, so I began to tell him the news. Just as I started the Dean walked into the room, so I began my tale again from the beginning. Warnie gaped at me open mouthed while the Dean muttered seriously, 'The news will have to be broken to the boys—very carefully, of course.'

'I think the Head is rather hoping that you will do that,' I said. Cowper nodded and said he would give some careful thought as to how it could best be expressed. Warnie and I then left him and hurried out to the gravel road behind the school.

We found Jack standing, deep in thought, over the corpse of Dave Fowler. Warnie was bubbling over with all the predictable questions.

Jack replied, 'We don't have the answers, old chap. All we have at the moment is a very strange puzzle.'

Warnie looked upwards at the stone balustrade that edged the roof of the Old School, and then muttered, 'Where on earth has this chap been since yesterday? How can he tumble off the roof and take hours to hit the ground? Dashed fishy, that's what I call it.'

Constable Bernard Butler came bursting through the rear doorway from the school, his uniform tunic unbuttoned and flapping in the morning breeze.

He stood and stared, open mouthed, at the body of Dave Fowler. Then he slowly did up his silver buttons and pulled a notebook from his pocket.

Jack and I had to repeat the events of yesterday several times before they finally sank in and ended up as scribbled notes in the policeman's small book.

It was during one of these repetitions that Dr Green arrived. He knelt down and felt the skin of the corpse, then lifted one arm, or tried to.

'Rigor mortis is fully developed,' the doctor said, 'and the body is completely cold. Death occurred at least eight hours ago. Constable, may I roll the body over?'

'Should we wait until Inspector Locke gets here?' asked the hapless policeman, clearly out of his depth. 'In fact, I need to go and call district headquarters—the inspector needs to be informed at once.'

Tucking his notebook into his tunic pocket he bustled away in search of a telephone.

'Well, I'm rolling the body over,' said Dr Green. 'I've seen the position of the corpse, and there's nothing to be gained by leaving it untouched.'

It was odd to see a human body being rolled over and not flapping flaccidly around, but moving as stiff as a piece of hardboard.

As the doctor pushed the body over onto its back, he said, 'Well, I think we have cause of death, gentlemen.'

There, protruding from the stomach of the corpse, was the handle of a long, narrow knife. The blade was completely invisible, being buried in Dave Fowler's stomach.

The long silence that followed was broken by Jack, who asked, 'Was it the knife wound that killed him then? Not the fall?'

'Actually, it could have been either,' Dr Green admitted, 'or a combination of both. The autopsy should tell us more.'

The doctor straightened up, blinking in the early morning sunlight, and then asked, 'Is this how you found him? I mean, when you discovered the body, was it in the position in which I first saw it? Face down?'

Jack and I both said yes, it was.

'That is strange then,' the medical man went on, 'because of the post-mortem lividity.'

'The what?' asked Warnie.

'The marks you can see that look like large bruises. That's where the blood pooled after death—post-mortem lividity. Those marks show that he landed on his back, and that he lay on his back for some time. But you found him lying face down. That's very odd.'

FIFTEEN

~

Detective Inspector Sexton Locke turned out to be a tall, thin man with a hawk-like face. He was accompanied by Sergeant Jack Drake, a solidly built, red-faced man. Both seemed unshaken by the sight of the dead body or by the strange tale that Jack and I had to tell.

Locke very quickly impressed me with his quiet, unflustered intelligence.

He paced around the body of Dave Fowler where it was still lying on the gravel road, looking and listening as Dr Green gave a brief explanation of what he'd found in his first, superficial examination. When the doctor had finished, Locke ordered two uniformed constables who'd come with him to borrow a stretcher and remove the body.

'Take the victim straight to the mortuary,' said Locke. 'And doctor, how quickly can you get the autopsy underway?'

'I can do it this afternoon,' Green replied, snapping closed the clasps on his Gladstone bag. 'There are a few patients I must see this morning, but I'll close the surgery this afternoon and attend to this matter.'

Locke thanked him and waited until the body had been removed.

'Now, Mr Lewis, Mr Morris,' he said turning to us, 'are you

sure that this wound we've seen on the corpse this morning is the wound you saw inflicted yesterday afternoon?'

'There's little room for doubt,' boomed Jack in his confident lecture room voice. 'There's room for unanswered questions, room for perplexing puzzles, but no room for doubt that Morris and I saw exactly this wound inflicted.'

Sergeant Drake scribbled this down in his notebook.

Inspector Locke stood for a moment in silent contemplation—and it wasn't hard to imagine what must have been racing through his mind. He had undoubtedly seen violent death before, but never like this, and never surrounded by the baffling story that surrounded this one.

'Drake,' he said, snapping out of his reverie.

'Yes, sir,' replied his faithful sergeant, all eager attention.

'We'll start by understanding something about the victim—and that means talking, in the first instance, to the Head Master. And gentlemen,' he added turning to us, 'if you'll hold yourselves available I'll have some more questions for you shortly.'

With these words the inspector and his sergeant strode off purposefully back through the archway to the close, leaving Jack, Warnie and me standing in the middle of the now deserted gravel road.

Jack relit his pipe, which had gone out, as Warnie scratched his chin and looked first up at the stone balustrade above our heads and then at the spot where the body had, eventually, fallen.

'John Dickson Carr,' he said at last. 'Detective writer fellow. Writes about "impossible crimes". This would suit him to a tee. A corpse that floats invisibly in mid-air overnight and then tumbles to the ground in the morning . . . huh . . . he'd come up with a cracking solution for that.'

'Unfortunately, he's not here to spin out some elaborate and clever explanation for us,' I grumbled.

Warnie started pacing down the length of the road, keeping a close eye on the gravel beneath his feet as he walked, perhaps hoping it might reveal its secrets if only he looked at it hard enough and long enough.

Left alone with Jack, I said, 'Did you notice how deeply that knife had been thrust into poor Fowler's stomach? That looked like a powerful, angry blow to me.'

Jack nodded as a look of deep sadness came over his face. 'That, young Morris,' he said, 'is what human nature at its most violent, most angry and most evil can do.'

'Come on, Jack!' I protested. 'Surely you can't really believe it's normal to do something like that to a fellow human being?' I paused to gather my thoughts. 'Who can do that? Who can strike a blow like that into the body of another human being? Despite what you say about human nature being defective, I just can't believe that a murderer is "normal" or has "normal human nature" in any sense of that word.'

'So you would describe murder as being "unnatural", I take it?'

'Yes, yes, that's a good word to use to describe such an act of evil—it's "unnatural". Not just murder—killing, any killing. In fact, any act of real, genuine evil, I believe, is against nature. At least against human nature.'

'We need to be quite clear about such things—so how, exactly, would you describe human nature when in its "natural" or unspoiled state?'

I thought for a moment before I replied. 'Our nature inclines us to want to see things go well, both for ourselves and for others. We are distressed by suffering we see in much the same way as we are discomforted by our own sufferings. From this, I take it, human nature, in the normal course of things, is kindly, sympathetic and basically . . . well, for want of a better word, good.'

'And you are not, of course, on your own,' said Jack. 'Many, perhaps most, would agree with you. Sadly, the evidence seems to be otherwise. Chesterton was fond of saying that the one doctrine that never needs defending is the doctrine of original sin—since the evidence for its truth surrounds us every day.'

'Well, Chesterton was a blockhead then! His doctrine of original sin is a gross insult to the whole human race. Furthermore, I refuse to accept that my own nature is fundamentally corrupt and disordered in some way.'

'Exactly, that's the rub, young Morris. What concerns us is that the Christian teaching about human nature is telling us something about ourselves that we don't want to know.'

'Something about ourselves that is quite untrue, you mean!' I protested vigorously.

Then Jack did something that quite surprised me: he clapped me gently on the shoulder and said, 'My dear chap, you mustn't think that because human nature—*all* human nature—is broken and defective in crucial ways that people aren't still likeable. You, for instance, are an extremely likeable young man. I always enjoyed teaching you when you were my pupil and I enjoy your company still. But that doesn't mean that you and I—and humans in general—are somehow basically *good*. That's a separate thing entirely.'

I admitted to Jack that I was now feeling confused.

'Which is completely understandable,' he responded. 'We take it that if people aren't good they aren't likeable and that everything they do is poisoned by their corrupt character. Our problem as human beings, however, is not of that order. We suffer from a corruption that we are, at some level, aware of and fighting against in all our best moments. But the very fact that we *have* to fight against it makes my case.'

Once again his pipe had gone out and he turned his back against the wind and struck a match to relight it. This action seemed to strike a thought.

'If there was no wind blowing this morning,' he said, his voice once again cheerful and hearty, 'I would not have to protect the small, flickering flame of the match. But I must because there is. We would not have to struggle with our consciences as often as we do if there wasn't a chill wind blowing through every human soul.'

I nodded thoughtfully as Jack continued, 'We would not be disappointed by our own small moral failures if it were not the case that we have to guard against such failures at every moment.'

Jack paused to look up at the roofline of the Old School and then back down at the gravel road before he added, 'When something like this happens, we are seeing that inner corruption—that "inner demon", if you wish—being unrestrained and allowed to break out in violent anger.'

SIXTEEN

~

Further discussion was interrupted by the brisk return of Detective Inspector Sexton Locke—this time without his sergeant, who was, I assumed, making enquiries elsewhere in the school.

'Now, gentlemen,' he said, 'I'd like you to accompany me to the roof—to the "scene of the crime", as it were.' With these words he turned and led the way.

As we passed under the Old School archway we encountered young Stanhope, running like a boy who was late for class— which indeed he was, the first bell having already rung.

When he saw us, he skidded to a halt and addressed himself to me.

'What's happened, sir?' he asked. This skinny, pale boy with his tousled blond hair blinked at me through his big spectacles, waiting for an answer.

'Did Dean Cowper talk to you at chapel this morning?'

'Yes, sir, he did, sir.'

'What did he tell you?' I asked, thinking it best if I knew what 'official' line of explanation was being taken in the school.

'He said Mr Fowler's had an accident, sir. He said he's dead, sir. Is it true?'

'I'm afraid it is, Stanhope. Now you run along or you'll miss your first class.'

He hesitated as if hoping for more details, but Inspector Locke snapped, 'Be off with you, boy,' and he took to his heels.

To get to the back stairs that would lead us up to the roof, our small group had to go down one of the long corridors. Here we found a group of Fifth Formers milling around outside their form room door.

'Off to class, boys,' I said. 'The first bell's already gone and the second will ring any minute. You should be at your desks.'

Hamilton, the leader of the group of boys confronting us, said, 'If you please, sir, we have a problem, sir.'

I asked him what the problem was.

'Well, we're supposed to have a mathematics lesson, sir, and Mr Fowler is . . .' His voice faded away, indicating that no further explanation was necessary.

'So who will do trigonometry with us this morning?' added Clifford, the keenest young mathematician in the group.

'It's not trigonometry this morning,' boomed a voice from the far side of the milling group of schoolboys. The group parted to reveal the school's History Master, Geoffrey Douglas, ambling towards us in his usual relaxed manner.

'It will,' he continued as he approached, 'be an hour on Roman Britain—so take your seats and get out your history books.'

The boys obediently filed into the classroom.

'Morning, Morris,' murmured the History Master as he passed. 'Difficult days, difficult days. The whole school is in uproar.'

'Morning, Douglas,' I replied. 'If there's anyone who can settle the boys down, it's you.'

He nodded in reply and went into the room.

As the form room door closed and a hush settled, our little group—consisting of Locke, Jack, Warnie and myself—proceeded on our way.

Rounding a corner we found ourselves confronted by the Head Master, Dr Rogers, looking more magisterial than ever.

'Ah, Inspector Locke. I was hoping to find you.'

Locke waited, expectantly and politely.

'I have just been engaged in telephone conversations with several members of our board of governors, informing them of this most . . . ah . . . unhappy . . . ah . . . incident. They asked me to do all I can to ensure that the police presence in the school, and any police disruption of the school, be kept to an absolute minimum.'

He stopped and raised one eyebrow until it almost curled into a question mark. Clearly he was hoping for some reassurance from the policeman. He didn't get it.

'We will, of course, do what needs to be done to investigate this murder,' Inspector Locke replied, with a quiet intensity.

'Oh, dear me, dear me,' murmured Dr Rogers gloomily. Then he brightened up as a thought occurred to him. 'You do know, don't you,' he asked rhetorically, 'that the Chief Constable is on our board of governors?'

'I do, Head Master,' replied the inspector. 'And knowing that, I made a quick phone call to Sir Edgar before I drove up to the school this morning.'

'Oh, did you?' muttered the Head gloomily, suspecting that this was not a good sign.

'And he assured me,' Locke continued, 'that I had his full support in taking whatever steps I deemed necessary. In his words, "The murder investigation must take priority." However, I'm sure that, for the most part, the school's activities can continue without being disturbed by us.'

A sour look came over the Head's face as he muttered, 'Very comforting, I'm sure,' then turned his back and walked off down the corridor.

Freed from the Head's concerns, Locke led us quickly up the rear stairs to the top landing.

Here we found ourselves facing the solid, ladder-like steps, bolted to the wall, that led from the landing to the roof.

'How did Fowler get his deckchair up these steep steps?' the policeman asked, speaking his thoughts aloud and directing the question at no one in particular.

'With some difficulty, I imagine,' said Warnie with a chuckle.

'He was a fit young man,' I volunteered. 'I think he could have easily enough manhandled something as light as a deckchair up onto the roof.

'And he clearly did,' Jack added.

Inspector Locke led the way up the steep, narrow steps, threw open the trapdoor at the top and clambered out onto the roof. We followed him.

By the time all three of us had emerged from the trapdoor, Inspector Locke was standing in the middle of the roof, his hands on his hips, looking around him.

It was an almost flat roof, covered with sheets of lead. There was a slight slope from one side to the other to allow for rainwater runoff. On the lower side was a narrow gutter to catch the rainwater and deliver it into a downpipe.

The deckchair still stood where we had seen it the day before.

'This is where you saw him?' the policeman asked.

'Exactly where the deckchair is now,' I replied. 'It hasn't been moved. We saw him—that is to say, Jack and I saw him—flopped down in his deckchair in precisely that spot, with a book and a straw hat resting over his eyes.'

'Where are they now?'

'Where are what?'

'The book and the straw hat.'

'The book,' I explained, 'is in my room. I picked it up when we were here on the roof, and somehow, absentmindedly, hung on to it. When I got back to my room I found it was still in my hand. It's still there. In my room, I mean, not in my hand.'

'And the hat?' Locke continued.

'We left it here,' said Jack. 'In fact, we didn't touch it.'

Locke looked around at the open, flat space. There was no straw hat.

'Perhaps the wind caught it,' Warnie suggested. 'Very exposed up here. Any gust of wind could whistle away something as light as a straw hat.'

Inspector Sexton Locke began to pace back and forth on the leads of the roof. Then he turned back to Jack and me and asked, 'Where, exactly, were you two when you witnessed this incident—or this attack, or whatever it was.'

By way of reply I walked over to the stone balustrade on the cathedral close side of the roof and pointed to the opposite side of the square.

'In the cathedral itself,' I explained. 'I'd been giving Jack the guided tour when David Evans arrived to practise that evening's anthem and invited us up into the organ loft.'

Locke patiently and thoroughly took Jack and me back over what we had witnessed the day before. Then back over it again—slowly and in detail. Nothing new emerged, so he finally said that he had learned all he could and we all returned to ground level.

Standing in the cathedral close, the inspector announced that he had to find Sergeant Drake and left us. I explained to Jack and Warnie that I had a class to take.

'In that case, Warnie and I might have a walk through the town,' said Jack, who loved any excuse to go for a walk. 'All right with you, old chap?' he asked his brother.

'Right as rain,' replied Warnie with a chuckle. 'Absolutely as right as rain.'

SEVENTEEN

~

My class was a difficult one. It's hard to get schoolboys to concentrate on Robert Browning when their minds are filled with the death of their Mathematics Master.

We were in the midst of working through 'My Last Duchess' when we came to the lines 'I gave commands; then all smiles stopped together.'

Jones, in the back row, eagerly thrust his hand in the air, and even before I could call on him asked, 'Does that mean she was murdered, sir?'

'Quite possibly,' I said. 'The young woman Browning was writing about, Lucrezia de' Medici, was only fourteen when she married the Duke of Ferrara and she died quite suddenly at the age of seventeen.'

'How was she killed?' asked Blake in the front row. He was the class dummy and was inclined to ask irrelevant questions with a look of blank innocence on his face.

'That's not really relevant to the poem, Blake, but there were suspicions at the time that she'd been poisoned.'

I thought this had got their minds off the school's own tragedy when a voice I couldn't identify, from somewhere in the back of the room, said in a stage whisper, *'Another* murder!'

And Jones, the class clown, joined in with, 'But this one wasn't thrown off a roof!'

After that they became more restless than ever.

At length the bell rang, and the mutual torture being enjoyed by the boys and myself—if 'enjoyed' is quite the right word—ended.

'Quietly, boys, quietly,' I urged as they packed away their books and filed out of the room for their morning break.

With time on my hands I tucked my own textbooks under my arm and headed back to the cathedral. I wanted to climb back up to the organ loft and see just how good and clear our view had really been from that position.

Leaving my books and class roll sitting on a small table inside the north door of the cathedral, I walked briskly to the steep stairs that led to the organ loft. Once I was up on this small platform, I went to the far end and opened the narrow window that looked out over the cathedral close.

The full width of the square lay between myself and the roof of the Old School where Dave Fowler had died, but the distance was not great, and from where I stood there was a clear view of what Inspector Locke had called 'the scene of the crime'.

As these thoughts were whizzing through my head I heard a clumping below and a moment later was joined in the loft by David Evans.

'Ah, Morris, I didn't expect to find you here.'

'Just replaying the events of yesterday,' I said, a rather glum tone in my voice.

'I see. And this is where you and Lewis stood and saw . . . well . . . whatever it was you saw.'

'Exactly! And the view from here is excellent, so I can't see how we could possibly have been mistaken.'

'It's all very grim indeed,' said Evans. 'Now, if you don't mind, Morris, I'll get on with my practice.'

'Practise all you like, old man. I'll just hang about for a bit.'

'Suit yourself.'

And with those words Evans opened up the console of the organ, spread out some pages of sheet music and began to gently play through something I recognised as Mendelssohn.

After a while I grew tired of staring out of the small window, trying to replay in my mind over and over again what I had seen and what it might mean.

I turned away from the window, leaned on the railing of the organ loft, and looked down into the body of the cathedral—allowing myself to be carried away on the wings of the music Evans was drawing out of the cathedral's beautiful Hill organ.

Then something caught my eye. Among the long shadows that filled the deserted church, a figure was moving—a dark figure, large and powerfully built.

Leaning forward a little over the railing, I squinted into the shadows. As I looked, the figure passed through a beam of light falling through the rose window, and in that brief moment I saw that it was McKell.

Now that may not have appeared startling to some people, but it certainly startled me. I happened to know, from one or two brief conversations I'd had with that prickly gentleman in my short time at Nesfield Cathedral School, that he was about as religious as I was. Which is to say, not very religious at all.

'Now what,' I asked myself in the silence of my own mind, 'is that blighter doing here?'

The cathedral was kept open for prayer, I knew that much. I also knew that folk from the town would, from time to time, drop in—to pray or to arrange flowers or whatever.

But McKell? That struck me as decidedly odd. This grumbling, taciturn man, and his equally ill-mannered sister, were among the least religious people I'd ever encountered.

And yet, here was McKell, coming to the empty cathedral on his own.

As I watched he made his way to one of the rear pews and took a seat. Clearly he was intending to settle down for a period. This was even more extraordinary. Somehow I simply could not imagine McKell engaging in silent contemplation, or meditation, or prayer . . . or, come to that, anything else in that vast, empty building that echoed to David Evans' exquisite organ playing.

It was while I was wrestling with this puzzle that I saw the south door of the cathedral swing open. This was the door on the town side of the building, the one that locals would use when they visited. It opened only slowly and cautiously. Then a small man stepped into the cathedral and closed the door silently behind him.

He was not a man I recognised. The light was poor in the body of the building, but I could see that he was short, slightly built and had a completely bald head. I could see enough, in fact, to place him if he was someone I knew. He was not.

He paced slowly and silently about halfway down the main aisle of the nave, looking around all the time. Then he appeared to spot McKell sitting, motionless, in a rear pew and hurried to his side.

I dared not move but stood stock still, leaning slightly forward, at the edge of the organ loft railings. I almost dared not breathe. McKell had always struck me as a slightly fishy character in some way, and now it appeared that he was having a fishy meeting with some unknown fishy character from the town. The whole thing smelled as strongly as a fisherman's pyjamas.

And sure enough—it was a meeting. McKell and the stranger had their heads together. From the bobbing of those heads in the dim shadows of the cathedral, it was clear they were talking to each other. I probably would not have been able to hear them from the height of the organ loft even if Evans had not been playing. As it was, there wasn't the slightest possibility of catching even a single word.

I comforted myself against this lack of possibly useful intelligence by imagining that they would only be speaking in whispers anyway, so even if there had been no music, and I had been downstairs, I would still—in all likelihood—not have been able to hear them.

Then McKell's hand darted into his coat pocket and he pulled out a small paper packet. This he handed over to the stranger. A moment later the visitor stood up and left, departing the same way he came in.

McKell waited until the stranger had gone and then made his own exit from the cathedral.

'Alice would have been able to describe this,' I said to myself. '"Curioser and curioser!" she would have said.'

EIGHTEEN

~

That night I was invited to dinner with Dean Cowper and his wife, Ellen—and since Ellen had a reputation as an excellent cook, I was delighted to accept.

Around the dinner table were Cowper and his wife and their guest residents—the two Lewis brothers—as well as myself.

The dinner was, as I had anticipated, outstanding: roast lamb with peas and potatoes followed by a baked rice pudding.

Once the table had been cleared by the maid, Ellen Cowper retired for the night and the Dean brought out a bottle of port and some glasses.

'Gentlemen,' he said, 'will you join me?'

We said we would and he poured out four glasses of the ruby red liquid.

'Very fine,' said Warnie as he took a sip. 'Very fine old port indeed.'

After finishing off his first glass and helping himself to a second, Warnie found a copy of the *Times* for that day lying on top of a small bookcase. He settled down in an armchair with his glass and the newspaper, leaving Jack, the Dean and myself to our conversation.

At first this revolved around the impossible murder of Dave Fowler. Those same questions that had popped into my head at the first sight of the body were now on everyone's lips. And, apart from wild speculations, there was no suggestion of any possible, and reasonable, explanation emerging.

'This strange matter,' muttered Dean Cowper, 'gives every appearance of having defied the laws of nature.'

Jack agreed. 'If Isaac Newton had been standing on that gravel road at the back of the school he would have found his law of gravity exhibited as effectively by the falling corpse as by a falling apple. But I suspect even Newton's giant brain would struggle to explain why gravity had not worked twelve hours earlier when we distinctly saw the body begin its fall.'

'Some of the boys,' said Cowper, shaking his head sadly, 'have managed to get hold of the details of this case.'

'In my short time here,' I said, 'I've discovered how efficient the gossip network in a small school can be.'

'Indeed,' Cowper agreed. 'That they have found out so much is not surprising. What alarms me is that some of the older boys have been trying to frighten the younger ones by claiming that the only explanation for this impossible event is occult nonsense—lots of stuff about ghosts and ghouls and things that go bump in the night.'

'If the children are being genuinely frightened,' Jack said firmly, 'that needs to be stamped out.'

'Quite right, Mr Lewis,' said Cowper. 'I intend to deal with it in my talk to the boys at chapel tomorrow morning.'

'And what insights can you give us,' I asked the Dean, 'into the mind of the murderer?'

Richard Cowper shook his head sadly. 'Who can understand what goes on in any human mind that drives it to such an act of savage violence?'

'Except,' I suggested, 'that it must be a badly diseased mind—a human mind that is unnatural, bent out of shape, in some way.'

Jack chuckled and said, 'Morris is trying to draw you into a debate he and I are engaged in over the truth concerning human nature.'

'I see,' muttered the Dean. 'Well, I'm afraid I have nothing original to add. In fact, I've sometimes thought that what is most remarkable about the doctrine of original sin is how unoriginal it is. Throughout human history the basic corruption in human nature keeps showing itself in the same horrible ways over and over again.'

'So it's two against one, Morris,' Jack grinned. 'You're outnumbered.'

'I take it you don't agree, Tom,' Cowper said as he refilled our port glasses and offered the bottle to Warnie.

'Surely,' I protested, 'all civilised people agree that human nature is basically, fundamentally, *good*!'

Jack and Cowper glanced at each other.

'I think,' said Jack, 'the Dean and I agree that your confidence in the goodness of human nature does you credit—it shows what a trusting and charitable person you are. But it also, sadly, shows that you just haven't been paying attention.'

'To what?'

'To the patterns of human history, to the stories in your daily newspaper, to the behaviour of those around you—and even to the inclinations of your own heart.'

'But I keep *seeing* goodness in human beings,' I thrust back. 'I see people behaving well and doing the right thing.'

'And the opposite, of course,' said Cowper gently. 'Or do you find you never need to discipline your class?'

'Well . . . of course . . .'

'And that's the whole point, young Morris,' said Jack, leaping gleefully into the battle. 'Human nature is this strange mixture. As a Christian, I believe we are made in the image of God; but this image is now sadly marred, deeply corrupted, by the rebellion of our primeval parents against God. Furthermore, their nature we have inherited, and hence we too are by nature corrupt.'

'But there's still good there,' I insisted.

'Chesterton put it best,' Jack responded, 'when he noted that the good that remains in human nature is like the goods Robinson Crusoe found on his beach—something salvaged from a wreck.'

'Pascal said something similar,' Cowper volunteered. 'He said that human nature contains these contradictory elements of nobility and wickedness.'

'Precisely!' Jack leaped in, seizing the point with delight. 'Pascal said something along the lines of *Quelle chimère est-ce donc que l'homme? quelle nouveauté, quel chaos, quel sujet de contradictions.*'

'I'm sorry, my French is not . . .'

'"What a chimera is man!" Jack translated. "What a novelty, what chaos, what a subject of contradiction."'

Dean Cowper was nodding enthusiastically as he added, 'Pascal's point is that man's greatness lies in his capacity to recognise his wretchedness.'

'But I *don't* recognise it,' I protested before he could go any further. 'Human nature is *not* basically wretched!'

'There is an apparent paradox here,' said Jack, putting down his port glass and reaching for his pipe. 'The seeming paradox is that human beings exhibit qualities of both greatness *and* wretchedness.'

'So what do you really think, Tom?' asked Cowper. 'Are human beings glorious, exalted creatures with tremendous potential or wretched beings desperately in need of rescue?'

'Well, listen to a Mozart symphony or look at a Rembrandt painting—you can see and hear how glorious the human spirit is,' I said.

Jack looked at me from under his lowered eyebrows and said seriously, 'Now look at the path of destruction wrought by Jack the Ripper and see the wretchedness.'

'But that's my whole point,' I said, seizing on the comparison. 'Mozart was normal—extraordinarily gifted, but normal— while Jack the Ripper was abnormal, unnatural.'

'I believe,' said Dean Cowper quietly, 'that Mozart was also an adulterer. Surely that corruption, that defect of character, is present in *every* human being?'

'Come back to literature, which we both know,' chimed in Jack. 'Charles Dickens, you and I agree, was a writer of genius. But in order to carry on an affair with a young actress, he expelled his wife from his home and even commanded his children not to visit their mother. There are clearly two sides to human nature.'

'But the most basic side is the nobility,' I insisted, determined not to surrender my argument. 'No one's perfect after all, even the best of us.'

'I think you've just given the game away, Tom,' Cowper said with a gentle smile. 'If nobody is perfect then the shadow of corruption lies across the human heart. There is a defect at the very core of human nature.'

'And that means that our murderer,' said Jack, leaning forward in his armchair, 'is no oddity of nature, but a normal human being showing what our nature is capable of.'

NINETEEN

~

The next morning I was busy with classes. At first I found the boys of the Fourth Form unsettled and restless. I could hardly blame them—the murder of a schoolmaster in such a baffling manner must mean that some of them would be losing sleep, some would be having nightmares, and all of them would be writing highly melodramatic letters to their parents at home.

To get them focussed on *Macbeth* I started a debate over the identity of Shakespeare's mysterious, unnamed 'third murderer'. This turned out to be the right manoeuvre, and soon they were throwing suggestions across the room that the third member of the murder squad might have been Macbeth himself, or possibly the bloodthirsty Lady Macbeth.

'But,' protested Stanhope, blinking furiously through his large, round spectacles, 'no lord of the manor would wun awound doing his own dirty work when he had paid servants to do it for him!'

This provoked howls of protest from other members of the class and debate was well and truly joined. So much so that after about ten minutes the classroom door swung open to reveal McKell frowning in the doorway.

'Keep your boys quieter, Morris!' he snapped. 'All this noise is disturbing my class next door.'

I apologised and hushed my class, insisting they continue their debate in lower tones.

At the end of third school I took my place in the hall for the school lunch. Unfortunately, we masters ate the same lunch as the boys, which that day was sausages and mashed potatoes followed by treacle pudding.

At the head table Dr Rogers told us that he had asked Henry Beard, our Classics Master, to take all the mathematics classes until the end of term—which was only two weeks away—and he was rewriting the timetable to accommodate this.

Beard, always a sullen and unhappy man at the best of times, then grumbled in a loud stage whisper, 'I wasn't *asked*, you understand—I was simply *told* I had to!'

'My dear Mr Beard,' said the Head Master in his heartiest manner, 'you are the only member of our current staff who has actually taught mathematics in the past. So it must, I'm afraid, be you. And, after all, it is only two weeks.'

'Two weeks of being overworked is still two weeks,' grumbled Beard.

Our History Master, Geoffrey Douglas, was sitting next to the grumpy Beard and tried to cheer him up.

'Come along, Henry,' he said warmly, 'you're wife's away at the moment, so you must have some free time in the evenings to do the extra prep.'

'Extra! Aye, that's the word. It's an extra burden is what it is.'

Dr Rogers ignored this exchange and went on to explain that he was making urgent contact with a retired mathematics teacher of his acquaintance to take the role for the next term, while the job was advertised and a full-time replacement for Dave Fowler was being found.

When I went back to my rooms after lunch, I found Warnie

in my front sitting room, seated in an armchair, reading a copy of Wisden.

'Ah, there you are, old chap. I've been waiting for you,' he said. 'We've been invited—or possibly summoned—to a meeting with the police.'

I asked him when and where, and he explained it was to be in the police cottage in the town in an hour's time. Then I asked him if he knew who would be there.

'Well, apart from us eyewitnesses, I gather all the police chappies involved in the case.'

So it was that three-quarters of an hour later Jack, Warnie and I were walking down Nesfield's high street in the direction of the police cottage.

In the front parlour we found Constable Butler serving cups of tea and a plate of digestive biscuits to Detective Inspector Locke, Sergeant Drake and Dr Green.

'Gentlemen, thank you for coming,' said the inspector. Then he cleared his throat and said hesitantly, 'This is, I realise, an unorthodox procedure—but this is an entirely unorthodox murder, and I thought it best to have something of a brain-storming session.'

He looked around the room slowly, perhaps waiting for objections, and then resumed, 'Dr Green, please get us started by bringing everyone up to date with the findings from your post-mortem.'

The doctor put down his cup of tea and said, 'Inspector Locke has my official report, but in summary I can tell you that it was a combination of the knife wound and the fall that killed poor Mr Fowler. The knife wound alone would have been sufficient given enough time. My estimate is that he was already dying from the trauma of the wound and from loss of blood, and probably losing consciousness, when he fell. But it was the fall that finished him off. He suffered a severe blow to the back of the head. And that blunt force trauma, added to the physical damage and the blood loss from the deep knife wound, resulted in his death.'

'And the time of death, doctor?' said Inspector Locke. 'Tell everyone your conclusion about the time of death.'

'In all probability death occurred at precisely the time you gentlemen,' said Green, nodding towards Jack and myself, 'say that you saw him attacked and saw him fall.'

'How did he fall? In what position or posture?' asked Jack. 'You talked yesterday about the position of the body—did you draw any conclusions as to how he hit the ground?'

'On his back,' replied the doctor. 'I have no doubt about that. I found small pieces of gravel embedded in his back—so he fell, on his back, face up, onto a gravel surface.'

'But the body was face down when we found it,' Warnie protested.

Inspector Locke came in at this point. 'You're beginning to see the dimensions of our problem. Clearly the body was moved. But when? And how?'

'I think he bounced,' muttered Warnie, almost to himself. 'Poor fellah came down with a terrible thump and then he bounced. Sort of thing a chappie in my regiment used to call a "dead cat bounce". Only explanation.'

Jack gave a rather grim chuckle as he said, 'Then he must have bounced to a considerable height, old fellow, bearing in mind he was invisible when Morris and I reached the spot just a minute or so after he fell.'

'Oh, ah, yes,' mumbled Warnie. 'See what you mean. That's tricky, isn't it? Quite a puzzle, eh?'

'In fact, it's the time element that makes it all so tricky,' Inspector Locke said. 'You two'—again he nodded in the direction of Jack and myself—'saw the wound inflicted (although exactly how that was done we don't as yet know), and you saw the wound bleeding freely. Then you saw him fall over the far edge of the roof.'

'And we ran to the spot as quickly as we could,' I volunteered.

'I have no doubt,' the inspector agreed, 'that you ran to his aid rapidly. The distance involved is not great. Sergeant Drake and I have timed how long it would take to climb quickly down the stairs from the organ loft, exit the cathedral, run across the cathedral close, go through the archway and emerge from the doorway onto the road behind the school. We think it can't possibly have taken more than a minute and a half. Even walking briskly you'd do it in two.'

'At the most, I would have thought,' Jack added. 'So the time period available for something to happen to the body is remarkably short.'

'So the method is a puzzle,' agreed Locke, 'but so is the motive.'

'Ah, yes,' Warnie said, 'method, motive and opportunity— that's what they all talk about in those detective novels I read . . . Agatha Christie and the rest . . . f'rinstance, Austin Freeman's Dr Thorndyke is always saying it . . . method, motive and opportunity.'

Sexton Locke nodded in agreement. 'And with the method remaining obscure, Drake and I turned our attention to motive—without, I'm sad to say, any greater success. Mr Fowler started with the school only at the beginning of this term, I believe. Is that correct, Mr Morris?'

'Yes,' I agreed. 'On the same day as myself.'

'So he's hardly been here long enough to make enemies, one would have thought. We're trying to track down his antecedents—his family background and where he was before he came here—so far without success.'

'That surprises me,' said Jack. 'I would assume his references and details of his previous employment would be in the school office.'

Inspector Locke ran his fingers through his hair in a gesture of frustration as a deep frown furrowed his brow. Then he said, 'There's a Scotland Yard officer, an old friend of mine, in the vicinity at the moment, and I'm hoping to consult him on this matter. He's a brilliant detective, so he may be able to help.'

TWENTY

~

Inspector Locke's brainstorming session continued for another half an hour but without producing any concrete results.

When it broke up and we spilled back out onto the high street, Warnie announced that he was heading for *The Pelican* to see if he could find some locals interested in a game of darts. Jack and I turned up the hill and began walking slowly towards the cathedral.

'Jack, let me ask you a question,' I said as we walked, 'and I want an honest answer.'

'Would I ever give you any other kind?' Jack replied with a warm smile on his face. 'Ask away, young Morris, ask away.'

'Do you think I am fundamentally a bad person?'

'It all depends on what you mean by "bad", my dear Morris,' replied Jack, making the same move he so often made in tutorials of going back to first principles and insisting on clear definitions.

'You know what I mean by "bad", Jack. When we speak of someone having a "bad character" we know exactly what we're saying—there's no ambiguity.'

'Actually, I think there is room for doubt and ambiguity,' Jack insisted. 'Since Chaucer's day we've used "bad" to mean "of defective quality or worth". And any such judgment depends upon the standard being used in doing the judging. When we describe someone as a "bad character", we mean his behaviour is defective, that is to say, he doesn't come up to the standard of most of our circle of acquaintance: he doesn't behave in the way most of our group think is proper.'

'But you seem to have been arguing,' I insisted, 'in this latest "great war" of ours, that *all* of us are "bad" in some way—basically defective and deficient in character. Yet we don't judge absolutely everyone around us as being a "bad character", so how can that be?'

'There is much in what you say, Morris,' Jack responded, using the words he employed in tutorials to express high praise. 'Let me explain by painting a picture for you. Imagine a tribe of pygmies living in the deepest, most remote jungles of central Africa. Among that tribe some are regarded as short and some as tall—quite correctly, in fact, since by their own tribal height standards some are, indeed, short or tall. Now imagine that tribe being encountered by Dr Livingstone or some other European explorer. By European standards he will see *all* the tribe as short. In much the same way, we distinguish among ourselves those of our acquaintance we call "good chaps" because they hit the mark of the general standard of acceptable behaviour. And there are some we call "bad" because their behaviour misses that mark. But when we encounter God, we discover that our mark was not nearly high enough.'

'In God's eyes we are all moral pygmies?'

'It sounds harsh when put as bluntly as that, but you're perfectly correct. We settle for lower standards because we are people of lower standards.'

'Which is why our murderer, in this case, is merely acting out of those lower standards of human behaviour inherent somewhere deep in all of us?'

'Precisely. Society and our own consciences both impose restraints on us, which results in us suppressing some of our impulses and acting like men in "the state of nature", to use Hobbes' expression.'

'And sufficiently provoked in some way, our true nature explodes through those restraints and violence results?' I asked.

Jack agreed.

'You almost make it sound,' I continued, 'as if we've inherited something defective and corrupt in our natures from our parents. Is that what you mean?'

By this time we had reached the top of the high street, but instead of walking through the gates into the cathedral close, we turned to one side to walk down a long, gentle slope to where the River Ness was making its lazy way around the town.

Jack lit his pipe, and then said, 'For the past fifty years or so there has been a movement called eugenics.'

'A rather unpleasant movement I would have thought,' I commented.

'I'm not recommending it, merely using it as an illustration,' Jack explained. 'The eugenics movement wants only people who will produce the finest offspring to be allowed to breed. They seem to think that if those they call the "criminal classes" were not allowed to have children, criminality itself could be bred out of the human race. The whole concept is both absurd and unworkable. However . . .'

'Ah, now we get to the point,' I said, rubbing my hands in anticipation of the idea Jack was about to spring.

'However, the word "eugenics" itself may enlighten us. It was coined only, as I said, about fifty years ago—put together from two Greek roots: from the word meaning "to produce" or "to breed" with the prefix *eus*, meaning—well you remember your Greek, don't you, Morris?'

'Of course—*eus* means "good".'

'So "eugenics" means "good breeding" or "well bred". On that model, I think, we can coin another word that means the opposite—a word that means "badly bred" or "bad breeding" in the sense of inheriting bad characteristics.'

'What would such a word look like?'

'If we take the Greek word *kakos*, meaning "bad" or "evil", we could coin the word "cacogenics"—and say that everyone in the human race is the product of "cacogenics". We have all inherited corruption from our parents just as pygmies inherit short stature from theirs.'

'And this goes back to having the right standard to judge against?' I asked.

'You follow my meaning exactly, Morris,' said Jack with a warm smile.

'You claim . . .' I began.

'No, Christianity claims,' Jack interrupted.

'All right, then, Christianity claims that by God's standards we are all born with some corruption within, which means that our human nature is damaged? We can't see it because we're all damaged in the same way?'

Jack clapped me on the shoulder and chortled, 'You always were one of my brightest students, young Morris. Among us damaged people I would call you a young man of "good character", not "bad character". That's the answer to the question you asked a moment ago. But we're still all fundamentally defective in some way.'

'In what way? What is the defect, the corruption, the damage in our souls?'

'We Christians call that defect "sin".'

'So it's all about sex then?' I asked.

Jack hooted with laughter. 'Morris, there are still parts of your brain that belong to the world of the university undergraduate. Of course "sin" is not just about sex. Our English word "sin" translates the Greek word *hamartia* in the New Testament. Now, you remember your Greek, so what does *hamartia* mean?'

'I think *hamartia* means "missing the mark" or something of that sort.'

'Indeed. It means missing the bullseye, missing the target. And the target in question is not socially acceptable behaviour but rather what God as our Loving Maker and Ruler requires of us. *Hamartia*, or sin, in fact means totally ignoring what God requires of us, plans for us and provides for us. And that fact gives us a clear, two-word definition of "sin".'

'Let's hear it then.'

'Sin means "ignoring God". And that's the defect, the corruption, that lives in the human heart—we, all of us, have this built-in bias, this inclination, to ignore God. To act as if God is not there, or is not paying attention, or has no interest in us and how we treat each other.'

I agreed that many, perhaps most, of my acquaintances never gave God a thought. They just lived their own lives, their own way, without God. So if sin meant 'ignoring God' they were sinners.

But then I added in protest, 'I still don't see it. How can ignoring God result in someone's committing a murder? I don't see the connection between the two.'

Jack chewed on the stem of his pipe for a moment and then said, 'Warnie once owned a radio, a small mantle radio, which he took from one army supply base to another when he was transferred around. It had a chargeable battery built into it.

It could run off mains power, or, if unplugged from the mains, it could run for a time off its built-in battery. We are like that radio. We are designed to run connected to God— plugged into God. When we ignore God, "unplug" ourselves from our life source, we continue to function for a while.'

'On the remnants of the power that God has built into us?'

'It's not a perfect analogy, but something like that. But if we ignore God, if we fail to turn back to God, to reconnect to God, eventually we fail to function properly.'

'And murder results?'

'Murders *are* committed by seemingly upright, perfectly normal citizens. Christianity says that sin—ignoring God—is the reason why.'

TWENTY-ONE

~

When Jack and I turned around and made our way back towards the cathedral close, we were joined at the gates by Warnie.

'I beat him,' he said cheerfully. 'I played a singles game against the publican, Trevor Travers. Nice chap. My hand has not lost its cunning. He is demanding a return match tonight.'

A delighted Warnie was chuckling as he told us this.

'But I'm afraid my brain might have lost its cunning,' said Jack, smiling grimly over the stem of his pipe. 'We have encountered the occasional puzzle in the past, but nothing like this.'

'Nothing like a body that floats,' I agreed, 'floats quite invisibly, in mid-air, for twelve hours or so and only then crashes to the ground.'

'To say nothing,' Jack added, 'of how the wound was inflicted. Both Morris and I saw Fowler quite alone on the roof—and then we saw him wounded, and then he staggered and fell. And during all that time there was, apparently, no one else on the roof within striking distance of him to inflict the wound.'

'Oh, ah, yes,' muttered Warnie into his moustache. 'A bit trickier than a game of darts.' He meditated for a moment and then continued, 'But I have complete confidence in you, Jack. Brain the size of the Albert Hall. You'll work it out. I'm certain you will.'

Jack put his hand on his brother's shoulder as he said, 'Thanks for your vote of confidence, old chap, but I might have met my match for once.'

'And then,' I contributed, raising an issue that was on my mind, 'there's the little matter of the motive. Inspector Locke told us that so far he hasn't found one. And based on what I've seen of Dave Fowler over the last few weeks, I can't even begin to imagine why someone would want to kill the blighter. I didn't particularly take to him, but he was hardly murder-victim material.'

As we talked we were walking slowly over the old cobblestones of the quadrangle in the heart of the cathedral close. Without having made a conscious decision to do so we were drifting in one particular direction. Somehow our feet were directing us towards the archway and the door that led out to the gravel road behind the school—the place where the body had been found.

Perhaps we were, instinctively, returning to the spot where the mystery had appeared, in the hope that another visit would send a shaft of illumination into our brains.

Pushing open the heavy wooden door, we stepped out onto the road behind the school—only to find that the Head Master, Dr Adrian Rogers, and the Dean, Richard Cowper, were already there, standing in the middle of the road, looking up at the roof of the Old School.

As we walked over to greet them, Dean Cowper said, 'This place does hold a sort of grim fascination at the moment, doesn't it?'

We all agreed it did.

Dr Rogers shook his distinguished thick, white hair as he murmured, almost to himself, 'The impossible simply doesn't happen. And certainly not in my school! This whole thing is disgraceful. And potentially very damaging for the school. It's both embarrassing *and* impossible. Most unfortunate. Most unfortunate indeed.'

It appeared that the Head Master saw himself, rather than Dave Fowler, as the real victim in this baffling crime.

'It's not impossible,' responded Warnie. 'It can't be—it happened!'

'Of course, my dear chap, of course,' Dr Rogers said. 'Impossible is entirely the wrong word. I should have chosen my words more carefully. Inexplicable is the word we want at the moment. Fowler's death is both inconvenient and inexplicable.'

'I keep wondering,' said Cowper, raising his eyes to the roofline, 'if there might not be some piece of masonry on the side of the building on which a body might have become lodged, only to fall off later—either from its own weight or from a gust of wind.'

Jack put his pipe back in his pocket and gazed off into the distance. On his face was the look I had seen many times before—the look that told me his mighty brain was at work.

With Jack distracted in this way I chipped in to offer my thoughts.

'You're not the first person to come up with that idea, Dean,' I said. 'But it doesn't really solve our problem. Jack and I looked up at the building as soon as we arrived here and saw that Fowler's body was missing from where we'd expected to find it.'

'Exactly!' Warnie added. 'If there was a body dangling from a protruding piece of masonry, Jack and Tom would surely have seen it. A body hanging off a cornice on a building of this size would certainly be visible to the naked eye.'

'There's a further problem with your admirable theory, my dear Dean,' said the Head Master. 'This part of the Old School is Georgian. There are many windows, but the building is symmetrical and has a smooth face. There simply are no protruding bits of stonework.'

'How far might it have fallen?' asked the Dean as he turned around and looked at the wide field that bordered the road. 'Might a gust of wind have carried it away from this road and into the long grass of the field?'

'Jolly interesting thought,' said Warnie. 'Hadn't occurred to me. Is it possible, Jack?'

I looked out across the field. On the far side were some workmen with picks and shovels and beside them a large, yellow earthmoving machine—standing idle at that particular moment.

'There was no wind on the day of the murder,' said Jack. 'Certainly nothing strong enough to carry a human body any considerable distance.'

'And Fowler was a very solidly built young man,' said Dr Rogers. 'I can't imagine any wind strong enough to lift such a weight so far as to be out of sight.'

'Not a very helpful suggestion, then?' concluded Dean Cowper.

'What's happening on the far side of the field?' I asked, pointing to the workmen.

'It's going to be a new housing estate,' the Dean explained. 'This field was part of the church property for the past two hundred years. About twelve months ago a builder approached us and offered a considerable sum of money for the field. He's planning a mixture of villas and smaller cottages. The Chapter wrestled with the question of selling or not selling for a long time. But eventually . . .'

His voice trailed away, as if he was still doubtful about the decision.

'I know you were never keen,' said the Head Master warmly,

'but we made the right decision. The cathedral repair fund desperately needed an injection of cash, and selling this field provided exactly what was needed.' Turning to Jack, Warnie and me he added, 'These old buildings look beautiful, but they cost a devil of a lot of money to maintain.'

A silence descended on our small group—a heavy silence that weighed upon us for several minutes. During that time we looked again at the facade of the Old School, and the empty gravel of the roadway—at that entire scene that was refusing to reveal whatever secrets it might hold.

Having read, marked, learned and inwardly digested what little these locations had to tell us, we silently made our way back into the school.

TWENTY-TWO

~

The rest of that afternoon I was rostered on to supervise prep. This involved patrolling the corridors that bordered the students' studies to ensure diligent quiet prevailed.

Only once did I have to exercise my authority when I heard subdued laughter followed by gasps of surprise in the Fifth Form corridor, coming from the study shared by Conway and Wynyard. Throwing open the door, I discovered them chortling over *The Hotspur*, a boys' story paper—which I immediately confiscated.

'But that cost me tuppence, sir!' Conway protested.

'We're in the middle of a story about Bill Samson of the British Intelligence Corps!' complained Wynyard.

'You'll get it back at the end of term,' I replied. 'Give you something to look forward to, won't it? Now, what are you two meant to be working on?'

'Latin,' growled Wynyard.

'Get your textbooks out then. Come along, quickly.'

Shakespeare has a line somewhere about the schoolboy dragging himself snail-like to school, and it was with snail-like slowness that those two produced their books. I left them in sullen silence with their Latin primers open on their desks and vacant expressions in their eyes.

Later that evening, school dinner in the hall was one of

those meals that made me hope that I never see a Brussels sprout again. Not that I have anything against Brussels sprouts personally—it's just that school dinners have made me happy to donate my lifetime supply to the starving poor of Africa.

After dinner I was walking across the close back to my room when I heard hurrying footsteps, and Henry Beard caught up with me.

'Morris, old chap,' he said, his grumpy face lit up by an ineffective attempt at a smile. 'About these extra mathematics classes I've been lumbered with for the next two weeks.'

I stopped in midstride and turned to look at him. Beard was not a warm and engaging man. In fact, if anything, he was usually silent, sullen and withdrawn. Someone had told me that he had had a 'bad war' and had never entirely recovered.

But I felt sorry for him having to cope with this extra burden. Schoolmastering, I had learned to my cost, was quite taxing enough without having extra tasks thrust upon one.

'If you could see your way clear to taking just a few of them—the extra maths classes, that is—' Beard began.

I interrupted him before he could go further.

'I'm afraid I'm not your man,' I said hastily. 'The reason I did English language and literature at Oxford was that I'm hopeless with numbers. Sorry, old man, but I could as easily teach trigonometry as fly to the moon.'

As Beard turned away he muttered loudly, 'I should have known you'd prove to be a broken reed.'

He shuffled off into the gathering darkness, and I was about to turn towards my own rooms when Jack and Warnie emerged from the Dean's house.

'Aah, ooh, Morris old chap,' hooted Warnie cheerfully. 'We're both off to *The Pelican*—I'm giving Travers the return darts match he asked for. Won't you join us?'

I thought about the papers sitting on my desk that required marking. I thought about them for a small fraction of a tenth of a second, and then I said, 'Yes, of course, I'd be delighted.'

In the warm, cheerful atmosphere of the local pub we ordered pints and stood watching for a moment while the publican, Trevor Travers, called on his barmaid to take over serving so that he could 'teach this visitor a lesson in darts'.

Warnie and he then rolled up their sleeves and tackled what was looking rather like a grudge match—with enthusiastic locals watching on, offering a constant running commentary along with coaching advice on the correct stance and the best wrist movement.

Neither of the two darts players seemed entirely to appreciate the contributions of the sideline experts.

Jack and I left Warnie to his game in the bar parlour and retired to a quiet corner of the snug to enjoy our pints.

After several silent minutes, Jack said, 'Why so quiet tonight, Morris?'

'Human nature,' I said, by way of cryptic reply.

Jack raised an eyebrow, so I continued, 'If this unknown murderer of Dave Fowler is not some freak, some sport of nature, but is simply an expression of all that is bad in ordinary human nature, then I feel most unhappy about my *own* nature. If my heart were an apple it would have a worm burrowing through it, slowly corrupting it. It's not a happy discovery.'

'It's better than the alternative,' said Jack firmly.

'Which is?'

'To live with the illusion that we have the hearts of angels.'

Jack was thoughtful for a moment, and then he said, 'Have you ever had the experience of seeing someone who's been discovered doing the wrong thing, acting badly towards another, and they respond with the explanation, "I made a mistake"?'

'Yes, yes, I've certainly heard that. I remember my landlady when I was in digs in Oxford. Her son was caught stealing from a local ironmonger and sentenced to a prison term. Her explanation to me was that her Albert had "made a mistake and I suppose he has to pay for it". But, Jack, stealing is not some sort of "mistake"—it's wrongdoing! Does a thief really say to himself, "What am I doing with this stolen money in my hands? Whoops! Bit of a mistake there!"'

Jack laughed heartily. 'I couldn't have put it better myself. The man who killed your Mr Fowler was not "making a mistake"—he was committing an evil act because he chose to. And that sort of honesty about human nature is better than living in an unreal dream.'

'But also very depressing. As a result of our discussions I'm finding my view of human nature to be rather bleak.'

'In truth the picture is not bleak, it's complex.'

'What do you mean?'

'Well, let me sketch out half a dozen or so factors operating in the human heart. I think you'll see that although human beings are defective, or corrupt, we are still complex beings.'

'Very well, let's hear your analysis,' I said.

Jack took a deep draft from his pint and then said, 'Firstly, human beings are rational. In our normal daily lives we trust our reason—we constantly use it to work things out. We know when we get things wrong because we know what it means to get things right.'

I nodded, so he continued. 'Second, human beings are moral because we have a moral nature and can glimpse an unattainable moral ideal. We know that God's law exists—and we know that we fall far short of it—because we fall far short of our *own* moral standards.'

I was feeling in a rather glum mood that night so I muttered in response, 'I wish I was a better person than I am. Well, some of the time anyway.'

'Third,' Jack continued, 'human beings are creative. This is one of the most interesting things about us. It's what makes my field of study possible. However, we're not just "creators" but what Tollers calls "sub-creators"—we were made *by* God *like* God. God is the Creator and we resemble him in being "sub-creators".'

'I hadn't thought of it like that before,' I said, staring into my beer and thinking about my secret ambition to become a novelist.

'Fourth, human beings are immortal. I know you and I have debated this in the past, and you don't entirely see things from my perspective. But it's immortality that gives our lives ultimate moral value. It's immortality that gives our lives consequence and purpose.'

'That's four,' I commented. 'You said you had about half a dozen.'

'Fifth, human beings have dignity,' Jack resumed patiently. 'Being immortal, rational and morally responsible gives us dignity. And finally, human beings are broken. Our moral grasp falls short of our moral vision, our reasoning can lead us astray, we can be "sub-creators" in dark and destructive ways as well as inspiring ways, and we can treat each other as beings without dignity. We do this because . . .'

'Because,' I offered when Jack paused, 'because of that Christian doctrine of "sin" you were throwing at me last time we debated this.'

Jack nodded and said, 'It certainly explains human nature, doesn't it? It explains *us*.'

TWENTY-THREE

~

As Jack finished I looked across the snug and was surprised to see a man I thought I recognised—a man I would not have expected to see in the small cathedral town of Nesfield.

'Jack,' I said as I pointed over his shoulder. 'Standing over there in the doorway—isn't that . . .'

Jack turned around to look. The doorway on the far side of the room, the door between the snug and the bar parlour, was dimly lit and the man standing there was in shadow.

'I believe you're right, young Morris. That is quite definitely our old friend Detective Inspector Crispin of Scotland Yard. Invite him to join us.'

I needed no more encouragement. Putting down my glass, I took the few steps across the room and tapped the man, whose back was towards us, on the shoulder.

He spun around quickly, almost defensively. That was, I guessed, the trained reaction of a professional policeman. Then he saw who I was and his face broke into a cheerful grin.

'Tom Morris!' he said. 'As I live and breathe—what are you doing here?'

'I teach up at the school,' I explained. 'But, rather more to the point—what are you doing here?'

The Scotland Yard man tapped the side of his nose and winked.

'I am involved in what we call "an on-going investigation",' he said.

'And look who else is here,' I said to the inspector. As I spoke I stepped to one side so that Crispin could see Jack, seated at our corner table on the far side of the snug. Jack raised his glass in a salute to the Scotland Yard man.

'Well, this is a delight!' he said as he strode across the room. Jack rose from his seat and the two men shook hands in a warm and hearty greeting. Then Jack invited Crispin to join us, and he drew up a chair at our table. We called over to the barmaid and ordered an extra pint for our guest, and fresh pints for ourselves, and then began the interrogation—although exactly who was interrogating whom was not exactly clear.

'Now how does it happen that I find you here in Nesfield, Mr Lewis?' asked the Scotland Yard man.

'Through the good offices of young Tom here,' Jack explained, 'I am guest speaker at the Nesfield Cathedral School's Annual Speech Night.'

'And when is that?'

'In two nights from now,' I explained. 'The event is open to the public. Why don't you come along, inspector?'

Crispin smiled thoughtfully and said, 'Yes, I just might do that. I'd like to hear you speak, Mr Lewis. What's your topic?'

'What I have to offer my unsuspecting hearers are some reflections on education with special reference to the teaching of English in the upper forms of schools.'

'Sounds a bit dry,' commented Inspector Crispin, 'if you don't mind my saying so.'

I laughed and said, 'The one thing Jack never is, is dry. One of the most popular lecturers in Oxford.'

'So how do you make the subject interesting, Mr Lewis?'

'When I explain the role of Morality, in the form of Natural Law, in education, I think I'll spark some interest—and even get a few backs up.' Jack chuckled at the prospect as he said this.

'Now, inspector,' I intervened, changing the subject, 'this tired old cliché about "pursuing on-going investigations" just won't do, you know. It won't wash—not with us. Why are you really in Nesfield?'

A sly smile crept across the Scotland Yard man's face as he said, 'As much as I might wish to discuss my work with you, Mr Morris, a police officer is not always at liberty to speak about certain things with civilians—at least not in the middle of an investigation.'

'I take it you've heard of our murder, inspector?' asked Jack.

'And most interesting, most intriguing it sounds,' said Crispin.

'Ah, the penny drops,' I cried. 'Our local man, Inspector Locke, said he had a friend from Scotland Yard in the district and he would consult this unnamed friend. I take it he was referring to you?'

'There's no harm in admitting that my old friend Sexton Locke has, indeed, taken me through the details of the Fowler murder case. But more than that I cannot say.'

'So is it the Dave Fowler murder that brought you down here then?' I persisted.

'No, as a matter of fact, it's not,' said Crispin firmly. 'I'm here making inquiries into an entirely different matter. It's just that this other matter has brought me to the district, and I was happy to sit down with my friend Sexton and talk over the bewildering murder mystery he's investigating.'

'And what exactly do you make of our intriguing little puzzle, inspector?' asked Jack.

'Very little so far,' the Scotland Yard man admitted.

'What help have you been able to give Inspector Locke?' I asked.

'Same answer, I'm afraid, Mr Morris: very little so far.'

'But you will be helping him to investigate?'

'No, this murder is definitely Inspector Locke's case,' said the Scotland Yard man, shaking his head. 'I have no intention of interfering.'

While this conversation was going on, I looked up through the doorway into the bar parlour. Judging from the noise coming from the front bar, the grudge match between Warnie and the publican was still going on—and was a close-fought affair.

As I watched I saw our esteemed Deputy Head Master, Gareth McKell, step up to the bar and place an order.

'Have you developed any theories, Mr Lewis?' Inspector Crispin was asking Jack.

'As it happens,' Jack replied, slowly and cautiously, 'the very beginnings of an idea have begun to develop in my mind.'

I was startled to hear Jack say this, and just as startled to see a large man approach McKell at the bar and tap him on the shoulder. McKell turned around to look at the looming giant who had thus interrupted his drinking. Was it my imagination, or did a look of fear flicker fleetingly across McKell's face?

That big man was speaking closely in McKell's ear and pointing towards the door of the pub. McKell downed the remains of his double whisky in a single gulp and followed the big man outside.

Meanwhile, Crispin was saying, 'Tell me about this idea of yours, Mr Lewis.'

Jack laughed and said, 'Ideas are sometimes rather like photographs: they start as negatives and only slowly, in solution, does the positive image appear. This seed of an idea that occurred to me this afternoon is certainly not yet developed. The positive image has not yet begun to appear.'

Jack paused to take a deep draught from his pint, and then said, 'Now, inspector, surely you can tell Tom and me—as old friends—a little more about this mysterious investigation that's brought you to Nesfield?'

Crispin finished his drink in thoughtful silence, and then said, 'Very well. But for your ears only, mind.'

He looked around as if fearing being overheard, and then said quietly, 'Diamond smuggling. I'm working on a diamond smuggling case.'

'What? Here in Nesfield?' I spluttered with amazement.

'I've already told you more than I should,' replied the Scotland Yard man. And despite my continued probing, he remained as tight lipped as a mussel in cold water.

TWENTY-FOUR

~

The next morning I was setting out across the cathedral close from my rooms when a window opened behind me and a head appeared. It was the sullen and grumpy Henry Beard, whose mission in life appeared to be providing a dark cloud to cover any sunshine that happened to be about at the time.

'Morris,' he called, 'can you spare me a minute?'

I said I could, and I did—mounting the front steps to his terrace house.

'Come inside, come into the study,' said Beard, trying, and failing, to be uncharacteristically hearty and welcoming.

As I strolled into his study I remarked, 'This place is certainly a mess.'

'I'm not much at housekeeping,' Beard admitted.

'Pity your wife's away,' I said, remembering he'd said she was off visiting relatives. 'She'd tidy this up in no time.'

Beard grunted in reply, but I wasn't really listening. I was surveying the shelves of his study and noticing something I hadn't seen before. I suppose I hadn't been in this room for more than a minute at a time in the past, but now I had the chance to look around.

The shelves were loaded with sporting trophies. All shapes and sizes of dusty monuments to past triumphs stood as mute testimony to Henry Beard's surprisingly athletic past. At least, it surprised me.

'Very impressive,' I said, pointing to the load of cups and shields that Beard had won as a young man. They were now collecting dust, grime and mildew and were sadly neglected, but there were certainly a lot of them.

'From before the war,' said Beard quietly, almost through clenched teeth. 'When I came back I was no longer very interested . . .' His voice trailed away.

'But look at them all: golf, tennis, archery, both long bow and crossbow, middle-distance running, and a fishing competition you seem to have won several times. Pity they're so dusty.'

'Samantha polishes them,' he said, reminding me of his wife's name. 'Or she will when she gets back. But look here, Morris, old chap. That's not what I asked you here to talk about. It's about this added burden, these extra mathematics classes.'

'As I've already explained, that's not my cup of tea. If you want me to teach a class on cross-sections of the cone I'm just not your man.'

'Yes, yes, yes,' muttered Beard impatiently, 'I understand all that. But very basic arithmetic, for the younger boys—you could manage that, couldn't you?'

'Well . . .' I hesitated.

'Look here,' urged Beard, seizing his moment, 'this is the revised timetable old Rogers has just brought around. If you could only take the Lower Third in this period here—this week and next week—it would be a small part of the load off my shoulders. And it's very basic, you know. So how about it, old man?'

I peered at the timetable, feeling divided. On the one hand, I felt bad about leaving the hapless Beard thrashing about trying to cope. On the other, I had a horror of trying to teach even the most basic mathematics. Then, as I looked down at the revised timetable, the light dawned and the weight rolled off my shoulders.

'Beard, old chap, that's when I take the Fourth for poetry. See—there's the class. It's a clash. I'm afraid I can't help you. Sorry about that.'

I added the last words as a look of devastated disappointment began on Beard's forehead and slowly crept over the remainder of his face—like a tide washing down a beach. When the entire acreage of his visage was thus covered, he lost interest in me and ushered me out as quickly as he decently could.

At the foot of the steps leading down from Beard's terrace I encountered the Head Master.

'Ah, yes, just the man I want to see,' said Dr Rogers, his distinguished head of thick white hair ruffling in the breeze as he spoke. 'I'm just in the process of assigning tasks to each of the masters for Speech Night.'

First school was about to begin and the cathedral close was filled with a gaggle of schoolboys trooping off to their first classes for the day. Some appeared eager—the swots, I suppose—while most ambled along, the snail-like stragglers more interested in talking to each other than getting into their classrooms on time.

'Now the task I'd like you to look after, Mr . . .' The Head's voice trailed away.

'Morris—Tom Morris,' I prompted.

'Of course, of course. You mustn't imagine I'd forgotten, Mr Morris. Oh, no, no, no. I'm not a man who forgets. Now, where was I up to? I was just saying—'

'What my task would be on Speech Night.'

'Ah, yes, of course, exactly. Now I've put you down to supervise the junior school. You are to ensure that all the junior forms are seated in the cathedral by a quarter to the hour—that should be well within your capacity, I imagine.'

The cathedral church, which loomed over our shoulders as we spoke, served as the school's assembly hall, as well as the school's chapel and the mother church of the diocese.

'Not a problem, sir,' I replied brightly. 'I'll see to it.'

'Excellent, excellent.'

The Head raised his noble chin and sailed off across the close with all the dignity of a flag-bedecked battleship cruising into a harbour.

I turned around to discover that Jack and Warnie had turned up at my elbow.

They were just heading out to take a morning walk along the banks of the River Ness. Jack was sniffing the fresh morning breeze with delight and eager to get started, but Warnie wanted to give me a blow-by-blow account of his darts match of the night before.

'Close fought thing, old man, very close. Went right down to the wire,' he said, puffing out his moustache. 'But I nailed him in the end. You see, what happened was . . .'

Warnie's charming voice, soft and mellow, rolled on as my attention drifted to the clusters of schoolboys still hurrying across the quad, now close to being late for their classes.

'We were level pegging at this point, you see . . .' Warnie was saying as McKell came out of his flat and began walking briskly across the close.

'. . . which gave him an extra fifty points,' Warnie was explaining. 'Then with my last missile I hit the twenty *in the triple ring*! Sixty points! Won again. How about that, young Morris?'

A smile as wide as the Strand spread across Warnie's face, so I clapped him on the shoulder and told him that he'd done brilliantly.

McKell was now approaching and I saw there was something odd about his appearance.

As he drew nearer I realised what it was—he had a black eye! And not just an ordinary black eye but a real whopper, with significant swelling that was turning a vivid purple colour. We all stared. It was unavoidable. It was like looking at a familiar landscape and discovering that a mountain had popped up in the middle distance overnight.

We three were standing immediately in the path he was taking across the close, so he could hardly ignore us.

He came to a halt, nodded good morning and was about to proceed when I said, 'What on earth's happened to your eye, McKell?'

His face crumpled into a sour expression.

'It's nothing significant,' he said.

'That's such a rich purple,' Jack said playfully, 'it's almost Episcopal.'

'Quite a blow you've had there, old chap,' murmured Warnie sympathetically.

'I had a fall, that's all,' McKell said through clenched teeth, clearly irritated that he had to offer any sort of explanation. 'Nothing serious. A small tumble. It'll clear up in a day or two.'

Then as he brushed past us and continued on his way I realised that he also had a cut down the side of his face and what looked like a graze on his chin.

As the Deputy Head moved out of earshot, I turned to Jack and Warnie and said, 'Now that's odd. In fact, it's very odd.'

'What's so odd about it?' Jack asked.

'McKell,' I explained, 'is a mountain climber. If there's one man in the school with an excellent sense of balance, one man who shouldn't have a fall—or a fall as serious as this one appears to be—it's McKell.'

TWENTY-FIVE

~

Just then a small boy came scuttling out of the archway, hurrying towards the schoolrooms, with his cap askew on his head and his blazer flapping open as he hurried along. He was hurrying like a cockroach that has just heard the dreaded step of the pest exterminator on the stairs.

It was, I saw, young Stanhope—clearly once again running late for first school. His arms were loaded with books, and every few steps he dropped one and had to stop to pick it up. Which was how Conway and Wynyard caught up with him, although they only appeared to be sauntering with their hands in their pockets, entirely heedless of whether they would be late for class or not.

Wynyard stepped forward and scooped up the Latin dictionary that had fallen from the bundle in young Stanhope's arms.

'This what you're looking for, Toffee Nose?' he sneered.

'Yes, please,' said Stanhope, stepping forward and blinking furiously through his large, round spectacles.

As the younger boy reached out for the dictionary, Wynyard held it high above his head, well out of reach.

'But I'm not sure if I should return it to you or not. What do think, Conway? Should I give this little squirt his dictionary?'

'Well . . . just let me think about that for a moment,' Conway snarled unpleasantly as he rested his chin on his hand in a schoolboy impersonation of Rodin's Thinker.

'Give me that dictionary,' demanded Stanhope furiously. 'I need it for second school.'

Wynyard held out the book as if to offer it to the smaller boy, but as soon as he reached for it, threw it to Conway.

'Now let me see what it is,' said Conway, turning the book over in his hand. 'Latin? You don't need a book on Latin, little Toffee Nose—you need a book on cricket. We got a wonderful laugh out of your performance at the nets, didn't we, Wynyard?'

'It was a hoot,' chortled the other of the two School Bounders. 'So it's time you gave up on Latin and starting swotting cricket, little Lord Muck.'

'Give me back my book!' demanded Stanhope, stamping his foot furiously.

'Then come and catch it,' taunted Wynyard.

Conway and Wynyard then started throwing the Latin dictionary back and forth as Stanhope ran from one to the other, trying fruitlessly to catch the book in mid-flight.

I had watched this entire performance with increasing annoyance and now decided it was time for me to intervene.

'Hey! You boys!' I called out as I walked over to bring an end to this unpleasant farce. 'Why aren't you in class? First school is about to begin.'

Thus distracted, the two Bounders took their eyes off the book they had been juggling back and forth and it landed with a solid thud on the cobblestones of the cathedral close.

'Conway and Wynyard, report to my study after third school. I'll think of some suitable punishment for you. Now get off to class.'

'Yes, sir,' they both mumbled in surly undertones, and with that they slunk away.

'Stanhope, pick up your book.'

'Yes, sir,' he said as he ran to where the battered tome was lying.

'Has it been damaged?' I asked.

'No, sir,' the boy replied, turning it over in his hands. 'It seems to be intact.'

I turned to go, but I was stopped by the sound of Stanhope's voice behind me.

'Sir,' he said.

'Yes, Stanhope?'

'They are wotters, sir. Conway and Wynyard are wotters of the first order, sir.'

'I can't disagree with you, Stanhope—they are thoroughly unpleasant boys. And they shouldn't be picking on you the way they are.'

'They are wotters, sir,' he repeated. 'And it's not just what they did to me now, sir. I mean at the nets, sir. They twicked me—they gave me a bwocken cwicket bat, sir.'

'Yes, we all saw that, young man,' said Warnie, sympathetically, for he and Jack were still standing by my side. 'We saw how the handle of the bat had been tampered with. A beastly thing to do.'

'Thank you, sir,' replied young Stanhope in his best lord-of-the-manor manner.

'This is Major Lewis,' I said, feeling obliged to make the introductions. 'And this is his brother, my old Oxford tutor, C. S. Lewis—who is to be guest speaker at our Annual Speech Night tomorrow night.'

Stanhope replied in the well-mannered way he had been taught to reply to formal introductions.

Then Warnie said, 'Would you like to get your own back on those two?'

This surprised me, and I wondered exactly what he had in mind. What he was thinking of quickly became clear.

'You don't have the hand-eye coordination to be a batsman, young fellah,' Warnie continued. 'You simply don't have the makings of a Douglas Jardine. However, if I gave you a bit of coaching you just might make a bowler. Now if you succeeded in bowling out Conway or Wynyard—in the nets or in a match—that would be a triumph, wouldn't it?'

Stanhope's young face lit up, and his eyes opened as wide as saucers behind his large spectacles.

'Do you think that's weally possible, Major? Do you think I could do it?'

'I don't see why not,' Warnie responded, beaming at the youngster's enthusiasm. 'It's all a matter of practising the correct wrist action. You and I could set up the stumps down in the nets, and we could both bowl at them. With a bit of time I'm sure I could teach you a few tricks—show you how to turn the ball and put a really devious spin on it.'

'Would you, Major?' Stanhope was now beaming as well. 'Twuly? You are twuly a gentleman as well as an officer.'

Warnie dug into the pocket of the jacket he was wearing and produced a cricket ball. He must have seen my look of surprise, for he explained, 'The ball I was using yesterday, when I was coaching some of the boys. Somehow it ended up in my pocket and I never returned it. But now I think I can put it to good use with this young man here.'

Warnie tossed the ball from hand to hand a few times, then gripped it with his fingers over the top of the curve with the seam parallel to his palm.

Crouching down he said, 'This is the grip for leg spin,

young man. Off spin is easier, feels more natural and can by quite effective. But leg spin, well done, is deadly. That's where the wickets are—in mastering leg spin. Now, if you and I could meet down the nets after third school and before lunch, I could show you . . .'

At these last words Stanhope's face fell.

'But everyone else will be there, watching me,' he said hesitantly. 'Could we get in some secret pwactice please? So that when I bowl to those two beasts, they'll be caught completely by surprise?'

Warnie chuckled and looked at me. 'That would be rather neat justice, wouldn't it?' he said. Turning back to Stanhope he continued, 'But young fellah-me-lad, you've got a class to go to now and I've promised my brother to go for a walk with him.'

Stanhope looked at me, a silent plea in his eyes.

'Very well, Stanhope,' I said reluctantly, 'you are excused from first school. You have one hour to spend with Major Lewis at the nets.'

'Thank you, sir. That's very good of you, sir.'

'Sorry, Jack,' Warnie began.

'Don't think twice. I see the value of what you've got planned,' replied Jack warmly. 'I'll have a walk along the river and up the hill on the far side while you turn this boy into a demon bowler.'

TWENTY-SIX

~

I was excused from school lunch in the hall that day and allowed
to join Jack and Warnie for a midday meal at the Deanery.
Cowper's good wife, Ellen, served a hearty lunch of roast lamb
and potatoes that made the switch from the routine fodder of
the school dining hall rather like switching from a comic book
to Dickens.

'Now, Jack,' I said as I scooped more lamb and gravy onto
my fork, 'how is your investigation going?'

'Explain yourself, young Morris,' Jack demanded in an
imitation of his old tutorial manner.

'Your investigation,' I explained, 'into the mysterious murder
of Dave Fowler.'

Jack chuckled as he replied, 'I am here to lecture, not to
investigate. Sexton Locke strikes me as an intelligent man and
I am quite satisfied to leave the working of the case entirely in
his capable hands.'

'Well said, Mr Lewis,' remarked the Dean. 'It's always best
if we leave these distasteful matters in the hands of the profes-
sionals to clean up.'

'But Jack,' I protested, 'you and I were eyewitnesses to what
appeared to be an impossible murder—and then to the equally
impossible disappearance and reappearance of the murdered

corpse. Have you no curiosity as to how those oddities came about? Or why? Or by whose hand?'

Jack looked thoughtful so I plunged on. 'And we are here, on the spot as it were, in the precincts of the school and the cathedral, in daily contact with the people and the place.'

'Morris is right, Jack, absolutely spot on,' Warnie volunteered. 'You don't lecture until tomorrow night, old chap. In the meantime, you ought to give Inspector Locke a helping hand by applying your giant brain to this puzzling problem.'

Jack didn't respond immediately. Indeed, rather than applying himself to problem solving, he applied himself to his plate of roast lamb and potatoes with increased vigour.

It wasn't until a good deal later, as he was pushing away the empty plate that had contained his bread and butter pudding, that he finally said, 'Very well, young Morris. Do you have your afternoon free?'

'I'm supervising prep at five, but until then I'm at your disposal.'

'Then let us follow the sound advice given to us on another occasion by Inspector Crispin. Namely, that to understand a murder you must first understand the victim.'

'Jolly good!' wheezed Warnie, almost rubbing his hands together with glee. 'Where do we begin?'

By way of reply Jack turned to me and asked, 'Did Fowler have any particular friends? Was there anyone he was close to? Anyone he spent time with? You and he must have been of an age—did he spend much time with you?'

'Now that you mention it, it's odd. Most of the masters are middle aged; only Fowler, myself, Ryan Carleton and Dave Evans, the organist, are on the younger side. But Fowler spent almost no time with any of us.'

'Who did he spend time with then?'

I closed my eyes and concentrated. Casting my mind back, I tried to picture Fowler as I had known him, letting him flash upon the inward eye in as many different situations as possible. Who could I most readily picture him speaking to? Who did he seem to spend time with? Those were the questions I asked myself. And the answer surprised me.

'That's odd,' I muttered. 'When I try to remember Dave Fowler, I seem to most often picture him speaking to McKell.'

'What? Your Deputy Head?' snorted Warnie. 'A rather sour gentleman that one. At least, that's how he strikes me, if you don't mind my saying so. Why would a young man hang around with that grim-faced relic?'

'Let's see if we can find out,' said Jack with a grin on his face.

Which is why, a short time later, Jack, Warnie and I were walking down the corridor towards the Senior Common Room in search of Gareth McKell.

We entered the comfortably furnished room to find History Master Geoffrey Douglas sprawled in a leather-covered armchair marking a pile of essays. He had often told me that he'd rather work in a room with company around him than alone in his flat. Douglas was rather like a large, elderly dog—perhaps an English sheep dog—but definitely a pack animal.

The school nurse, Mary Flavell, was at the coffee table pouring herself a cup of tea, and in the far corner there was someone who was largely invisible behind a copy of the *Times*. But the legs that protruded from beneath the spreading newspaper were legs I recognised. So I walked up and said, 'Afternoon, McKell.'

He lowered the paper, revealing a more fully developed and deeply purple bruise around his eye, glowered at me for a moment, muttered, 'Afternoon, Morris' and went to raise his newspaper again.

But before he could do so, Warnie, in his most affable manner, said, 'Dreadful business this, isn't it? Shockin' business. Oh dear me, yes, just shockin'.'

'What on earth are you talking about?' growled McKell, looking puzzled.

'The murder, of course,' said Warnie, pulling up a chair.

'Oh, that,' spat McKell in disgust. And he would have gone back to his newspaper reading if Warnie had let him. But he didn't.

'Young man,' Warnie continued, 'prime of life and all that sort of thing. Who could have wanted to kill a young chap like that, eh? Got any theories, McKell?'

Common decency compelled the Deputy Head to lower his newspaper and engage with the three of us, who were now seated around him.

'No,' said McKell. 'I have no "theories", as you put it. I leave all of that to police.'

'But he was a friend of yours, wasn't he?' I asked, trying to make my question sound as innocent as possible.

'A friend? Of course not! Whatever gave you that idea?'

'Just that I seem to remember him talking to you rather a lot.'

'He was a pest, I grant you that much,' said McKell. 'He was always hanging around—trying to engage me, or poor Muriel, in conversation.'

His description of his sister as 'poor Muriel' amused me, as my experience had always been that she was a dragon lady who was even more ready than her brother to snap one's head off at the slightest provocation.

'So he was trying to cultivate your friendship, was he?' asked Jack, making the question sound entirely innocent.

'Perhaps,' McKell conceded. 'Perhaps he just wanted company.'

'But you didn't encourage him?' Jack continued.

'He was a nuisance,' grumbled McKell. 'A junior master in his first year? Why did he imagine I might be the least bit interested in him?'

'Well, if you weren't Fowler's special friend,' Jack asked, 'who was?'

McKell rustled his newspaper loudly as a hint that it was time for us to leave him alone, and he was even starting to raise the paper once more as he said, 'Ask Beard. He was always dropping in on poor Henry.'

With that the paper came up and the bruised visage of Gareth McKell disappeared from sight.

Jack, Warnie and I then took off in search of Henry Beard—and this time we struck lucky.

As we stepped out into the cathedral close, Beard and the Head Master were standing in the middle of the cobblestone square engaged in a quiet, but intense, conversation.

At least it was intense on Beard's side. His arms were flapping and his head was nodding back and forth, as if he was engaged in attempting to plead or persuade.

Dr Rogers, on the other hand, was his usual, unflappable self.

We walked across towards to them in time to hear the Head's response to whatever Beard had been saying.

'I'm sorry, Beard,' said Dr Rogers, 'but there's no point in our discussing this matter any further. I simply have no time on my hands to personally pick up any of Mr Fowler's mathematics classes. You know, my dear chap, that I would help if I possibly could. But I am far too busy—far, far too busy. No, I'm very much afraid you will simply have to cope with the load for the next two weeks. I'm quite sure you can do it, my good chap—quite sure.'

With those words, rather like a ship catching the wind in its billowing sail, the Head Master turned and cruised across the square.

TWENTY-SEVEN

~

A red-faced Henry Beard stood there, quivering slightly, then noticed us approaching.

'Still not having any luck then?' I asked before he could turn and flee.

'I'm still stuck with Fowler's classes, if that's what you mean!' he growled in response.

'Oh, ah, poor young fellah,' said Warnie. Then when Beard's eyes opened wide in astonishment, Warnie went on, 'Oh, not you, old chap. Sorry if you thought I meant you. I was thinking about the murder victim. Such a young chappie to die so violently. Terrible business.'

Beard more or less snorted in reply, as if his sole concern was the extra workload he had to carry, with Fowler's death being significant only as the incidental cause of this truly major disaster.

'Did you know him well?' asked Jack affably.

'Know him? Know who?' asked Beard, whose mind was still on other matters.

'The murder victim,' Jack explained.

'Him? No—barely knew him at all.'

'But McKell said that he often dropped in to visit you,' I said.

'Rubbish!' snapped Beard. 'Complete rubbish. McKell's a fool if he's saying things like that. Now if you'll excuse me, I have a mountain of work to do.'

And with those words Beard stalked angrily away across the quad. With his short stature and broad shoulders, his retreating back gave him the appearance of an angry dwarf spoiling for a fight.

'Didn't get too far with him, did we?' wheezed Warnie, puffing out his moustache. 'Where to next, Jack?'

'Morris,' said Jack turning to me, 'whereabouts is the school office?'

'On the ground floor of the Old School building—at the far end,' I replied. 'Why?'

'When he applied for a job here, Fowler must have supplied some references, some information about himself. I wonder if his staff file would tell us anything about the man?'

The school secretary was a lady, now somewhat beyond middle age, by the name of Edith Carter. She had devoted her whole life to the school, and she was known to the boys as a 'soft touch'. When they wanted money for confectionary or comic books, if they went to her with a tear in their eye and a sad story about their latest postal note from home being held up, she almost always came good with a 'loan' of a few pennies, or even, on special occasions, a sixpence.

She looked up from clattering away on her typewriter to say, 'Oh, Mr Morris, what can I do for you?'

I introduced her to Jack and Warnie, and then said, 'As you know, we've spent a lot of time talking to the police about the murder of Dave Fowler.'

'Oh, yes, a shocking business. I do hope the whole matter is resolved very soon, otherwise a shadow will hang over the school—and that would never do.'

'To that end,' said Jack carefully, 'we are doing all we can to assist the police with their enquiries. With that in mind, may we have a look at Mr Fowler's staff file, please?'

A cloud passed over Miss Carter's face as she said doubtfully, 'Well, I'm not sure if—'

Warnie chimed in to say brightly, 'We have just been with the Head Master . . .' He left the sentence hanging as if to imply official approval, without bothering to mention that all we'd had was a brief, chance encounter in the quad.

'Well, in that case,' said Miss Carter. She turned around, slid open a filing drawer and pulled out a manila folder. 'And anyway,' she said as she produced the file, like a magician producing a stout rabbit from a top hat, 'the police have already looked at this and made their notes.'

I took the folder from her outstretched hand and flipped it open. It contained very little. There was a London address for Dave Fowler—presumably the place where he'd been living before coming to the school. There was a letter of application saying he was a graduate of the University of Liverpool, and one letter from a previous employer.

'Only one reference?' Jack asked Miss Carter.

'Well, he was a young man, only at the beginning of his teaching career. In that case one reference is all that can be expected.'

Jack turned the letter of reference over in his hands. It was a single sheet, typewritten. The address at the top said 'Crichton House, Rodwell Regis' and the signature at the bottom said 'Grimstone'. In between were a few brief paragraphs saying only that Fowler was of good character and was an excellent mathematics teacher.

'I knew a chap named Grimstone some years ago,' said Jack thoughtfully. 'There was a Grimstone who was an undergraduate with me. In fact, we were both members of an undergraduate society called the Martlets. He became a schoolmaster. I wonder if it's the same chap? It's a pity I don't have his phone number here—I know I had it once.'

'Ah, but I almost certainly will have it,' huffed Warnie with a cheerful grunt. Then he turned to me and said, 'One of us has to be properly organised, so I keep track of things.'

Out of the top pocket of his coat he pulled a small, thin, black-covered booklet. He opened it up, revealing a long list of names, addresses and phone numbers.

'What's the name again?' he asked, and then began searching for 'Grimstone' in his list. A few moments later he cried triumphantly, 'I'm sure this is it.' He handed the small book over to Jack, pointing, as he did so, to a particular entry.

'Miss Carter,' said Jack, 'may I impose on you once more, please, to make use of your telephone?'

'Certainly, Mr Lewis,' said that agreeable lady. 'The telephone is next door in the Head Master's office. But as Dr Rogers is not there at the moment, I'm sure he wouldn't mind if you used it.'

Jack thanked her effusively and went through the door she held open for him.

He returned five minutes later with a thoughtful look on his face. He thanked Miss Carter for all her assistance and led us outside.

In the corridor he handed the black booklet back to Warnie and said, 'Now that is very interesting. It's the same Grimstone, all right. He seemed pleased to hear from me again, and was happy to answer my questions—until I raised the name of Dave Fowler. Grimstone said he'd never heard of any such man and never employed a teacher by that name. Then, when he learned where I was calling from, he went silent and was reluctant to tell me any more.'

'Do you think he knows any more?' I asked.

Jack said that, yes, he almost certainly did know something that he believed he could not, or should not, pass on.

This was one more puzzle to pile on top of the already complex web of puzzles that were making this murder mystery so utterly inscrutable.

'A forged reference?' I asked as we walked back out into the cathedral close.

'Almost certainly an unreliable and untrue reference,' Jack replied.

'But why?' asked Warnie, his voice filled with exasperation. 'And who was Dave Fowler really? And what was he doing here?'

'And what,' I added, 'does Grimstone know that he won't even tell his old colleague?'

'Well, I never . . . well, I never . . .' Warnie muttered to himself several times. Then he stopped and said, 'I can tell you one thing for nothing—this murder mystery is making my head hurt. I think I need a drink. Shall we walk to the village, Jack?'

TWENTY-EIGHT

~

Later than night, after another evening meal of school sludge, I was sitting alone in my room trying to sort out the confusing, interlocking pieces of an increasingly complicated puzzle.

My mind kept drifting back to our Deputy Head Master, Gareth McKell, and his sister, Muriel. They both had personalities as indigestible as cold toast. But was that sufficient reason to suspect them of involvement in the murder of Dave Fowler?

I was supposed to be preparing a lesson on Matthew Arnold and *Sohrab and Rustum* lay open before me. But I was as restless as Sohrab in the Tartar camp and gave up my fruitless efforts at concentrating on the task at hand. For a while I paced around my study, then I decided that a pint at *The Pelican* might settle my unquiet heart and grabbed my coat.

I emerged into the moonlit cathedral close and came to a halt in the doorway to my terrace house. Standing there in the shadowed stoop, I was facing the flat occupied by the McKells—directly opposite me on the far side of the quad— and what I had come to think of as the 'The McKell Mystery' once again started thumping away at my brain.

I rather fancied walking across, knocking on the door of their flat, fixing them with a frosty glare and demanding,

'Now, then, just what are you two up to, and why did you kill Dave Fowler?'

However, good sense prevailed and I chose not to follow this attractive scenario.

As the moon drifted behind scudding clouds, the door to the McKells flat opened and both brother and sister emerged. They looked around but failed to see me standing as still as a statue in the distant darkness. Then they headed for the gateway leading out of the cathedral close and into the town.

I decided to follow them.

Exactly why I made this decision I couldn't have explained. Except that I felt certain that in similar circumstances Sherlock Holmes would have instructed Watson to 'follow those two suspects, and don't let them out of your sight'. So I chose to follow my Holmesian instincts, and my two suspects.

The night was chill, the clouds were coming and going across the face of the moon—as if uncertain as to where exactly in the sky they were meant to be—and the breeze was rising. My mind went back to the lesson on Alfred Noyes I'd taken my junior form through the week before. The wind had, indeed, become a torrent of darkness among the gusty trees, and the moon now clearly resembled a ghostly galleon tossed upon cloudy seas.

I buttoned up my coat, pulled my scarf out of the coat pocket and wrapped it around my throat.

The McKells had now left the quad, so I slipped as quietly as I could across the cobblestones. At the gateway I stopped and looked ahead.

The mysterious couple were well ahead of me, on their way down Nesfield's high street. As I watched, they passed through the pale patch of light cast by a street lamp. The dim glow, roughly the colour of clotted cream, seemed to penetrate the gloom only some six feet from the lamp and no further.

Keeping a safe distance, I followed.

Now I must admit there is nothing particularly mysterious about walking down the high street of a town in the evening hours in the general direction of the nearest pub. However, I wanted this to be a moment when I uncovered some startling new fact about this pair of—well, the only proper expression was 'suspicious characters'.

I think I was under the influence at the time of a book I had confiscated from a schoolboy a week earlier. It was called *The Purple Gang*, and it involved the hero, a tough detective type, doing a lot of following of suspects down dark streets. I hadn't meant to read the wretched book, of course, but it lay on my desk and tempted me from doing more serious things. Now it came back to haunt my imagination like a ghost that refused to be exorcised, keeping me hot on the heels of the pair ahead of me.

By now the McKells had reached *The Pelican*, where they paused for a moment. Then, to my surprise, they continued just a little further up the high street. One shop on, and well out of reach of even the feeblest of street lamps, they stopped again. And this time they stayed stopped.

As a precaution I crossed to the other side of the street and kept moving silently forward, keeping well within the shadows, until I was directly opposite where they stood. There was no sign of movement on the McKell side of the street, and just as I was trying to make up my mind as to what my next move should be, the town taxi (Geo. Weekes, prop.) trundled slowly past.

In the brief yellow glow of the taxi's headlights I now saw that huddled opposite was not a group of two people but of three. The McKells had been joined by someone. Whoever it was, they were now in whispered conversation with this third party.

This activity I was engaged in was called 'shadowing' suspects in the *Purple Gang* book, and over the next fifteen minutes or so I discovered how chilly and boring this 'shadowing' lark could be.

In fact, I was close to giving up and going back to my nice warm room at the school when there was movement on the footpath opposite. The little group started walking, fairly briskly, up the high street—still moving away from the cathedral.

I followed them on my side of the street until they reached the Nesfield railway station. Here I caught my first glimpse of the third man in the group—and a glimpse was all it was. He was tall and thin, wore a dark overcoat and had a fedora pulled firmly down on his head, the broad brim covering his face with shadow.

At the entrance to the railway station Gareth McKell shook the man's hand. The stranger entered the station while the McKells turned around and retraced their steps back up the street.

I waited until they were gone, then I began to cross the street just as a train pulled in with a wheezing hiss of steam and a clang of steel wheels.

By the time I had crossed the railway footbridge to reach the platform, the guard was raising his flag and the train was about to pull out. The McKells' mysterious friend was clearly already on board, so I failed in my attempt to get a better look at him.

The guard's flag dropped, and with a heavy chuff-chuff-chuffing sound the huge wheels slowly began to turn. As the train pulled out of the platform, I turned and looked at the destination board: the train was headed for London.

I turned around and slowly made my way back up the high street to Nesfield Cathedral School. Had I, as I wanted to think, seen the McKells engaged in something suspicious—some part of their nefarious activities, whatever they might be? Or was this entirely innocent? Had the McKells merely been seeing a friend off on the train?

In the end I decided that reading confiscated books such as *The Purple Gang* was not good for me and went to bed.

TWENTY-NINE

~

The next afternoon the Head Master and the Dean jointly hosted a high tea to officially introduce the school community to the man who was to be their guest speaker that night.

'Mr Lewis is a distinguished Oxford scholar,' the Head was saying as I slipped into the room a little late.

The room in question was the Head Master's large drawing room, and it was filled with staff and members of the board of governors. Also present were Brenda Rogers, the Head Master's wife, young Julia Carleton, Ryan Carleton's wife, and the sour-faced Muriel McKell.

A maid was carefully negotiating her way around the crowded room balancing a tray of sherry glasses, rather like a small pushbike weaving through the traffic in Regent Street. I whipped a glass of sherry off her tray as she passed.

'A very distinguished scholar indeed,' Dr Rogers was rumbling on, addressing himself to a small group of town worthies gathered around him, all of them governors of the school. 'He lectures chiefly on Mediaeval and Renaissance Literature, and he tells me he's been commissioned by the Oxford University Press to write a book on late mediaeval allegory. Oh yes, a most distinguished man—we were very fortunate to get him.'

'And what will he be speaking on?' asked one of the town dignitaries.

'Ah, well, yes, he did tell me, and to be perfectly honest, my dear fellow, I simply cannot recall,' responded the Head with a disarming smile. 'So you'll just have to be here tonight to make the discovery for yourself. Ah, there you are, Sir Edgar—so good to see you again . . .'

With these last words the Head detached himself from his group and sailed through the crowd to greet a middle-aged, military-looking gentleman who was just arriving.

I turned around to find myself part of a small group that included both Jack and Warnie. The latter had seized upon one of our town visitors, also an ex-army man, and the two of them were sharing memories of bad army food.

'The only thing you need to remember,' said Warnie with a chuckle, 'is that the standard army nickname for the base cook was "The Poisoner". That tells you everything you need to know.'

His interlocutor hooted in appreciation of this reminder just as Henry Beard cruised into the orbit of our little group, a sherry in his hand and a grumpy expression in his face.

'I just wish this whole charade would end,' he grumbled, 'so I could get back to my work.'

Knowing I could make no contribution to easing his additional workload, I changed the subject.

'Pity your wife couldn't be here, Beard,' I said. 'I only met her once or twice myself but she struck me as a delightful young woman.'

'She's very shy,' muttered Beard. 'She wouldn't like this sort of bun fight.'

Jack chimed in to ask Beard where his wife was, and he gave the same answer he'd given to me the day before—visiting her sick mother up in Whitby.

'How long has she been gone?' Jack asked.

'A couple of weeks,' mumbled Beard indistinctly. 'She left as soon as news came through that her mother was ill.'

'Nothing serious, I hope,' I said, making polite conversation.

'I don't know,' Beard replied. 'I haven't heard from Samantha since she left.'

We were interrupted by the Head Master, who introduced some local worthies to Jack.

He politely shook hands with them and then turned to the Head and asked if the absent Dave Fowler had been a helpful sort of man on special occasions such as this—in social situations, and helping out with events such as Speech Night.

'Ah, there you touch upon a sore point, Mr Lewis,' replied Dr Rogers, shaking his distinguished grey head sadly. 'Young Fowler was not what one could call a very helpful young man. Your friend Morris here is much more useful.'

'So,' Jack persisted, 'despite the unhappy and dramatic way in which Mr Fowler shuffled off this mortal coil, you will not really miss him?'

Dr Rogers leaned in closer and quietly confided that he found 'young Mr Fowler' to be something of a 'disruptive influence'.

Jack asked in what way, and the Head replied, 'Now that you ask me directly, I can't exactly put my finger on it. But things were never quite settled from the moment Mr Fowler joined the staff. Somehow he seemed to set people's nerves on edge. No one was quite themselves when Fowler was around. To tell the truth, I would have dispensed with his services quite soon after his arrival if that had been a practical step. Of course, what held my hand was the difficulty of finding a replacement quickly.'

The Head then surged off towards another group, to make

his presence felt and to ensure the social wheels were all turning smoothly. I also wandered away and became engaged in desultory conversation with my fellow schoolmasters, who were inclined to grumble at being made to attend these events. Except, as always, for the relaxed Geoffrey Douglas, who seemed to find it all rather amusing, in a detached and remote sort of way.

Shortly after this I saw Jack using the general hubbub to slip way unnoticed and make his escape. I followed, and caught up with him on the steps of the Head Master's house.

'I had done my duty,' said Jack, by way of excuse, 'and I don't really engage in small talk. Hence my quick escape.'

I fell into step beside him, striding quickly across the cathedral close, before we could be spotted and called back, and out through the main gate. There on the road we slowed down and turned towards the river.

'When Warnie was coaching that boy yesterday, I took a walk across the bridge and up that far hill,' Jack said. 'Delightful countryside, and a most enjoyable walk. But that hilltop opposite us is not the peak it appears to be. When you reach the crown, you discover another and higher peak beyond it, and another beyond that.'

I asked him if he'd gone far, and he said he'd walked for an hour and then retraced his steps.

'Talking about retracing steps,' I said, 'can I retrace our steps to our "great debate" on human nature?'

'With pleasure, young Morris, with pleasure,' said Jack as we walked down from the road towards the towpath that ran along the river bank.

'You keep telling me that human nature is not basically good but basically corrupt. Is that correct?'

Jack nodded.

'But where could that come from? It's altruism—caring for each other—that builds communities and therefore that has survival value. How could corruption go on being passed on from one human generation to the next?'

'The Christian answer, of course, is what is called the doctrine of the Fall. It's a good name for a difficult concept. It conveys the notion of starting on a higher level and falling to a lower one.'

'But is there any evidence for what you call the Fall?'

'The evidence can be found in any day's newspaper or any book of human history. You'll recall Chesterton's line— I mentioned it earlier—that the one Christian doctrine that never needs arguing for, because it's so obviously true, is the doctrine of the Fall.'

'But what bit of us is actually corrupted by the Fall— whatever it is?'

'I would think every bit. St Paul talks about the flesh being corrupt, and we all know the experience of what should be normal, healthy appetites being corrupted in unhealthy directions—towards gluttony or adultery or whatever. And we know that our minds can easily be corrupted towards accepting specious arguments for that which we wish to believe. And above all—the heart.'

'What do you mean by the heart?'

'Clearly not the blood pump but rather that inner self that contains out deepest longings.'

'So you say the corruption of human nature functions at that deepest of all levels?' I asked.

'Not just me,' replied Jack . 'Do you trust Jesus as one of the greatest teachers of history? Yes, I know you do, for you've told me so before. Well, Jesus says: "Out of the heart proceed evil thoughts, murders, adulteries, fornications, thefts, false witness, blasphemies." That, young Morris, is why you, and I, and all of us struggle to do what we know we ought to do.'

Here Jack paused while I took in these words, then he added, 'And why we so often do what our conscience, in its best moments, tells us not to do.'

THIRTY

~

When we returned from our walk, we found the shadows lengthening and the cathedral close deserted—except for four boys: Hamilton, Clifford, Redway and Cardew. This was the group known around the school as 'The Famous Four'. They were huddled together like a rugby scrum. They were deep in conversation, and there were worried expressions on all four faces.

When the boys saw us enter the close, they turned and began walking towards us.

As they drew closer, Jack took his leave to go in search of Warnie.

'If I know my dear brother,' he said, 'he'll stay until the last guest is ejected. I had better relieve Dr and Mrs Rogers of his presence so they can get ready for tonight.'

With those words he left, and I turned to the schoolboys who were approaching me.

'Excuse me, sir,' said Hamilton, the leader of the group. 'May we have a minute of your time, please?'

'Yes, of course.'

'It's about young Stanhope.'

'What about him?'

'We think Conway and Wynyard might be planning more trouble for him.'

'They're absolute bounders, both of them,' Redway contributed.

'We've had trouble with them before,' said Clifford.

'When I first arrived they tried to make my life a misery,' Cardew explained. 'Until these other chaps told them where to get off, that is.'

I couldn't disagree with anything Hamilton and Co. were telling me. I had taken classes in which Conway and Wynyard had sat at the back of the room, not paying attention to the beauties of Wordsworth but trying to flick inked darts at other boys when they thought I wasn't looking.

In any class that contained Conway and Wynyard there was an inherent danger in turning to write on the blackboard, because that meant having one's back to the class. And the moment the teacher's back was turned, those two seemed to think they had a licence to indulge their baser instincts.

In fact, in my 'great debate' with Jack about human nature, if Jack had known of the pattern of behaviour displayed by Conway and Wynyard, he would probably have trotted them out labelled 'Exhibit A for the prosecution'. It certainly appeared to be the case that 'the corruption of human nature' of which Jack spoke was paraded—with trumpets and drums and all flags flying—in their conduct.

'My estimate of the character of those two,' I said to the Famous Four, 'is exactly the same as yours. But I take it you have some specific concern?'

'We suspect, sir,' Hamilton replied, 'that those two are planning to come down on young Stanhope rather like the wolf on the fold.'

'But unlike the Assyrians,' said Clifford, 'their cohort won't be gleaming in purple and gold. In fact, there'll be nothing open or obvious about whatever attack they're planning on young Stanhope.'

'They are not only bounders, sir,' Hamilton explained, 'they are also sneaks.'

'But why their special focus on young Stanhope?' I asked.

'It's the young blighter's own silly fault,' Cardew said. 'He keeps going on about his Pater, and about his family estates and so on. He's still young, sir. Give him another year and he'll get over that and be just one of the school.'

'But in the meantime,' I said, 'you think that Conway and Wynyard are planning something to take him down a peg or two.'

All four boys nodded in agreement.

'You surprise me,' I admitted. 'We saw the incident at the nets, with the cricket bat that snapped in two. And we all had no doubt that Conway and Wynyard had tampered with the handle. But surely they've had their triumph now. Why would they launch another attack on the same small boy?'

I was genuinely puzzled. Both in my short time at school-mastering and in my memories of my own school days, it seemed to me that the pattern of behaviour—for there was a Conway and Wynyard in every school—was to plague one boy for a while and then move on to the next victim. Surely, I thought, Conway and Wynyard had had their fun with young Stanhope, so why weren't they moving on to some other game?

'It seems that at the cricket nets, sir,' Hamilton explained, 'Stanhope got all the sympathy. Conway and Wynyard, and their few friends, all hooted with laughter, but the rest of the school didn't join in.'

'We have the impression, sir,' said Clifford, 'that those two villains feel they didn't win on that occasion—and so they intend to try again.'

'I see. Do you have any idea what they might be up to this time?'

A worried look was exchanged by the Famous Four. Then Hamilton said, 'We fear they're planning something more serious this time, sir.'

'Serious? In what sense?'

'It may be that rather than just trying to make Stanhope a laughing stock, they are planning to get him into serious trouble,' Hamilton explained.

'Possibly serious enough to get him sent down,' Redway added.

That was a worry. If Conway and Wynyard were intending to trap young Stanhope into something that would result in his expulsion from Nesfield Cathedral School, that was serious indeed.

'Are you sure about this?' I asked.

Four faces looked slightly uncomfortable until Cardew explained, 'We weren't snooping, sir. It's just that I'm shorter than the high windows in the Old School building, so Conway and Wynyard couldn't see me passing when they were standing at the window talking about their plot.'

'What did you hear?'

'Not much, sir,' Cardew admitted. 'Just a few words, really. But enough to make me think they're planning to steal something and plant it on Stanhope.'

I shook my head in disgust at the grubby villainy of the two School Bounders.

'So I told the others, sir,' Cardew resumed, 'and Hamilton said we should tell you.'

'Why did you pick me?' I asked Hamilton. 'There are other more experienced masters.'

'We've noticed that you've been keeping an eye on him, sir—on the sufferings of young Stanhope, that is,' Hamilton explained.

For a long moment I was lost in silent thought. Clearly we couldn't let Conway and Wynyard get away with whatever they were plotting. The problem was, we didn't know exactly what that was.

My prolonged silence prompted Clifford to say, 'We did notice, sir, that you stepped in to protect young Stanhope the last time Conway and Wynyard were being unpleasant, so we thought you might be able to suggest something.'

'The problem is that I can't,' I said. And again I lapsed into silence, with my brain racing at a hundred miles an hour.

'Look,' I said at length, 'I'm going to assign you four to a task.'

Four eager faces looked at me.

'Unfortunately it has to be a rather vague task,' I continued. 'Would you four be able to play the role of "guardian angels" to young Stanhope? What I mean by that is simply to be very aware of what Conway and Wynyard are up to, and of what Stanhope is doing that might make him vulnerable. He is capable of being a foolish boy—as I know only too well.'

'I take it you just want us to keep our eyes and ears open, sir?' Hamilton asked.

'That's it exactly,' I said. 'Watch for trouble, and keep me informed. At this stage, I think, that's all any of us can do.'

THIRTY-ONE

~

I went to find Jack and Warnie in their digs at the Deanery. We three were invited to dine at the Head Master's house that evening prior to the big occasion of Speech Night—with the members of the board of governors and their wives also being present at the feed trough with us.

I found Jack in the Dean's sitting room, on his own, reading a well-thumbed copy of *Tristram Shandy*. There was no sign of Warnie.

'He's slipped off to the nets again,' Jack explained, 'to give some more coaching in spin bowling to that young schoolboy. And I have a proposal for you, young Morris.'

'What sort of proposal?'

'We have some time before we need to start changing for dinner, and I would like to spend that time paying a visit to each of the masters in their respective studies.'

I raised an eyebrow as I wondered out loud why. Jack pointed out that I was the one encouraging him to involve himself in the investigation into the impossible murder of Dave Fowler, and this was part of that.

I, of course, readily agreed.

We started with Ryan Carleton, the young Music Master in the school and Choir Master in the cathedral. He and his wife

Julia occupied the top floor of the same terrace house that held the apartment of Henry Beard and his wife, Samantha.

When we approached the front door of the house we found it unlocked and let ourselves in. The ground floor apartment—Beard's—was empty. At least there was no response to our echoing calls asking, 'Anyone at home?'

So we climbed the stairs and found the Carletons' flat to be in a state of cheerful chaos.

'Julia!' Ryan was calling as we knocked on the door. 'Have you seen my other black sock?'

A shouted reply came from an inner room as Carleton opened the door.

'We've obviously come at an inconvenient moment,' I said apologetically.

'Not at all, not at all,' insisted Carleton. 'You've very welcome, as long as you don't mind the mess and the general chaos.'

We stepped into his front sitting room.

'Ryan, would you zip me up, please?' said Julia as she bustled into the room. 'Oh, I'm sorry, I didn't know we had guests.'

'You've met Mr Lewis, haven't you, dear? Oh yes, this after-noon at tea. I'm afraid we're rather at sixes and sevens. Richard and Ellen Cowper invited us to dinner with them tonight, before the big event—seeing as how they were losing you to the Head and his big bun fight with the governors and their wives. What can I do for you?'

'We only wanted to ask about Mr Fowler,' said Jack. 'We're still trying to help the police with their investigation—but this is clearly the wrong time . . .'

'I didn't like him at all,' said Julia Carleton.

'Really? Why not?' Jack asked.

'He was . . . creepy. I know you're not supposed to speak ill of the dead, but he really was creepy . . .'

'Julia!' Carleton protested, sounding shocked.

'Perhaps,' said Jack, 'in the case of murder victims the principle of *De mortuis nil nisi bonum* doesn't apply. Understanding the victim is often the key to understanding the murder.'

Then I chipped in and asked, 'In what way exactly was he "creepy"?'

Julia Carleton suddenly looked doubtful. She glanced at her husband, then slowly said, 'I shouldn't have spoken so quickly. That's always my trouble—I speak before I think.'

'But you had something specific in mind, didn't you?' Jack pressed her.

Again she looked at her husband, who said, 'You might as well tell them. You never know, it might even prove helpful.'

'You mean tell them what I said to you . . . ?'

'Yes, tell them that. The very first time we ever met Fowler,' Carleton said to us, 'the same day we met you, Morris, at the afternoon tea for staff on the first day of term, we came back here and Julia used that same word, "creepy", to describe him.' Then he quickly added, 'But she quite liked you, Morris.'

I said thank you, and then pressed them both again for what lay behind the word 'creepy'.

'Well, what she said was . . .' Carleton began, and then said, 'You tell them dear.'

Julia Carleton hesitated, blushed and then said, 'I told Ryan when we got home that day that I didn't like Dave Fowler because he . . . it was something no man would ever notice, only a woman . . . because, you see, when he looked at a woman . . . he undressed you with his eyes.' Those last few words came out in an embarrassed rush.

'And nothing after that day caused you to change your opinion?' Jack asked.

'Certainly not!' Julia was firm on the matter.

We talked to them for a little longer and then left them to their preparations. As we were going back down the stairs, we could hear Carleton saying, 'Dear, have you seen my collar stud anywhere?'

Henry Beard was still not home, so we headed across the quad to the flat occupied by the odious McKells.

It was the sister, Muriel, who answered our knock. She swung open the door and looked at us as if we were a pair of ill-smelling lepers of whom she was not especially fond. In fact, judging by the look on her face, our appearance at her front door seemed to have given her a sudden toothache.

'Yes?' she demanded, in a tone that implied that if we were drowning she'd throw rocks at us.

'Sort of a social visit,' I began, smiling and trying to counter the chill in the air.

'And to ask about Fowler,' Jack added. 'The murder investigation is continuing, and we are doing our bit to help.'

This was greeted by a long silence, eventually broken by Muriel McKell saying—in a voice like a buzz-saw attacking a piece of rotten timber—'We can't help you, I'm afraid.' She didn't sound afraid. She sounded rather pleased to be unable to help. 'And just at the moment we're busy.'

With that she closed the door. She didn't slam it loudly in our faces because this was a polite school in which that sort of thing didn't happen. But she closed it with a swift, silent movement that implied the loud slam we couldn't hear.

Jack and I stood in the corridor looking at each other for a moment, smiled and then started to leave, intending to visit Geoffrey Douglas in his bachelor establishment.

However, when we got to the corner in the corridor, we heard knocking on the door behind us. We turned around and saw Conway and Wynyard trying their luck where we had failed.

I laid a hand on Jack's arm, indicating that we should wait and see what happened.

We were standing in the shadows at the far end of the corridor, and I was intrigued to discover why those two young villains should be knocking at McKell's door.

After a moment the door was opened—not, this time, by Muriel but by our Deputy Head himself.

'Yes?' he demanded curtly.

'Please, sir,' said Conway, 'we thought, that is to say, Wynyard and I thought, that perhaps you'd like us to clean your hiking boots for you, sir.' Since there was no immediate response he added, by way of explanation, 'The ones you brought back from your last trip, sir.'

'No,' snapped McKell impatiently. 'Just clear off, the both of you.'

Then he swung the door swiftly closed and the two School Bounders slunk away into the distance.

'What was that all about?' Jack asked.

'There's an end-of-term exam next week,' I explained, 'that McKell is setting. I suspect those two, who have wasted most of the term not studying, are trying to curry favour with him.'

'Given the man's personality, an impossible task, I would have thought,' Jack commented.

'Quite correct,' I agreed. 'But desperate schoolboys will try anything.'

THIRTY-TWO

~

When we arrived at our History Master's flat, we were welcomed in and offered brandy. While fetching glasses and finding a bottle of Napoleon, Geoffrey Douglas expressed his hearty dislike of all school speech nights, and all formal occasions in general, and his intention of putting off getting ready for the coming 'awful event', as he called it, for as long as possible.

Hence he entered into the game of answering our questions enthusiastically.

'What did I make of Fowler?' he asked, scratching his chin. 'It's a good question, mainly because I don't have any real answer. I found him to be something of an enigma.'

'In what way?' Jack pressed.

Douglas was silent for a while, puffing on his pipe, and finally said, 'He never gave anything away, if you understand what I mean. Everyone else on the staff, even our ice-cold Deputy Head McKell, will occasionally illustrate an argument or make a point by telling an anecdote from their own experience. Fowler never did that.'

He continued to puff away in silence for a while. Jack joined him and lit up his own pipe while waiting patiently for the next revelation.

'Fowler was like a man who was blank,' said Douglas at last. 'He never mentioned family, or friends, or his university, or previous employment, or hobbies, or sports he played. I spend a lot of time in the Senior Common Room—I'd rather work there than here in isolation. And in all that time I can't remember Fowler ever telling us anything about himself. That's why I call him an enigma.'

Jack pursued this line for a while, drawing out further details from Douglas, but all in the same vein—namely, that, for Douglas, Dave Fowler was an unknown quantity.

This thought had never occurred to me until I heard Douglas say it aloud, but the moment he did, it rang a bell. As I looked back I realised with a shock that I had never heard Fowler tell us anything about himself.

Leaving Geoffrey Douglas to his pipe, his brandy and his leisurely preparation for the evening, we made one final attempt to visit Henry Beard.

This time he was at home and he let us in in response to our knock. His manner was again impatient and sullen. He looked like an ill-tempered tapeworm that had just received bad news in the post.

Once again he showed us into his untidy, cluttered study, where he had to remove a pile of essays from one chair and books from another to give us somewhere to sit.

Jack drew attention to Beard's vast and impressive, if somewhat dusty, collection of sporting trophies, just as I had done on my last visit.

As a way of making conversation, I asked Beard if he had kept any of his sporting equipment, and by way of answer he threw open a cupboard which proved to be packed with golf clubs, fishing lines and all the rest of the equipment the trophies referred to.

Anxious to get beyond small talk, Jack said, 'I'd like your honest and frank opinion, please, Mr Beard. What did you make of the dead man, Dave Fowler?'

'Not much,' Beard shot back quickly. Then he added after a longish pause, 'I suppose he struck me as a bit of a low-life . . . an untrustworthy man lacking in decency.'

And although Jack pressed him to expand on this for the next few minutes, that was all Beard was prepared to say.

As we were leaving, Jack noticed a photograph of Beard and his wife on the hall table and remarked, 'She's looks to be a lot younger than you.'

To which Beard only said that he got married later in life than most men—because of the war, he said. Then he urged us to leave as he had to get changed.

I left Jack at the Dean's front door and went back to my rooms to put on my dinner jacket.

The dinner itself was one of those affairs best passed over in silence. Warnie turned up in full dress uniform, which made the dinner jackets worn by Jack and myself almost shabby by comparison. Dr Rogers was most impressed by the display of medals and brass buttons and the crown indicating his rank. He immediately decided to shift Warnie up several places in the rows of dignitaries to be seated at the front of the cathedral during the official proceedings.

The conversation over dinner was of the kind that Jack always labelled dull. There was no talk of literature, no challenging ideas, no wit and no word play. So Jack applied himself to his meal and made such polite remarks as were required of him.

Dinner ended with coffee and cigars. Then the Head dispatched me on my way to take care of my assigned task of rounding up the junior school, while the official party made their leisurely way to the robing room at the rear of the cathedral, from where they would, in due course, process down the main aisle.

I went back to my room to drape my academic gown over my dinner jacket, and then began rousing the boys out of the junior school dormitories.

The more responsible boys, the floor monitors, had already done their job of chivvying the lads along and making sure they were dressed neatly in full school uniform in time for my summons to gather in the quad.

In the corridors of the dorms the boys were scurrying around me, and order was slowly forming out of the chaos, when I looked down and saw young Stanhope at my side.

'Excuse me, sir,' he said, in that half strangulated voice of his that always sounded as if he had a hot potato in his mouth.

'As you can see, Stanhope, I'm busy right now.'

'Just one question, sir,' he persisted.

'As long as it's a quick question.'

'It's about the building going on in the field behind the school.'

'What about it?' I asked impatiently.

'Do they work all night, sir?'

'Of course they don't!' I snapped. And then I stopped and thought again—I had no idea at all what their working hours might be. So I added, 'I don't really know when they work. Why do you ask?'

'One of their trucks woke me up, sir.'

'Really? When was this?'

'Two nights ago, sir. It was in the middle of the night. It was still dark. But it was all right really, because it woke me up from a nightmare.'

Just then Blake, the floor monitor, arrived to announce, 'All the boys are assembled.'

'Very well, Blake—march them downstairs and tell them to line up, in two straight lines, in the cathedral close. And Stanhope—you should be with your class group. Step lively.'

A long, winding snake of boys made its way down the stairs and out into the close. There I ordered them to line up in their Forms, and conducted my own inspection to ensure their uniforms were in order. For small things like unbuttoned blazers the Head had an eagle eye, and I didn't want to get into his bad books.

This done I checked my watch, and then marched them to the cathedral. We halted at the door until the verger, old Ashley Brown, indicated he was ready for us. Then we processed, in a more or less orderly fashion, down the main aisle to the seats, just behind the front rows, reserved for the juniors.

THIRTY-THREE

~

With my boys settled I made a leisurely patrol of the whole cathedral to see that all was in order.

The senior boys were allowed to sit with their parents—those, that is, who had chosen to honour us with their presence for Speech Night. People were still drifting in. The big doors on the town side of the cathedral were standing open, with knots of parents gathering, gazing up and down the vast building looking for their sons. Others were ambling the length of the main aisle and the side aisles, looking for a vacant pew with enough room for their (often large) families.

I made my way down the full length of the main aisle to the back of the building. Here the door to the robing room was standing open and the Head Master was watching the crowd slowly gathering.

'Everything in order, Mr Morris?' he asked. I was impressed that he appeared to have learned my name at last.

'The juniors are all settled, Head Master,' I replied. 'And I have the floor monitors seated at the end of each pew to keep an eye on them.'

'Jolly good, jolly good,' he murmured, then something else seemed to cross his mind and he wandered off deeper into the robing room. His place at the door was taken by Jack, now with his Oxford academic gown draped over his dinner jacket.

'All prepared?' I asked. By way of reply, Jack patted the jacket pocket that contained the text of his speech.

'How long before we begin?' he asked.

I looked at my watch and told him at least ten minutes, possibly fifteen.

'Then I'm going to take the weight off my feet,' he said as he lowered himself into the vacant back pew. I sat down beside him.

'I think I agree with Geoffrey Douglas,' I said. 'I'm not overly fond of these big events, these formal occasions. At least, not in my role as a schoolmaster—too many small boys to keep an eye on all at once.'

Jack asked, with a mischievous twinkle in his eye, if I thought he could get away with smoking his pipe in the cathedral. Then he chuckled with delight at the shocked expression on my face.

'Human nature can't be basically bad,' I said, to steer the conversation in other directions. 'Look at those small boys from the junior school. They're full of energy and always hard to control, but tonight they're on their best behaviour and sitting quietly—no doubt bored to their back teeth, but doing as they're told and waiting for the show to begin.'

'That, my dear Morris, is exactly the point,' Jack responded. 'It's discipline and the rule of law that makes human behaviour orderly and decent. Take that away and pride and selfishness take over, and, inevitably, the strong exploit and hurt the weak.'

'This is, I take it, that bizarre doctrine you call "the Fall",' I remarked, finding it hard to keep the sneer out of my voice.

'Not I, young Morris—the whole of classical, mainstream Christianity. The Fall is at the heart of the Christian explanation of why the world is the way it is, and why human nature is the way it is.'

'Very well then, explain the Fall to me,' I challenged.

'In effect I've already done so—when you and I read Milton's *Paradise Lost* together in tutorials. You'll recall that in the poem Milton simply follows Saint Augustine, who in turn says what the church as a whole believes.'

'Yes, I remember you making me read *De Civitate Dei* to understand Milton!' I complained.

'And thereby expanded your intellectual horizons,' said Jack with a warm smile.

Then he continued, 'God, Milton tells, created all things good—everything, without exception. Which is why, in the world around us today, there is much that is good, much that we can delight in, much that gives us joy. But the sad truth is that this world is not good enough.'

'How does the Fall explain that?'

'Because Good is a positive while Bad is a negative. Bad is the absence of Good. The Fall might be thought of as the Great Subtraction—the negative action withdrawing Good from human hearts and from the human world.'

I waited patiently until Jack resumed—as always, weighing each word carefully.

'The Fall consists of disobedience—of human beings withdrawing themselves from the ultimate Good, from God. The Fall was humanity rejecting the notion of being subject to God by rebelling against God's authority. The Fall was the human race's cosmic cry of "No!"—the Great Negation, the Great Subtraction, that brought Bad out of Good.'

We fell into silence at this point—Jack watching me keenly while my mind was racing. Around us was the hushed murmur of people finding their places in the cathedral, but within, upon the 'inward eye' as Wordsworth put it, I was seeing a much bigger picture.

'One way of putting it would be to say that the Fall broke the supply chain,' Jack continued. 'Warnie could explain how an army depends on its supply chain. And we broke our "supply chain".'

Jack pulled the papers containing his talk out of his pocket, contemplated them for a moment and then said, 'By rejecting God's authority over him, man lost his own authority over all that he should be controlling: including his emotions, his mind and his own body. Look down the length of this cathedral, Morris, and imagine the authority of the school over those young boys ceasing to exist and being replaced by anarchy.'

'Unpleasant thought.'

'Unpleasant for you as a master—but, in the end, also unpleasant for the boys themselves. Anarchy would, in the long run, deliver more pain than pleasure. It would be a case not just of the punishment fitting the crime, but of the crime and the punishment actually being the same thing. That's what happened in the Fall. Our primeval parents desired anarchy by rejecting God's authority. And God allowed them to have it.'

In silence I chewed this over until Jack resumed by saying, 'The anarchic world that resulted was a world in which the Good was marred by the Bad—in which the Great Subtraction of the Fall "hollowed out", so the speak, both human nature and the human world. The garden ceased to be Eden and became, in Milton's words, "these wilde Woods forlorn". It was disobedience driven by pride that gave us all the fallen, corrupt human nature we now have.'

'Pride?'

'Our primeval parents were too big for their boots. Their disobedience consisted of announcing that "No one tells me what to do, not even God". Addison says somewhere that "the great moral which reigns in Milton is the most universal and most useful that can be imagined, that Obedience to the will of God makes men happy and Disobedience makes them miserable". That explains the corruption of human nature. That explains those ghastly bounders Conway and Wynyard. But it also explains the snobbery of young Stanhope, and it explains you and me, Morris.'

'Us?'

'The prosecuting attorney at our trial before the High Court of Heaven, Morris, will be our own conscience. This is the dazzlingly simple fact about human nature.'

The Head Master opened the door of the robing room and beckoned.

As Jack rose to go he said, 'Conscience does not, as Hamlet would have us believe, make cowards of us all—it makes convicts of us all. It convicts us of our faults of pride and disobedience. The truth is that the human heart is not now as it once was. The fact of disobedience, driven by pride, has produced corruption.'

THIRTY-FOUR

~

The Head Master now stood beside us, interrupting our conversation. As he and Jack walked away, I heard Dr Rogers say, 'We're about to begin, Mr Lewis.' Then he turned and looked at me and said, 'And Mr Morris, would you do a final sweep of the cathedral close please, and the school buildings, so as to ensure there are no boys lurking elsewhere who should be here?'

Jack took his place beside the Head Master in the procession down the aisle while I made my way through the north door into the chill evening air outside. Walking quickly across the quad, I entered the dormitory building and checked both floors, finding them completely deserted. Next I mounted the stairs to the Old School and walked swiftly down one corridor after another. I pushed open closed doors and glanced into every study cubicle. Every wing of the building I found to be empty.

It appeared that even the School Cads and Bounders had fallen into line and joined the rest of the student body in the cathedral.

Coming back down the stairs from the Old School, I found myself on the far side of the quad, facing the cathedral across the empty expanse in between.

The cathedral itself was glowing with light, and I could hear the school hymn being sung as I stepped out into the cool evening air. Between me and the cathedral building was an ocean of darkness—deep purple shadows fading to utter blackness in corners and crevices.

The cloud cover was heavy that night, and a thin sliver of moon made only fleeting appearances. The quad presented the appearance of shadow falling upon shadow, like waves rolling upon each other on a low shoreline.

I began to make my slow way around the close, doing a thorough job of the 'final sweep' that I had been asked to do. Slowly my eyes adjusted to the blackness of the night, and I could just make out the slinking form of the cathedral cat slipping through the town gates—presumably bent on a night on the tiles.

The cat's name was Alfred—short for Alfred the Great. This name was bestowed upon him in recognition of his gigantic size. Alfred was pampered—and, more significantly, fed—by the Dean and his wife (the theoretical owners of the feline) as well as by the staff in the school kitchen and most of the boys. The result was a cat that waddled even when it slinked.

I won't say that Alfred was the fattest cat in Christendom, but he would certainly have been in the running for the title. In fact, any halfway decent bookie would have given good odds on his winning.

Alfred was a cat with secrets. He certainly believed himself to be vastly superior to the mere humans that surrounded him. I always thought it was a pity cats don't have eyebrows, since that would have allowed Alfred to look sarcastically at the rest of us from behind lowered eyebrows.

And there he was, slinking, in a wobbling sort of way, in the direction of the town, probably, I thought, intending a bohemian night of debauchery interspersed with occasional fights which Alfred—as the heavyweight in the scrap—would easily win.

I was standing in the shadows in front of the Head Master's house as these thoughts trickled idly through my mind. They were interrupted by a slight noise from the far side of the quad.

I turned and stared into the purple shadows, looking for any sign of movement. I kept very still and very quiet for what felt like half a lifetime. And then I was rewarded. I saw a dark figure move cautiously in front of the dorm building opposite, slinking in front of the windows; slinking not with an Alfred-like waddle, but in a sleek and surreptitious way.

At least, this is what I imagined I saw.

The moon and clouds were not really helping much at that point, the moon having faded as if its batteries were running down, and the little illumination it provided being obscured by patches of cloud, rather like gloved fingers covering a lantern.

Then there was another sound. It was not much of a sound—merely the scraping of leather on cobblestones—but it was enough.

Rather than reveal myself by walking boldly across the intervening space and demanding 'Who's there?', I decided to embark on an undercover operation.

Keeping close to the buildings, in the deepest and darkest of the shadows, I began moving cautiously in the direction of the scraping sound and shadowy movement opposite.

As I moved I lifted my feet and employed the 'cat-like tread' so well described by Mr Gilbert.

I reached the place where I thought there had been an intruder and found—nothing.

But I was certain that someone had been there and I had just missed them. I was standing quite close to the windows of McKell's flat. Perhaps, I reasoned, the intruder (or intruders—could there have been more than one?) had avoided me by slipping into the building.

I followed.

The corridors of the dormitory building were brightly enough lit and I blinked as I stepped in out of the dark. A quick patrol back and forth showed the ground floor to still be completely deserted. Then I checked out the floor above.

Which is how I came across a closed study door (odd— I thought I had opened all the study doors a short time before) with the sound of whispered voices coming from behind it.

Stepping forward silently, I stood and listened, trying to pick up the thrust of the indistinct conversation. But the conspirators were speaking far too softly for this to be possible.

At one point I thought I heard the word 'paper' but nothing else.

So I pushed the door open and discovered—huddled in secret conference—the odious Conway and Wynyard.

'What are you two doing here?' I demanded ferociously.

Their mouths opened, flapped a bit and then fell silent without uttering a syllable.

'You both know where you should be—in the cathedral. I'll speak to you about your punishment tomorrow. In the meantime, get a move on. Now!'

I almost barked the final word, and Conway and Wynyard stood up and took off like a pair of startled rabbits who'd just heard the local poacher loading his shotgun.

I looked around the deserted study they had left behind. Was there any clue here to what devious plan they might be plotting? I could see nothing but a jumble of untidy school books and half-completed assignments.

I could hear their footsteps clattering hurriedly down the stone staircase. I followed them, still deep in thought. Had it been these two I had caught a possible glimpse of in the cathedral close—suspiciously close to the windows of McKell's flat?

If so, what had they been up to? Had I come across them at the beginning or end of their scheme?

And what had that whispered conversation meant? What 'paper' had they been talking about? And where had they been when I'd conducted my main search of the school buildings?

It was with a head full of questions rather than answers that I hurried out of the building, intent on taking my assigned seat in the cathedral.

THIRTY-FIVE

~

I caught up with Conway and Wynyard at the foot of the stairs and marched them across the darkened quad.

'What were you two talking about in there?' I asked. 'I heard the word "paper" mentioned—what paper?'

Conway and Wynyard looked at each, and I realised I was not about to get the truth. It was the glance of co-conspirators desperately trying to work out where to go with this.

'It was a piece of paper, sir,' said Wynyard.

'Yes, I'd worked out that much,' I responded sarcastically.

'It was a paper that . . . that had . . .' mumbled Conway, trying to extemporise inventively, '. . . that had . . .'

'His sister's address on it,' offered Wynyard with a stroke of inspiration.

'I see,' I said, coming to a halt and putting my hands on my hips. 'You wanted to write to your sister and you'd forgotten your own address, is that it?'

'Yes, sir . . . I mean, no, sir . . .' Conway fumbled, failing to catch the ball that had been flicked to him.

'It was his married sister, sir. He had her new address on a piece of paper,' volunteered Wynyard, his brain working a little faster than his colleague's.

'That's right, sir,' yelped Conway, gleefully seizing the rope that had been flung to him. 'My married sister, sir. Her new address, sir. And I'd lost it somewhere in the study. And we were looking for it, sir. So I could write her a letter, sir.'

'About what?'

This produced a blank stare, and then a jumble of words, 'Oh, just about . . . well, school . . . and what I'd been doing . . . and that sort of thing, sir.'

'When you were supposed to be in the cathedral for Speech Night?'

This reminder generated no reply but made both Bounders pick up their pace and hurry into the cathedral.

Wynyard mumbled, 'We're late, sir,' over his shoulder as they fled.

I went in after them.

As I took my seat—at the back so as not to disturb anyone— the Head Master was just introducing Jack.

'As I'm sure many of you will know,' he was saying, 'Mr Lewis is one of the most distinguished scholars of Medi-aeval and Renaissance Literature at Oxford University. We are most fortunate to have him with us tonight. And I call upon Mr Lewis to deliver his talk, which, he tells me, is entitled "Reflections on education with special reference to the teaching of English in the upper forms of schools". Mr Lewis . . .'

There was a polite rattle of applause as Jack stepped up to the lectern.

As always Jack seized his audience's attention at once and kept it with the vigorous rumble of his voice, his carefully chosen words and the intelligent gleam in his eye.

For me it was a delight to be hearing Oxford's best lecturer once again. For a moment I drifted away as I realised how much I'd missed hearing Jack speak to an audience like this. Then

I shook myself into consciousness again, to focus on what he was saying.

And it turned out to be about Natural Law—those basic moral principles knowable by all people, and written upon all hearts. With great clarity, and with common sense, he defended the existence of an objective moral code that applies at all times, in all places and in all cultures.

He supported this by quoting not only from the Ancient thinkers Plato and Aristotle, and the Christian thinkers Augustine and Aquinas, but also from eastern thinkers such as Confucius and the sages of Hinduism.

He spelled out the common thread that ran through them all—the thread that used common sense and uncommon wisdom to draw upon the same universal, objective moral code.

Then he took deadly aim at some of the English textbooks used in the upper forms of our schools. These, he said, often set out to undermine the objective, universal morality of the Natural Law.

As he spoke I remembered a philosophy lecture I'd heard at Oxford, promoting a concept called 'emotivism'—the idea that all moral statements were just expressions of an emotion. Praising something as morally good, or condemning it as morally bad, is nothing more—said the lecturer on that occasion—than a grunt of pleasure or a growl of pain. There was no rational content to any moral utterance, he told us. This struck me as an odd, and possibly dangerous, idea at the time.

Jack hammered home his case that moral relativism is, in the end, self-defeating. The moral relativist can never protest to the friend who lies to him or cheats him that such actions are 'morally wrong' since he has reduced all moral judgments to mere subjective sentiments.

Then Jack targeted the textbooks that taught exactly these ideas. These books, in sly and suggestive ways, he said, were debunking objective moral virtues such as courage and honour as nothing more than meaningless sentiments that may change from time to time and from culture to culture.

The damage this does to the younger generation was Jack's real concern. These destructive textbooks fail the purpose of education, he said, because they fail to link the great timeless moral virtues to those proper emotions, found in great literature, that will encourage the younger generation to resist their base appetites and take responsibility for each other and for preserving what is best in human society.

The result, Jack suggested, would be a civilisation that had ceased to be a flourishing, growing garden and had become instead a bunch of cut flowers on display in a vase. Cut off from the soil that nourishes them, flowers will eventually wither and die—and that, he said, is what will happen to our civilisation if we cut off the virtues of decent living from the soil of Natural Law out of which such virtues grow.

The result would be a new generation from which we could never demand—or expect—decent civilised behaviour.

Teaching moral relativism makes moral behaviour impossible.

It would be like, he said, castrating a ram—turning it into what sheep farmers call a 'wether'—and then sending it into a field full of ewes and telling it to breed. Without an objective moral foundation, the virtues of decent living become barren and die.

Hinting, I thought, at the rising shadow of Hitler in Germany, Jack said that, without timeless morality and objective truth, everything is reduced to a struggle for power. We end up in Hobbes' famous 'state of nature' where the powerful rule over, and exploit, the powerless. And in such a state, as

Hobbes said, 'the life of man is solitary, poor, nasty, brutish, and short'.

Jack concluded that we must stop using textbooks in the senior school that claim to 'explain away' all our rational moral instincts. Such 'explaining away' ends with nothing left to explain, and with the whole notion of explanation becoming a hollow mockery.

As Jack sat down, applause rippled across the building. Looking at the faces of our senior boys, I thought they looked interested and startled by what they'd just heard. Their parents, however, tended to look more puzzled than anything else— interested but puzzled. Perhaps, I thought, they'd get their sons to explain it to them later.

Various votes of thanks followed, and the evening concluded with us all rising to sing the national anthem. I was pleased to discover that during my sweep of the school buildings I had missed the whole of the dreary presentation-of-prizes part of the evening.

The official party on the platform processed out, leaving the rest of us free to rise from our pews and start the slow shuffle to the doors.

I eased my way through the crowd of parents and hurried forward to take charge of the junior school. I kept them seated until most of the cathedral had cleared and then mustered them out into the quad. Here I lined them up, counted them off and sent them back to their dorms.

As the juniors made their way to their staircase, I turned around and saw the Famous Four emerging from the cathedral. I caught their eye and called them over.

'Something more on the Conway and Wynyard front,' I told them. I explained that I had caught those two rotters cutting Speech Night, slinking around and whispering about some 'paper' or other.

'My concern,' I explained, 'is that those two have somehow got their hands on the term paper that they—and all the middle school—will be examined on next week.'

'How can we help, sir?' asked Hamilton.

'Keep an eye open for what they're up to,' I replied.

Little Cardew leaped in to say, 'We're already doing that, sir.'

'Yes, I know you are, and I appreciate it. But now you need to step up the surveillance. Watch those two like a hawk—or, rather, like four hawks.'

They all agreed enthusiastically, and as Hamilton, Clifford, Redway and Cardew walked off, I could hear them planning a roster between them for keeping watch.

THIRTY-SIX

~

The next morning, between second and third schools, I made my way to the Senior Common Room for a cup of tea. I was surprised to find Detective Inspector Locke and Sergeant Drake waiting for me, and with them, Jack and Warnie.

'Good morning, inspector,' I said, 'what are you doing here?' Sounding, I thought, like a bit of bad dialogue from one of those BBC radio plays.

'Ah, Mr Morris,' responded the policeman, 'just the man we were waiting for.' With these words he patted a brown paper parcel he had tucked under his arm and said, 'I'd like an opportunity to talk to you and Mr Lewis in private about this—if you can spare the time?'

This, of course, made me thoroughly intrigued. Would I mind a private conversation about his mysterious parcel? Of course I wouldn't mind! In fact, I was rather looking forward to what the inspector would produce from the strange package.

'Why don't we go back to my rooms?' I suggested. 'We won't be disturbed there.'

Jack and Warnie rose from their armchairs and I was about to lead our little group out of the Senior Common Room when I found the doorway blocked by Gareth McKell.

I have to say that he was looking no prettier, the purple bruise on his face now being in full bloom and showing no sign, as yet, of starting to fade away.

'I was told the policeman was here . . .' McKell began, then he spotted Locke over my shoulder. Pushing past me, he said, 'Inspector, I have been the victim of a theft.'

I was about to protest at this rudeness, but when I turned around I saw that the inspector was responding quite differently.

'Really, Mr McKell? What has been stolen?' he asked as if his plans for continuing the murder investigation were of no consequence, and nothing could interest him more than investigating a minor theft to please our odious Deputy Head.

We all went back into the heart of the Senior Common Room and sat down. All except McKell, who restlessly paced the carpet.

'My haversack has been stolen!' McKell complained.

'Your notebook, Sergeant,' said Inspector Locke. Sergeant Drake obediently whipped his small black notebook out of his top pocket and began writing down McKell's complaint.

'It's the haversack I take on walking and rock-climbing expeditions. Only two weeks ago I took it with me to the Continent.'

'And it's now missing, is it, sir?' asked Sergeant Drake, his pencil poised.

'Of course it's missing! That's why I'm here complaining!' growled McKell.

'Where was it taken from, sir?' Inspector Locke asked.

'From my flat. In between trips it sits in the bottom of a wardrobe. But I went to fetch it this morning and it's gone.'

'So someone has broken into your flat, sir?'

'So it would appear, and I want you to do something about it!'

'Sergeant Drake,' said Locke, 'would you accompany Mr McKell back to his flat and conduct a thorough investigation, please?'

Drake pocketed his notebook and rose to his feet.

'You're not coming yourself?' McKell protested to the inspector.

'I assure you, sir, Sergeant Drake is a thoroughly competent investigator—he will find out whatever there is to be found out.'

McKell reluctantly led the sergeant out of the Senior Common Room.

'Now,' Inspector Locke said, 'if you would lead the way please, Mr Morris.'

I led the small group across the cathedral close and into my ground floor flat. Once we were there, the door was securely closed, and Jack, Warnie and I were seated, Inspector Locke produced his parcel from underneath his arm and placed it on the coffee table.

Then he proceeded to carefully unfold the brown paper wrapping to reveal—a blood-stained knife.

Warnie let out a long, low whistle. 'Is that what I think it is, inspector?' he asked.

'Yes, sir—that is the murder weapon.'

Without thinking, I reached out my hand to pick it up, but then stopped and drew back.

'It's all right,' said the policeman, 'it's safe to touch it. The weapon has been dusted for fingerprints.'

Given permission, I picked up the blood-stained weapon, delicately—holding one end of the hilt between my fingertips.

'It's very light,' I said, surprised by the weapon's lack of weight.

Jack, who had been sitting very quietly taking all this in, suddenly said, 'Could it be a throwing knife, inspector?'

'Ah, my good friend Crispin of Scotland Yard told me what a sharp brain you have, Mr Lewis. That same thought crossed my mind, so I consulted an expert. It turns out that this weapon doesn't have the balance that a throwing knife needs. So, no, to anticipate your next question—it rather looks as though this knife could not have been thrown into the victim from a distance.'

'Why are you showing this to us?' Jack asked.

'Since you two are the only eye witnesses to the actual murder,' said Locke, nodding at Jack and me, 'I was hoping the sight of the weapon might trigger some memory, some detail of that moment that you'd forgotten until now.'

I let the knife or dagger or whatever it was dangle from my raised hand—turning it around and examining it from every angle.

'No,' I said at length. 'This tells me nothing more . . . opens no hidden doors of memory. I'm afraid I can't add anything to what I've already told you.'

Jack, meanwhile, was staring very closely at the knife.

'Morris—turn it around again, will you?' he said. 'When the light caught it, I thought I noticed something.'

'Quite observant of you, Mr Lewis,' commented Inspector Locke. 'We, of course, noticed the same thing in the police laboratory.'

Then I looked down at the spot on the hilt Sexton Locke was pointing at. It was a small protuberance sticking out at right angles to the hilt.

'That's odd,' Warnie remarked. 'Jolly odd. I've seen a few weapons in my time, but never a knife with a little rod, or notch, or whatever it is sticking out like that.'

'That's what my people in the police laboratory thought,' said Locke, nodding his head in agreement. A long silence followed, broken by the policeman when he asked again, 'No memories? No inspiration? This triggers no thoughts?'

I shook my head, as did Warnie. Jack looked puzzled and thoughtful.

'In that case,' said the inspector, 'I'd better be going across and seeing how my sergeant is coping with Mr McKell and his stolen rucksack.'

He carefully wrapped the knife back in its brown paper covering and took his leave.

Jack was quiet and seemed to be deep in thought when Warnie looked at his watch and exclaimed, 'Ah, there's another try-out at the cricket nets this afternoon. Will you join me there? I'm rather hoping my young protégé, Stanhope, is given a chance to bowl at either Conway or Wynyard.'

Jack and I agreed that we would be there to see the results of Warnie's coaching.

As we walked down the stairs from my front door, I said quietly to Jack, 'You've thought of something, haven't you?'

'It's just possible that I have, young Morris,' he said with a smile, '. . . just possible.'

THIRTY-SEVEN

~

Third school was followed by lunch in the dining hall (the usual: sludge with potatoes followed by sludge with custard). After this I dug Jack out of the Dean's house—where he'd been quietly reading Trollope's *Barchester Towers*—and dragged him off in the direction of the cricket nets. Jack was not a man for games, but he was a stout supporter of his brother and so came without protesting. Warnie, he told me, was already at the nets.

As we ambled slowly across the quad, I said, 'That weapon—the one Inspector Locke showed us this morning—did that strike you as a weapon that had been specially prepared?'

'Well done, young Morris,' Jack responded. 'That's exactly the thought that crossed my own mind.'

'So the murder was no outburst of sudden anger but something planned in cold blood?'

'And, I would suggest, meticulously and carefully planned.'

'But that's horrible!' I protested. 'After our recent discussions I'm prepared to grant that there's some deep, subterranean level in human nature that is ugly and dangerous—and it may spontaneously erupt if sufficiently provoked. But this is different. This is someone sitting in an armchair, quietly plotting and planning a murder—and perhaps carefully crafting that murder weapon we saw.'

'And that sheds deeper, darker light on human nature, doesn't it?' said Jack. 'That's a demonstration of how corrupt human nature basically is at its very heart—would you agree?'

'No, no, no,' I said, shaking my head. 'Anyone who can coldly plan a murder is not normal—and what they're displaying is not normal human behaviour.'

'Not, you claim, the nature that all human beings are born with?'

'Certainly not!' I said emphatically.

Jack paused to light his pipe and then said with a smile, 'I remember being at tea at Tolkien's house once, and after the adults had been served there was only one piece of cake left to be shared between his two boys—both quite young at the time. His wife—very wisely, I thought—told one boy to cut the cake and the other boy to choose first which piece he wanted. She was carefully allowing for the natural human tendency towards selfishness.'

'Yes, all right then,' I responded a little irritably. 'We've all seen children behave selfishly—refuse to share toys and so on. But that's childishness, not corrupt human nature.'

'Really?' said Jack with a smile. 'So you're saying that very young children have been shaped by culture and not by nature?'

'Well . . . not very young children. No, I suppose not.'

'So what we see in the very young must be the human nature we all come equipped with?'

I could see I was walking into some sort of trap, but I felt I had to say, in all honesty, 'Yes, I suppose that must be so.'

Jack seized the opening and plunged in. 'The Hardwoods—Cecil and Daphne—told me a story about one of their children. This child was only about three years old when this happened.

Cecil and Daphne walked into the kitchen to see the boy sitting in the middle of the floor with his Teddy Bear clutched tightly in his arms. On the floor beside him was a spreading pool of thick, sticky syrup next to an upturned bottle. The Harwoods said nothing for a moment—they just looked at the child. Finally he said, "Teddy did it!"'

I laughed and said, 'Well, that's small children for you.'

'Exactly,' said Jack, seizing the point. 'That's what small children are like. No child ever needs to be taught to lie. They all do it automatically, naturally. Lying is just part of human nature, because human nature has this built-in level of corruption.'

I opened my mouth to respond but couldn't think of anything to say. I was rescued from the need to counter Jack's argument by our arrival at the cricket nets.

McKell, still nursing his swollen, purple eye, was sitting in a canvas chair supervising proceedings. Warnie was waiting patiently on the sidelines.

We saw several batsmen, and several bowlers, come and go. Then McKell called on Conway to go to the crease and take his stance in front of the wicket.

As he did so, Warnie leaned over and whispered something in McKell's ear. The Deputy Head appeared to be surprised by what Warnie was suggesting. There was a look of utter astonishment on his face as Warnie went on quietly and insistently saying whatever it was he was saying.

I caught the last four words of Warnie's soliloquy: they were, 'Trust me on this.'

McKell apparently decided that he would indeed trust Warnie because, to the surprise of all the boys gathered at the nets, he called out, 'Stanhope! Come over here and take the ball. I'd like to see you bowl to Conway.'

Young Stanhope, blinking furiously through his large glasses, did as he was bid. He accepted the ball from Hamilton, who had bowled the last over, and advanced towards the nets.

Conway grinned triumphantly at his friends behind the netting as he called out, 'This should be good! Watch this!'

As a slow bowler Stanhope took only a short run up and let fly with a ball that was straight and accurate—aimed directly at the off stump, on a yorker length. But to my surprise there was no spin, no deviation, no turn at all—and Conway had no difficulty in whacking the ball decisively.

I looked over to Warnie and shrugged my shoulders as a way of asking a question.

In response Warnie gestured with his hand and mouthed the word, 'Wait.'

So I waited.

The same thing happened with the next ball, and the next few balls after that. But then, on the second last ball of the over, Stanhope did something different. I saw him adjust his grip and glance down at his fingers.

And when he released the ball, it hit the pitch just behind Conway's legs, bounced, skidded and turned sharply around the batsman's legs straight onto the stumps. Middle and off stump both went spinning out of the ground.

Conway stared behind him unable to believe what had just happened. He stood there, frozen to the spot and looking completely bewildered.

Seeing him fail to move, McKell raised one finger and called, 'Out! Next batsman.'

The boys around the nets who were not friends of the Conway-Wynyard group broke into spontaneous applause—and Stanhope was grinning from ear to ear.

Warnie wandered over to say, 'That's what I told him to do—lull the batsman into a false sense of security and then hit him with a demon ball.' Warnie rocked back on his heels with a big grin on his face as he added, 'And it worked! By golly, did it ever work!'

Jack was smiling too as he remarked, 'That does seem to be an entirely suitable form of revenge.'

'Stanhope!' called out McKell, 'who taught you to spin the ball like that?'

'It was the Major, sir. He taught me the tricks of the spinner's trade, didn't you, Major?'

Warnie just chuckled.

'Let's see you do it again, boy,' said McKell, 'against another batsman.'

And he did do it again. And again.

Finally McKell said, 'I think we've found someone to play at number eleven in the school team. We can't have you bat any higher than eleven, boy—you're a rabbit with the bat. But as a bowler you might just be our secret weapon against Greyfriars.'

THIRTY-EIGHT

~

Conway and Wynyard, I noticed, had their heads together. Conway's face was black with fury, and the two were muttering conspiratorially.

After their intense whispered conversation they approached McKell.

'Sir, sir,' said Conway with an urgent ring in his voice.

'What is it, boy?' growled McKell. 'That was a perfectly legitimate ball Stanhope bowled you with.'

'That's not it, sir,' Conway said. 'It's something else, sir.'

'Well, what is it? Spit it out, spit it out.'

At this point I suspected something serious might be up. Turning around I caught Hamilton's eye and beckoned him and the other members of the Famous Four to gather closer. I wanted them within earshot of what was about to be said.

'It is about Stanhope, sir,' Conway began.

'But not about his bowling,' Wynyard added.

'It's another thing altogether, sir,' Conway resumed. And then he seemed to hesitate.

'Well then, out with it, you two,' McKell insisted, becoming impatient.

I was standing about two yards away from McKell as this conversation was going on, with the Famous Four at my back. We could clearly hear every word.

'It's about the term exam paper, sir,' said Wynyard.

'Next week's term exam, sir,' Conway added unnecessarily. Then the pair of them again lapsed into silence as if reluctant to continue.

I looked around for Stanhope, but he was on the far side of the nets surrounded by a small group of well-wishers.

'Well, sir . . .' said Wynyard, 'we saw Stanhope outside your study window, sir.'

'So? What about it?' McKell was becoming more and more irritated by this piecemeal announcement that had to be extracted, it seemed, one slice at a time. 'Anyone in the cathedral close might pass in front of the windows of my flat, so why do you think Stanhope's presence there is significant?'

'It's just that it looked to us . . .' Conway said, still feigning reluctance to name the crime of which he wished to accuse young Stanhope, 'it seemed to us . . .'

'It seemed that Stanhope,' said Wynyard, taking up the tale, 'was coming out of the window of your flat, sir!'

'What? You're saying he'd been inside my flat? Creeping out like some sneak thief? Is that what you're saying? What possible motive could he have for doing that?'

'Next week's exam paper, sir,' said Wynyard.

'He asked us to sneak it for him, sir,' Conway added in as shocked a tone as he could manage.

'And when we refused,' Wynyard added hastily, 'it did occur to us, sir, that he might sneak it himself.'

'Are you accusing Stanhope of having stolen the term paper from my study?' demanded McKell.

'It's just our suspicion, sir . . .' Conway said slowly, as if fearing he had gone a step too far.

'Well, this can be settled very quickly,' said McKell firmly. 'You two will accompany me to my study immediately. We'll see if next week's term paper is still in my desk where I left it. If it's not, we'll investigate your suspicions—we'll search Stanhope's study. But if the exam paper's not missing—let me warn you—then you two will be in trouble. Come on, both of you. With me. Now.'

As McKell, Conway and Wynyard marched off, I turned to the Famous Four and asked, 'What do you four think is going on here?'

'We have a fair idea, sir,' said Hamilton. Then, with a glance at the others, he said, 'Leave it to us, sir, we can take care of things from here.'

'Off you go then,' I said, and at my words of dismissal all four of them took off at a trot.

What happened next I was not an eyewitness to, but when it was all over, the Famous Four came to my study that night and reported to me. From what they told me I think I can piece together a fair account of the sequence of events as they unfolded.

Hamilton, as leader of the Famous Four, had come to the conclusion that Conway and Wynyard had stolen the term paper—probably under the cover of darkness on Speech Night—gone into Stanhope's study when the younger boy was absent and hidden the exam paper there. They had probably, he thought, copied it for their own convenience first.

But this was more than a mere schoolboy prank. Hamilton, Clifford, Redway and Cardew all knew that if a stolen exam paper was found in Stanhope's study, he would be expelled in disgrace.

Disgusted at what Conway and Wynyard were doing, they knew they had to foil the plan, and they had to act quickly.

They were certain that McKell would go to his study and discover the term paper to be missing. He would then respond to the poisonous suggestion from Conway and Wynyard that Stanhope must have it, and the boy's study would be searched at once.

The Famous Four knew they had only minutes to act. If the paper was in Stanhope's study, they had to retrieve it before McKell came storming in, demanding the study be turned over and a thorough search conducted.

The four of them hurried to the first floor of the dorm building where, to their dismay, they found Stanhope's study door was locked. Stanhope himself was nowhere in sight. The last time they had seen him, he was being carried off in triumph to the tuckshop to celebrate his newly discovered skills as a spin bowler.

'The window,' said Hamilton, as the Famous Four stood in the corridor outside the locked study door. 'Clifford, you need to spring off to the caretaker's shed and borrow his ladder—top speed, lad, off you go. And Redway, you're the smallest and lightest of us—you need to be waiting at the foot of the wall when Clifford comes back with the ladder. Shoot up and see if the window's unlocked.'

'And if it's locked?' asked Redway.

'Then we're sunk—and so is Stanhope. But if you can get in, you'll have just minutes to find that exam paper that Conway and Wynyard planted and get it out before McKell arrives breathing fire.'

Two minutes later, Redway was on the back lawn underneath Stanhope's window. A minute after that the muscular Clifford arrived, lugging with him the caretaker's ladder. It was the work of a moment for the two of them to prop the ladder against the wall and for Redway to scramble up.

'It's unlocked!' he called out to Clifford below when he

reached the window sill. Without wasting precious seconds, he pushed up the window and squeezed into the study.

Then he began his desperate search.

As he did so, he called out through the locked door to Hamilton and Cardew, still waiting in the corridor outside the study.

'I'm in, but I can't find the paper,' he said through the timbers of the door.

'Keep going, old chap,' urged Hamilton, 'and hurry.'

From inside the study came the sound of drawers being opened and furniture being shifted.

Then the two in the corridor heard the dreaded thump of boots, and McKell emerged from the staircase and began marching towards them. Hamilton gave two thumps on Stanhope's study door as a warning to Redway to make his retreat.

'Out of the way, you two,' demanded McKell as he arrived. Close behind him, and smirking in an unpleasant way, were Conway and Wynyard.

McKell tried the study door. Finding it locked, he produced his master key from his key ring, turned it in the lock and swung the door open.

Hamilton and Cardew anxiously looked inside. There was no sign of Redway—so at least he had made his escape. But had he found the missing exam paper?

'We're doing no good hanging around here,' said Hamilton quietly to Cardew, 'let's go and find Redway.'

They left McKell launching his search of Stanhope's room and hurried down the staircase. At the foot of the stairs they found Redway.

'Did you get it?' asked Cardew.

By way of response Redway patted his pocket and smiled.

'Where's Clifford?'

'Returning the ladder. What do I do with the paper?'

'Do you think you can get it back into McKell's study without being seen?'

'Let's try,' responded Redway, heading for the open space of the cathedral close.

Clifford joined them to report that he had returned the caretaker's ladder and it hadn't been missed. Then the Famous Four hurried over to the windows of the Deputy Head's flat.

Fortunately for them, McKell's desk stood just underneath an open window. Hamilton hurried from window to window to see where McKell's sister was. When he saw her in the sitting room, knitting, he gave Redway the thumbs up. The smaller boy stepped over the garden and dropped the stolen term paper back inside McKell's study. He saw it flutter to the floor just underneath the desk.

'Mission accomplished, skipper,' he said as he hurried back to Hamilton's side.

And with that announcement the Famous Four exchanged grins and handshakes all round. Then they headed off to the tuckshop to join Stanhope's celebration.

THIRTY-NINE

~

It was the following afternoon that Jack, Warnie and I went for a walk into the town. We were at the top of the hill heading down the high street with no particular objective in mind, but with the strong possibility of ending up at the pub at the foot of the hill—from the force of gravity if nothing else.

Jack paused to light his pipe and to draw our attention to the sky, where pale grey clouds were rolling in from the west, piling one upon the other like shape-shifting rocks rolling into a jumbled heap at the foot of an avalanche.

Warnie broke into Jack's poetic monologue, saying, 'There's that unpleasant woman.'

'What woman?' I asked.

By way of an answer Warnie pointed the stem of his pipe at a thin, angular woman who was just emerging from the small jewellery shop next door to the pub.

'It's the sister of your Deputy Head Master,' Warnie continued. 'Whatever her name is.'

'Muriel,' I explained. 'Muriel McKell.'

'Yes, that's her. Strikes me as a most unpleasant woman.'

I agreed with Warnie that Muriel McKell was the sort of person who, given half a chance, would howl at the full moon, eat broken glass for breakfast and devour her young.

Jack interrupted my character analysis to say, 'Look on the other side of the high street.'

At first I couldn't see anything of interest in the direction Jack was indicating, so he added, 'Sitting in the bay window of that little teashop opposite the pub. Isn't that our old friend Inspector Crispin of Scotland Yard?'

I squinted at the figure sitting in the sunlight in the window of the teashop and then said, 'Yes, I do believe you're right.'

'And,' said Warnie, 'he appears to be taking as much interest in that odious McKell woman as we are.'

This prompted me to look again at Muriel McKell. She was still standing in front of the jeweller's with her handbag open. She was rummaging inside this, her hand thrust deep into its innermost recesses.

'Forget about the pub,' said Jack with a smile. 'I propose we have afternoon tea.'

'Tea? Really? Afternoon tea?' Warnie responded. 'Oh, ah well, I suppose so. If that's what you want, then tea it is.'

Jack led the way across the road, and we stepped up our pace down the high street until we reached a twee little shop done up in a half-timbered mock Tudor style with the sign *Nesfield Tea Rooms* over its front door.

As we entered, a small bell on the door tinkled musically. Crispin was so occupied with his close observation of Muriel McKell—still hovering on the footpath outside the jeweller's shop—that he didn't look up to see who had come in.

It was Warnie who interrupted him by saying, 'Now this, inspector, resembles what those American detective novels I read would call a "stakeout".'

Crispin glanced over his shoulder at us, then resumed his steady gaze at the Nesfield high street.

'Good afternoon, gentlemen,' he said without taking his eyes off the street. 'Popped in for a spot of tea?'

'May we join you?' I asked.

Crispin waved his arm in a welcoming gesture at the spare chairs around his table. We pulled out the chairs to sit down, and as we did so, on the opposite side of the street, Muriel McKell—still unaware that she was under observation—snapped closed the clasp of her handbag and strode purposefully away, heading up the hill towards the school.

Seeing his target disappear, Crispin swung around in his chair and gave us his full attention.

'And how are you getting on with your murder mystery?' he asked as he signalled to the waitress. When she arrived, he ordered another pot of tea and said, 'Do you have the whole puzzle neatly solved now, Mr Lewis?'

'Hardly!' snorted Warnie. 'This one's dashed impossible. Body killed by invisible assassin, sails off a roof, floats in the air unseen and tumbles to earth the next day. I mean, even for a giant intellect like Jack's, that's a tricky one.'

A frown creased Crispin's brow as he said, 'Tricky is certainly the word for it.'

'Have you been offering the local chap, Inspector Locke, any of your thoughts on our mystery?' I asked.

Crispin shook his head. 'No, no, no—I have my own little matter to focus on.'

'A matter which involves the McKells, I see,' said Jack with a knowing nod.

For a moment Inspector Crispin looked uncomfortable. Then he turned to me and asked, 'What do you know of the McKells, both brother and sister, Mr Morris?'

'Almost nothing,' I replied. 'Bear in mind I only arrived at the school at the start of term. And they're not very approachable people. Not exactly warm and welcoming.'

At that moment the waitress arrived with a fresh pot of tea and a tray filled with cups and saucers, a bowl of sugar and a jug of milk.

As we were helping ourselves to cups of hot tea, Crispin asked me another question. 'Have you noticed anything at all odd about the McKells—or about their behaviour?'

'They have all the charm of a couple of ill-tempered mastodons thumping about in a primeval swamp. That's all I've noticed really. Unless you count McKell's constant dashing off to rock-climbing conferences. And I'm told he spends every holiday skipping up and down vertical rock faces all over the Continent. Fellow's a regular mountain goat apparently.'

Crispin stirred his tea in thoughtful silence, and then said, 'I'll take you gentlemen into my confidence. I trust you—and you might be useful as my eyes and ears inside the school.'

A lingering silence followed, broken by Jack asking, 'What do you suspect the McKells of being involved in?'

Crispin said, 'Diamond smuggling.'

Warnie hooted with laughter. 'Preposterous! That sort of thing happens in London, not in small cathedral towns. And it's done by international gangs, not by schoolmasters.'

'That's what's made their operation so difficult to detect,' Crispin admitted.

'I must admit,' I said, 'my impression is that both the McKells are thoroughly unprincipled and would stoop to anything.'

Warnie raised a questioning eyebrow, so I explained. 'He clearly hates schoolmastering, so if he thought he'd found a way to make enough money to retire in comfort, I think he'd seize the opportunity with both hands.'

'Whatever the motive,' said Crispin, 'and however it got started, we're now convinced it has being going on for some time. Long enough to earn the McKells enemies.'

This interested Jack. 'What enemies?' he asked.

'We believe a London gang has become aware of the McKells' small but efficient operation. We suspect the gang wants to take over.'

'There was,' Jack reminded us, 'that very large man we saw in conversation with McKell at the pub two nights ago.'

'And,' I added, 'it didn't look like a very friendly conversation.'

'That's it!' said Warnie. 'That explains McKell's black eye. He "had a fall", he told us. Poppycock! The man's a mountain climber. Had a fall indeed! He was thumped by that visiting thug from London.'

'It might also have been,' I suggested, 'one of the London gang who stole McKell's rucksack.'

'How long have you been aware of this?' Jack asked.

Crispin explained that Scotland Yard had first become aware of the Nesfield connection, and the McKells' involvement in black market diamonds, some months before.

'What's held up our investigation is just how they do it. Because we've had our eye on McKell, we've tipped off customs and his baggage has been very thoroughly searched every time he's come back from the Continent. But we've found nothing. Despite this, our sources have told us a fresh supply of diamonds has appeared on the black market just after each of those trips. So how does he get the diamonds in? Even allowing for the small size of gem stones, we've been very careful, very thorough. We have no idea where he hides the stones in his luggage, or how he gets them into the country. That's the puzzle.'

Jack asked Inspector Crispin what steps Scotland Yard had taken so far to uncover McKell's mysterious method of diamond smuggling.

'We put a man here,' said the inspector, 'to watch McKell at close range. Firstly with a view to discovering his smuggling method, and then to collect enough evidence to convict him.'

'An undercover operation,' said Warnie, puffing out his cheeks in delight. 'I've read about those in my detective novels.'

'Did you place your man here in town or in the school?' Jack asked.

'Right in the school itself,' Crispin replied.

He stirred his tea for a moment and then said quietly, 'Your murder victim, Dave Fowler, was an undercover police officer.'

This explosive revelation, delivered in Crispin's quiet, thoughtful voice, bowled us over, and we were silent for the next minute absorbing this startling news.

'That explains a lot,' said Jack, 'including his lack of references and job history.'

Warnie was still sitting at the tea table in stunned silence when suddenly his face lit up.

'That's why he was killed, wasn't it? Somehow McKell tumbled to the fact that this chappie was an uncover police officer and murdered him! That must be it.'

'You may very well be right, major,' said Crispin. 'And Inspector Locke knows the full truth about Dave Fowler and his role here. However, there's not a shred of proof. Not one scintilla of evidence against the McKells at this stage.'

'Is Muriel McKell also involved in the smuggling operation?' I asked.

'We believe she plays some role, yes,' the Scotland Yard man replied. 'But the connection of either of them to the murder—well, all we have is speculation, just that and nothing more.'

'And you think we might play a useful part in this?' Jack asked.

'Now you know this much,' Crispin explained, 'I'm rather

hoping that if you keep your eyes and ears open you might pick up some useful fragments of information for us.'

'Happy to help, if we can,' I said. 'But the problem, as I see it, is that none of this gets us any closer to a solution to our impossible murder.'

Crispin sipped on his tea in silence for a moment, and then said, 'My own belief, Mr Morris, is that in this case the key is the method by which the crime was committed. If we discover the method, we'll discover the murderer.'

FORTY

~

We tossed theories back and forth for the next five minutes without getting any closer to a solution. At least Warnie, Crispin and I did. Jack was mostly silent. I suspected he was chewing over some idea of his own and was waiting until he had developed it, and collected more information to support it, before he told the rest of us.

Stepping back out into the afternoon sunshine, Warnie announced that he thought he might pop across to *The Pelican* for a pint, 'and possibly another game of darts'.

Jack was in the mood for walking so I fell into step beside him.

We got to the end of the high street then branched off into a country lane. The road was bordered by high hedges, and beyond them, fencing the fields, was a line of poplar trees thick with green spring foliage, standing as straight and tall as guardsmen at Buckingham Palace.

'There it is,' I said, 'nature clothed in beauty. That's the stuff that knocked Wordsworth sideways.'

Jack chuckled. 'I'm glad you never used those exact terms in the essays you read to me in tutorials. However, Wordsworth would agree with your sentiment—he saw the splendour in the grass and the glory in the flower.'

'And human nature shares in this beauty,' I exclaimed. 'That's the point I've been trying to make: what is natural is beautiful and good, and when people behave wickedly they are acting against nature.'

'Mind you,' said Jack, pausing to light his pipe, 'Wordsworth also said: "I have learned to look on nature while hearing the still, sad music of humanity." I'm not sure he was quite as sanguine as you about human nature.'

'But just look at that peaceful scene,' I said, sweeping my arm in a wide gesture that claimed everything from our heels to the horizon.

'In those fields,' Jack responded as we continued to stride purposefully along, 'rabbits dwell, safe at the moment in their burrows. But tonight they'll creep out to feed and be hunted by predators—hawks and owls. Nature is not all serenity; it is also red in tooth and claw.'

'So now you're saying the whole of Nature is corrupt! Is that it?'

'Far from it: rather it seems to me that Nature is neither the perfection that God first made nor merely evil and corrupt. It is much more complicated than that—a good thing spoiled.'

'But if God is good, how can God's creation not be good? How can it be spoiled?'

'The doctrine of the Fall is the only intellectually satisfactory explanation. If the Materialist Darwinians are right, Nature—and our life within Nature—has been a bitter competition from the beginning. For them there is no right or wrong, only survival. But our moral instincts reject that cutthroat view. Our intuitive understanding that there is a Natural Moral Law which holds us accountable tells us there is more to life than survival. There is also good and evil—right and wrong.'

'And this natural world around us, you say, is a mixture of both good and evil. So how can it come from the good God you believe in?'

'As I said, the doctrine of the Fall makes sense of this as nothing else does. What God created was perfectly good. And that included our primeval parents—and his good creation included genuine free will for those ancestors of ours. Not pretend freedom, not sham freedom, but real freedom. They were not puppets—nor, to use Karel Capek's word, were they "robots". They were truly free people. And they used that freedom in such a way as to damage themselves and damage creation.'

'So you're saying they chose evil over good?'

'Not at all. Our primeval parents became primeval sinners not by choosing evil but by choosing a lesser good—choosing themselves—and in so doing rejecting a greater good, God. It was pride that did the damage.'

I didn't respond immediately, so Jack continued, 'That original freedom was genuine, but not infinite. Each choice confines the range of available choices from then on. Each choice draws the margins, the borders as it were, and so channels the direction of our future choosing. There came a time when those first humans were fully shaped and fully directed by the path they had chosen. Their choices meant they would end up irrevocably attached to either the Heaven of God or the Hell of rebellion against God. What they chose was the latter: the cold, dark fire of self-imprisonment.'

Jack stopped to relight his pipe, which had gone out, then said, 'And this Nature around us was caught up in the rebellion of humanity against God.'

'How so?'

'Picture it like this: a kindly landlord builds a cottage.

Everything about the cottage and fittings and fixtures is perfect. To keep it that way the tenants need only follow the landlord's instructions for maintaining and managing the property. But if the tenants are wilfully rebellious—if in their pride they think they know better than the landlord—they may well make a mess of the cottage and the gardens. After they've splashed paint on walls that needed no paint and tipped garbage down the well in the backyard and allowed weeds to overtake the flower beds, the original beautiful perfection is still there, but seriously damaged—it is a good thing spoiled.'

'Hence all of this—Nature itself—is a good thing spoiled?'

'Exactly. And even more importantly, human nature itself is now a good thing spoiled. You know yourself that if you make a habit of doing something unhelpful—let's say, gambling away your week's earnings every Friday night—as time goes on it becomes harder and harder to break away from that habit. Habits are first cobwebs and then cables.'

'And it's pride that drives this?'

'Pride is the original sin.'

'Aha! That's the doctrine of Original Sin.'

'Although in a sense,' said Jack, 'only our primeval parents were guilty of truly original sin. The rest of us are guilty of the less inventive, but still serious, offence of plagiarised sin!'

We walked on in silence for a bit, then Jack said, 'Even scientists now admit the universe has a history. Just as nations are shaped by their history, so our natures are shaped by human history. And that history began with the first humans telling God to buzz off. They were too big for their britches. They thought they knew better than God. And in their pride they decided that creation should be all about them, not all about God.'

'My head is starting to ache with this flood of big ideas, Jack. Let me see if I'm understanding you here. Are you saying that the choices we make—particularly the big choice made by the first humans—is directing our nature down a particular channel?'

'Not a bad picture, young Morris. We'll make a poet or a novelist out of you yet! Yes, human nature should be a crystal clear mountain stream bubbling over the ancient rocks of its river bed. Instead it's a meandering river, spreading across soft, peaty soil and picking up all kinds of impurities along the way.'

Our feet were crunching on the gravel of the country lane as we walked and talked. Without our making any conscious decision, somehow our path had led us in a wide circle, and we were now approaching the Nesfield railway station again—this time from a slightly different direction to that in which we had departed from it.

'That's human nature?' I said. 'A good thing spoiled? It's still a flowing river—the water is still there, the hydraulic power is still there—but the river is now heavily polluted?'

'Sadly, my dear chap, that's the case.'

FORTY-ONE

~

A train was standing at Nesfield station, the locomotive wheezing and hissing like an elderly asthmatic uncle trying to catch his breath after a brisk walk up a steep hill.

The air was filled with the distinctive smell that all working locomotives have: a mixture of hot oil, steam and coal smoke. It's a smell I've loved since I was a small boy. We stood at the rail crossing and watched as the guard on the platform lowered his flag and the big brass piston rods began to slowly turn the steel wheels. With a steady chuffa-chuffa-chuffa, the train slowly picked up speed and pulled out of the platform.

As it disappeared around a curve, I turned back to the station and saw a figure I thought I recognised.

'Jack—that young woman on the platform, the one with the small suitcase . . . I think that's Henry Beard's wife.'

'The one who's been away visiting her mother?'

'Yes. Now what was her name again? Ah, yes—Samantha.'

As she came down the steps from the platform we caught up with her.

'Hello, Mrs Beard,' I said.

She smiled shyly and said, 'Good afternoon, Mr . . .'

'Morris. Tom Morris. And this is my friend, Mr C. S. Lewis— he's here as the guest speaker for Speech Night.'

We fell into step beside her as we walked up the high street towards the distant cluster of old stone buildings on the hill above the town—the cathedral and school.

'And how is your mother?' asked Jack politely.

Samantha Beard looked puzzled.

'Your husband told us your mother was unwell and you'd been taking care of her,' I explained.

'Oh, yes . . . yes, of course. Mother is much better, thank you.'

'And did Henry write to you,' I asked, 'and tell you our news?'

'What news?' enquired the young woman.

'Why, the death of Dave Fowler, of course,' I replied.

Samantha Beard stopped suddenly in her tracks. Her face went pale and her small suitcase fell from her limp fingers onto the footpath.

'Dead? He's dead?'

'You hadn't heard then?' I asked as Jack stooped to pick up her suitcase.

'No . . . I hadn't . . . What happened? Was there an accident?'

'Worse than that,' I said, feeling pleased, in my ignorance, at having a dramatic story to tell. 'He was murdered.'

The young woman opened her mouth as if to say something, but no sound came out. Then she started to sway, and she appeared to sag at the knees.

I reached out an arm and took her weight before she could fall in a dead faint onto the footpath.

'I'm sorry, I shouldn't have said it like that,' I gabbled. 'Too much of a shock. I'm really sorry.'

She groaned and her eyes flickered open.

'Are you all right?' asked Jack, deep concern in his voice.

She tried to stand upright, wiped a hand over her face and

said in a faint voice, 'I'll be fine in a minute. Just give me a minute.'

Her eyes were moist and she was blinking rapidly as she asked, 'Have they arrested the . . . the murderer?'

'Not yet,' I said. 'The murder is still unsolved. We have no idea who did it.'

'Oh. Oh, I see,' she murmured.

'Look, you're clearly very shaken up,' I said, 'and I feel it's my fault. You need a brandy or something.'

'An excellent idea,' said Jack heartily. '*The Pelican* is just a few steps away. Morris, you take Mrs Beard into a quiet corner of the snug, and I'll go and fetch a small brandy for her from the bar.'

As we walked up the steps of the pub, Samantha was still leaning heavily on my arm.

'I just need to sit down for a little while,' she said in a quiet voice that was little more than a whisper.

The snug was deserted, so I settled her in a corner and then took a seat facing her. She sat very still, her hands clasped in her lap, trembling slightly.

Jack came into the snug, carrying her small suitcase in one hand and a glass of brandy in the other.

'Here,' he said as he offered her the glass and placed the suitcase on the floor. 'Sip this very slowly—it will make you feel a little better.'

Samantha raised the glass to her lips, sipped and then coughed. She put the glass down on the table in front of her and blinked her eyes. Tears were starting to run down her cheeks.

I picked up the glass and held it out to her. She accepted it with trembling hands and drank a little more.

When she put it down she groaned aloud, 'Oh . . . oh . . . this is . . . this is . . .'

Then she buried her face in her hands and began to sob uncontrollably.

Jack and I looked at each other, both feeling awkward and embarrassed. As single men we felt uncomfortable in the presence of a crying woman. If we could have thought of how to comfort her without embarrassing her—or ourselves—we would have done so.

But we couldn't, so we just sat and waited until the sobbing subsided.

After a few minutes Samantha dug a small, lace-edged square of fine linen out of a pocket and dabbed at her eyes.

'I'm sorry,' she said as she wiped her nose. 'You must think me very foolish. It's just that the news came as such a shock.'

'That's my fault, I'm afraid,' I confessed. 'I suppose we've lived with this—well, this tragedy, really—for so long that it didn't occur to me what a shock it must be hearing about it for the first time.'

'It's not your fault, Mr Morris,' she said. 'You mustn't blame yourself. I'm just feeling a little delicate at the moment. Tell me: how . . . how did it happen?'

'Mr Fowler was on the roof of the Old School building,' Jack explained. 'He'd gone up there to catch some sun and read a book.'

'Yes, he did that sometimes,' said Samantha quietly.

'Morris and I were, as it happens, in the organ loft of the cathedral so we could see him—and we saw all that happened. He appeared to be attacked.'

'Who by?' she asked anxiously.

'Well, that's part of the problem—we could see no one on the roof with him. Despite which he appeared to be stabbed and then to fall off the far side of the roof. Morris and I, of course, hurried to the gravel road behind the school where his body should have fallen—'

'But it wasn't there!' I said, leaping in to contribute my piece to the narrative. 'But the following morning it turned up, lying exactly where it should have fallen the afternoon before.'

'I don't understand,' murmured Samantha, looking puzzled.

'None of us understand just at the moment,' said Jack. 'That's the whole point. Inspector Locke is leading the investigation, and he confesses himself to be as baffled as we are.'

'Was it the fall that killed him?' she asked.

'He was stabbed,' I said. 'So it was a combination of the knife wound and the fall that killed him—at least that's what we've been told.'

She finished off the brandy with one last, large gulp and then asked, 'And no one knows who killed Dave?'

'Not at this stage,' Jack admitted. The colour had returned to her face, so he said, 'If you feel up to it, we can walk you back to the school.'

She said yes please, rose from the table and picked up her small suitcase.

We walked beside her in silence as far as the cathedral close and saw her enter her front door.

'She was very shaken,' I said, turning to Jack.

'Yes,' he nodded, a thoughtful look in his eye. 'Very shaken indeed.'

FORTY-TWO

~

Later that day it was my turn to supervise prep. As I walked down the corridors making sure the students were in their study cubicles with heads down over books, I once again encountered the odious Conway and Wynyard.

They were walking towards me carrying a pair of old boots.

'Why are you two not in your study?' I demanded. 'And where did those boots come from?'

The two Bounders knew they were late for evening prep but at least they had the grace to look embarrassed at being caught.

'Ah, they're M-M-Mr McKell's boots, s-s-sir,' stuttered Wynyard.

'He told us to clean them for him,' added Conway hurriedly. 'Truly, sir.'

'But he didn't mean clean them during prep,' I snapped. 'Get off to your study now, both of you, and get to work! There's an exam tomorrow, in case you've forgotten.'

'Yes, sir.' 'Yes, sir,' came their rapid responses as they hurried away with their heads down.

When I saw their study door close behind them, I continued on my way.

Just as I was completing the last of my rounds I saw McKell at the far end of the second floor corridor.

'Excuse me, Deputy Head Master,' I called out. McKell turned around, displaying his usual welcoming expression of a dark scowl. Somehow he managed to create the impression that he'd eaten a bad oyster and the taste lingered.

'I've just encountered Conway and Wynyard,' I explained as I caught up with him, 'and they were carrying a pair of boots: your boots, so they told me.'

'Yes, I'm trying to work out what punishment to give them for that tarradiddle of lies they told about young Stanhope. While I consider what sentence might be appropriate, I'm making them fag for me—giving them all the unpleasant little jobs I can think of.'

We fell into step beside each other, walking towards the Senior Common Room where, at this time of day, we should find a fresh pot of tea.

'Those two bounders seem to be set in their ways,' I said. 'I'm not sure that any punishment will reform their characters.'

This was greeted by a moment's silence broken by McKell, surprisingly, asking for my opinion on the subject.

'What do you think, Morris? What can be done about them? What steps can be taken?'

'It's too late,' I said, shaking my head sadly.

'Too late?'

'They both should have been strangled at birth,' I explained. 'A golden opportunity missed.'

McKell actually raised a wry smile at my words.

Thus encouraged I continued, 'Surely the real problem here is that they might have actually, temporarily, absconded with that exam paper they accused Stanhope of taking. It might have been in their possession for some time.'

I didn't let on that I knew more about the history of the exam paper and its travels than I had revealed. Instead I continued,

'If they had their hands on that paper they will certainly have written out a copy of the questions, and they'll be planning to cheat in tomorrow's exam.'

'That possibility had occurred to me, Morris,' McKell replied dryly, 'so I've taken steps.'

I asked him what steps and he explained that since there had not being sufficient time to write a whole new paper, he had dug out an old paper from some five years ago.

'None of these boys were in the school then, so the questions will be unfamiliar to them,' he added. 'The answers, however, should be no problem—as long as they've been paying attention in class and doing their prep.'

This old paper McKell had given to the ever-efficient Edith Carter to type out and duplicate on her Gestetner machine.

'With the result,' McKell said, 'that tomorrow in the exam room Conway and Wynyard will be faced with an unfamiliar paper. That will block their cheating and really test their mettle.'

The following morning I had the task of invigilating that particular term exam.

Fifteen minutes ahead of the starting time I had the classroom monitors top up the ink wells and put a supply of paper on each desk. Then I placed a copy of the exam paper, face down, on each pile of writing paper.

As the clock tower on the cathedral stuck half past nine, the classroom doors opened and a parade of glum-faced, nervous pupils filed into the room and took their seats.

Conway and Wynyard, I noticed, sat together on the far side of the room with cocky expressions on their faces. When everyone was seated and settled, I checked the time on my watch and told them they could turn over their exam papers and have ten minutes reading time before they started writing.

I kept an eye on Conway and Wynyard as this process

began, and I was delighted to see their cocky, over-confident expressions disappear to be replaced by pure, wide-eyed panic. One moment they were swaggering bulldogs, the next they were rabbits caught in the headlights of life.

They looked at each other and began a tense, whispered conversation.

'Silence at the back there!' I called out sternly, delighted at being able to put those two in their place.

A few minutes later I looked at my watch again and announced, 'Reading time is over—you may now begin writing.'

Across the room heads went down and pens began scratching across pages. All, that is, except for Conway's and Wynyard's.

Conway was squinting at the Gestetnered page of questions in front of him—apparently wondering if the instruction at the top of the page, 'Five questions only to be attempted', could possibly be reinterpreted to mean 'or none at all, if that's how you're feeling'.

Wynyard, meanwhile, was displaying a settled gloom closely resembling, in the weather forecaster's nicely turned phrase, an 'intense low-pressure system'.

Their punishment, I thought, was entirely just since, if their scheme against Stanhope had worked, the younger boy would have been expelled. They had gone beyond mere schoolboy japes into an action of real wickedness. This, of course, reminded me of my ongoing debate with Jack—and, if anything, seemed to strengthen his case, not mine.

For the next hour and a half I patrolled that classroom relentlessly, walking down the narrow aisles between the desks and keeping an especially sharp eye on Conway and Wynyard.

Finally the ordeal was over, and I was able to announce, 'Time's up. Pens down. Stop writing.'

I walked around the room distributing paper pins as I explained, 'Pin your pages together, and be sure to write your name in the top right hand corner of the top page—if you haven't already done so.'

A few minutes later this was done and the boys were sitting quietly—some confident and others looking anxious or depressed.

I dismissed them and walked around the empty room collecting the completed exams. Most boys, I noticed, had managed to write ten or twelve pages. Conway and Wynyard, on the other hand, had managed to write three and four pages respectively.

I sorted the exam papers into four bundles so that McKell, Beard, Douglas and I could share the marking equally. This is the point where exam depression shifts from the boys to the masters.

I put the bundles into manila folders and set out to distribute them, looking forward to telling McKell that the trap he had set for Conway and Wynyard had sprung tightly closed with a satisfying clunk.

Those two young gentlemen could look forward to nothing but bad news when the exam results were posted on the school noticeboard.

FORTY-THREE

~

It being an exam day, with normal classes suspended, I had an hour to spare before lunch, so I roused out Jack and invited him to join me for a walk along the banks of the River Ness.

Jack should, according to the original timetable, have returned to Oxford by this time, but Inspector Locke had asked both him and Warnie to stay on for a few days in case he needed to interview them again.

We left the cathedral close through the main archway and headed down the slope, not towards the town this time but in the other direction, heading for the fields that fell gently down to the water's edge.

Small, white clouds were sailing through a mostly blue sky, spreading moving patches of pale shadow amidst the yellow, buttery sunshine across the valley that morning.

As we walked, I talked to Jack about the behaviour of Conway and Wynyard.

'But you see,' I concluded at the end of my story, 'most of the boys in our school don't behave like that. There are many decent boys—Hamilton, Clifford, Redway, Cardew and count-less others. I can't accept that Conway and Wynyard are a good example of normal human nature.'

'So you're telling me,' replied Jack with a twinkle in his eye, 'that if you walked out of your classroom and left your class alone and unattended, unsupervised, they would do the right thing? Are you saying they would all put their heads down and do whatever work you'd left them to do? All of them? Or even most of them?'

'Well . . . not necessarily. Not in those circumstances.'

'Isn't it more likely that you'd come back to find your classroom in chaos, the work being ignored and ink darts being tossed back and forth?'

I would have liked to have strenuously denied Jack's calumny on the character of the schoolboys I taught. But I was rather restrained by my memory of an incident that occurred early in the term—more or less along the lines that Jack was sketching out.

'Most schoolboys are like most adults,' said Jack. 'They behave well not because they have no inclination to indulge themselves but because they fear being caught.'

'But we all do have good instincts within!' I protested vigorously.

'Exactly!' Jack replied, seizing on my words. 'We have both good and bad instincts within—we are "a good thing spoiled".'

Pointing at a Guernsey cow grazing peacefully in a field on the other side of the river, he said, 'It's not all brown and not all white—there are patches of both. Your claim that human nature is basically good falls at this fence: namely, when we see that human nature is *both* basically good *and* basically evil. Human nature consists of both characteristics.'

I chewed this over in silence for a while as we climbed over a stile and into a sloping field that led down to the river's edge.

'Do you think,' I asked at length, 'that most people would

acknowledge the mixed component—good *and* evil—in human nature?'

'I don't know about "most",' Jack said, 'but certainly many have done so, and many still do.'

'For instance?' I challenged.

'Perhaps the most famous example,' said Jack, 'is in Stevenson.' He stopped to relight his pipe and then resumed, 'Have you ever read his *Strange Case of Dr Jekyll and Mr Hyde*?'

'I confess I haven't. The only Stevenson I ever read was *Treasure Island* and that was when I was a boy. Is it a good novel?'

'Not bad. It's not long—perhaps little more than an extended short story—but once read it grips the imagination. Hence its popularity.'

'Well, I certainly know the premise behind the story: the concept of the good man who takes some sort of chemical potion and turns into a cold, callous, murdering fiend.'

'Yes, even for those who've never read it the expression "Jekyll and Hyde" has become proverbial.'

We reached the water's edge at this point and turned onto the towpath that followed the curve of the stream towards the town of Nesfield.

'The story begins with an encounter,' Jack said as he puffed vigorously on his pipe, 'with an exceedingly ugly and brutal young man, Edward Hyde, who in his haste tramples over a young child. It turns out that this Hyde has a mysterious connection with kindly old Dr Henry Jekyll, who had made a will in Hyde's favour. Later Hyde is seen to commit a murder—beating a man to death with a heavy cane. The police come searching for Hyde. He's vanished, but he's left behind his heavy cane—the murder weapon. This turns out to be the property of Dr Jekyll.'

A flock of wild ducks came swooping in over our heads. They circled slowly against the wind and then landed in feathery splashes on the gently flowing waters of the River Ness. They looked around as if checking their surroundings. Apparently satisfied that all was in order and no dangers loomed, they began ducking their heads under the surface—feeding on the water weeds that grew densely along the river bed.

We watched in silence for a moment, and then Jack resumed his tale. 'Well, old Dr Jekyll assures his friends that Hyde has gone, and that all connections with him have been severed. Dr Jekyll resumes his old life, but the improvement doesn't last. His servants become alarmed when he locks himself in his laboratory and refuses to come out. His friends eventually break in to discover Hyde, wearing Jekyll's clothing, dead from suicide.'

'And as I understand it,' I said, 'the friends quickly discover that the two—Hyde and Jekyll—were the same man.'

'Yes. Jekyll left a letter explaining everything. He had discovered a medical potion of some sort that allowed him to transform himself, both body and mind, to unleash the suppressed and ugly self-indulgent side of his nature. The "science" in the story is pure fiction, of course, but it works as a device to make Stevenson's point about every man being, in truth, two men: one better and one worse.'

'Is he making a moral point or a psychological point?'

'Oh, there can be no real doubt that his point is a moral one. Apparently the seeds of the story came to him in a nightmare. But dissatisfied with it as a mere story, he rewrote it intending an allegory.'

'The point being that I am *both* Jekyll *and* Hyde?'

'And so am I, and so are we all. That's the brokenness that exists in human nature.'

'So it's not just a matter of bad life experiences making bad people?'

'No indeed. There is that seed within us all that, given sufficient provocation or a lack of restraint, will flower into evil deeds.'

'Such as killing Dave Fowler?'

'Such as murder, yes. But not just murder. We all of us do evil deeds every day. For the most part these are small in scale and non-criminal. But we still succeed in hurting other people in the process.'

'And this is from within us? This is not some dark shadow that comes on us from without?'

'Precisely. Remember that Jesus said, "For from within, out of the heart of men, proceed evil thoughts, adulteries, fornications, murders." And I think, in our most honest moments, we all know this is true of ourselves.'

Then Jack burst out into his typical hearty laughter as he added, 'I certainly know it's true of me!'

I was becoming a little uncomfortable with where the conversation was going, so I did what I always do in such circumstances—I deflected.

'Come on, Jack, it's almost lunchtime, and this afternoon I have exam papers to mark. We should be getting back to the school.'

FORTY-FOUR

~

In acknowledgment of the continued presence of our Speech Night guests, the Head Master invited us to dinner that night. When I say 'us', I mean Jack, Warnie and all the masters and their wives (those that had wives).

This had the delightful (for me) result of giving me one night free from eating the standard school dinner served up to the boys. That night was 'cottage pie night'—meaning brown, vaguely beefy slosh topped with white gooey slosh. I was more than happy to give that a miss for properly cooked roast beef and Yorkshire pudding.

When the company was gathered in the formal dining room of the Head Master's house, Dr Rogers tapped a spoon on his wine glass. A respectful silence fell, and the Head launched into his little speech.

'This year's Speech Night, I think we can all agree, was an unqualified success. And for this we can thank our speaker, Mr C. S. Lewis of Magdalen College, Oxford.'

A small ripple of applause followed this formal statement.

'It has been a delight having Mr Lewis and his brother, Major Lewis, staying with us here at Nesfield Cathedral School. And we are more than happy, of course, to extend our hospitality for as long as the . . . ah . . . the police deem it necessary to have their . . . ah . . . witnesses close at hand. That goes without saying.'

Which is why, of course, the Head Master said it.

'For as long, as I say, as it is deemed necessary. Nevertheless, it seems appropriate to think of our gathering here tonight as a farewell dinner to both Mr Lewis and Major Lewis. Not, of course, that they will be leaving at the crack of dawn tomorrow. Ha, ha.'

That odd little sound at the end was a signal that the Head Master had made a joke. A very small joke. And a joke that was not actually funny, as such. But a joke nonetheless.

'However, I'm sure the police will very soon . . . ah . . . release them to return to their home in Oxford. Hence, tonight's little farewell "do". So if you will kindly take you seats around the table, our cook tells us that the staff are ready to serve up.'

'Is,' said Jack to me *sotto voce* as we shuffled towards our places, like cattle shuffling towards their evening feed in the barn.

I raised an eyebrow, so Jack said, 'The staff "is" ready to serve up.'

'Collective noun singular,' I responded, also in a low voice.

Once we were settled in our designated places I found myself between Warnie and our History Master, Geoffrey Douglas.

This gave me the interesting experience—during the Brown Windsor Soup phase of the proceedings—of hearing the extraordinary sound effects that resulted when Douglas collided with the soup in question. His method of consumption sounded like a buffalo pulling its hoof, very slowly, out of a bog. He carried on this interesting performance oblivious to the looks he was getting from around the table.

The Head Master sought to distract us from the liquid sounds rolling around the room by telling a long anecdote about someone called Lord Worpseldon. This old buffoon was, I gathered, a member of the school council. The anecdote, I think, was meant to be amusing and it may even, at some point, have reached a punchline. However, I didn't have a sufficient attention span to discover the point of the whole thing.

Seated opposite me was Henry Beard, looking as grumpy and dyspeptic as ever. So deeply was he sunk in gloom that he reminded me of one of my fellow students when I was an undergraduate. The look on Beard's face exactly resembled the look on my friend's face as he stood in the dock of the magistrate's court, heavily hung-over, waiting to be slapped with a five pound fine for nicking a policeman's helmet on boat race night.

Then it was, I suppose, inevitable that sooner or later someone would raise the topic of Dave Fowler's murder.

It was McKell who did it.

'Are the police any closer?' he asked, addressing his question to Jack who was seated beside the Head Master at the head of the table. 'Any closer, that is, to solving Fowler's murder?'

I thought it was like his cheek to ask since I had decided that he was almost certainly the murderer. Either him or the odious Muriel. Or possibly both of them together.

'Really, McKell!' protested the Head. 'Do we need to discuss such . . . such . . . grubby matters over dinner?'

'It's what is occupying all our minds,' said McKell, speaking, I thought, more sharply than he normally spoke to the Head. 'And until it's settled it will be impossible for life to get back to normal—both for us and for the boys.'

Dr Rogers wearily shook his grey head and muttered, 'I suppose you're right.'

'Well, Mr Lewis,' McKell continued, 'you seem to be

particularly friendly with the police—can you tell us anything about how their investigations are proceeding.'

'I'm not privy to their secrets,' boomed Jack robustly as plates of roast beef, Yorkshire pudding, baked potatoes and peas were slid in front of us by the domestic staff.

'However,' he continued, still apparently explaining the obvious to the dull boy at the back of the room, 'Detective Inspector Sexton Locke strikes me as a most intelligent and capable officer who has the matter well in hand. And a friend of mine, Inspector Gideon Crispin of Scotland Yard, is in the district and is lending his long experience to the investigation as a consultant. I would not be surprised if an arrest was made in the next day or two.'

Really, I thought? Personally I would have been astonished if an arrest was made in the next month or two. What did Jack know that I didn't?

The conversation rolled on, reviewing the familiar—indeed, overly familiar—facts of the case and puzzling once again how Fowler was killed and how his corpse had floated unseen for some hours before hitting the ground.

As this was happening I glanced across the table at young Samantha Beard. And I was surprised. When Jack and I had broken the news to her of Fowler's murder, she was grief stricken, unable to contain her tears. There was no sign of that now. What I could see in her young face could only be called terror.

She had gone white, was glancing down at her plate and was avoiding eye contact with anyone in the room. In fact, she stopped eating, seemingly frozen to the spot. Her face, her whole demeanour, suggested to me that she was paralysed with fear. But fear of whom? Did she fear that our unknown murderer might strike again?

Later, after the dessert, the ladies left the room, and over the port and nuts we gentlemen rose from our seats and ambled about, chatting quietly in small groups.

This was how I came to find myself in a quiet corner, in front of a bookcase, with Jack. In the relaxed, late evening atmosphere I began rambling on about Conway and Wynyard and the problem they continued to be for the school.

In the course of my monologue I mentioned that McKell had given them his boots to clean. The effect on Jack was electrifying.

'Are you sure they didn't take the boots?' he asked.

'No, McKell definitely handed them over to be cleaned,' I explained. 'He told me so.'

'I have to go into town,' said Jack grimly.

'Now? At this time of night?'

'Immediately. It shouldn't be hard to find Crispin—he told me he's staying at *The Pelican*.'

'But what do you need Crispin for? And why so urgently?'

'Because the smuggled diamonds are now in the jeweller's shop in Nesfield, and Crispin must act swiftly before they're shipped to London to be disposed of.'

FORTY-FIVE

~

The next time I saw Jack was the following morning after chapel. I was at chapel because I was rostered to supervise the younger boys, and Jack was there because he liked to be there: 'flying the flag', he called it.

'Well?' I said as we walked across the cobblestones of the cathedral close after chapel had ended. 'What did Crispin say?'

'He saw immediately the significance of what had happened.'

'But what *had* happened?' I almost squeaked in utter amazement. 'McKell gave his boots to Conway and Wynyard to be cleaned. How can that possibly be significant?'

But at that point Jack fell silent. He closed up as tightly as a deep-sea clam nodding off for its nightly eight hours. I knew there was no point in trying to prise information out of him when he had decided not to give it, so I changed the subject.

'Back to the School Bounders—Conway and Wynyard. How on earth, Jack, do we get them to change?'

'What would you like to see happen?'

'I'd like them to see the light!' I protested. 'I'd like them to see there's a better way to be part of any human society than the way they've chosen.'

'Your goal is a modest one, young Morris. To achieve it, all you need do is to show them that society is organised in such a way that certain behaviours are rewarded while other behaviours are not. In the end, the Conways and Wynyards of this world are not very bright. Their corrupt souls are obvious because they haven't the wit to hide them.'

'We, on the other hand—you and I—well, I suppose we have learned to be cleverer, more cunning, in the face we show the world.'

'You always were very fast to see the point, old chap,' said Jack with a warm smile. 'Yes, but we have to be honest enough to admit that "good" behaviour, socially acceptable behaviour, is not enough.'

'Enough for what?'

'Enough to satisfy our deepest longings. The corruption that's eating away at the human heart needs to be dealt with more deeply, more effectively, more powerfully. By the way, my dear chap, do you need to go on class shortly?'

'No, no, I don't have to take first school this morning.'

'Excellent!' Jack almost rubbed his hands with glee. 'Then let's continue our walk in the fresh morning air and see if we can reach some sort of satisfactory conclusion in our "great war" over human nature.'

'Nothing would please me better,' I said. And I meant it.

We walked across the cathedral close and out through the wooden door to the gravel road behind the school, then followed the road in the direction of a distant stand of trees. Off to our right were builders working on the new housing development the Dean had told us about. But they were far enough away, and their work was quiet enough, not to disturb us.

'If there really is, as you have argued, a basic corruption in the human heart then what is needed is a repair job,' I suggested cautiously as we walked.

'Precisely!'

'So what I need to do for myself is what prison life is supposed to do for convicted criminals. I need to rehabilitate myself.'

'Sadly, young Morris, that's not enough,' said Jack.

I was surprised and asked him to explain.

'Well,' he said, carefully weighing, as he always did, every word, 'rehabilitation does what you're planning to do for Conway and Wynyard—it teaches corrupt hearts to wear a new face; it teaches the problem people in our society to function differently. But it does nothing to change the basic corruption itself.'

'I suppose what it really teaches is suppression.'

'And suppression alone, of course, can never be enough.'

'Meaning . . . ?'

'Imagine a red-headed Irishman born with a fiery temper. He is, by inclination, likely to fly off the handle at the least provocation—and either verbally or physically abuse his provoker. To function normally in society he will suppress his natural inclinations. But they will still be there. He still feels the deep hurt and hatred—he just stops showing it.'

'And you're proposing instead,' I said tentatively, 'some sort of treatment that deals with the source of the problem, not just the symptoms?'

'That's what Christianity has taught from the beginning. Remember that quotation from Jesus: "Out of the heart proceed evil thoughts, murders, adulteries, fornications, thefts, false witness, blasphemies." We can suppress those things, but the problem is the heart from which they spring.'

I asked with a sarcastic laugh, 'Are you suggesting some sort of cardiac surgery?'

Jack smiled and said, 'Perhaps we could call what we need "spiritual cardiac surgery". Our hearts are distant from God. More than that, our hearts are rebellious against God.'

'And by "heart" we mean—?'

'Our core—our life stance. Life consists of our relationships, with each other and with the creation around us, but we act as if all of life is about *us*. And that life stance, that "heart", never satisfies, because it is a corruption of the way we were designed to function.'

I asked Jack to explain further, so he went on, 'People are still people. They hunger for eternal life and for fellowship with God, yet at the same time they flee God and try to replace him with idols of their own making. But the replacement does not satisfy. Christ as the Saviour addresses the whole human being, in the heart, at our core—not merely one side of us.'

'Do you think I worship an idol?'

'I don't imagine that you keep a small, carved statue in a cupboard in your room and bow down to it, laying gifts at its lifeless feet.'

'Well then . . .?'

'In our modern world the most common idol that each of us treasures, worships and serves is—himself.'

'So you're saying the idol I worship is Tom Morris?'

'And the idol I worship is Jack Lewis. That is the corruption in the human heart. The murderer of Dave Fowler worshipped himself enough to feel motivated to end another human life. Dave Fowler had somehow defiled the murderer's altar of Self, and so Dave Fowler had to die.'

We were now nearing the copse of elm trees that lay at the end of the field, and I thought about Jack's words for a moment before replying, 'Your case, if I understand it well enough, is that fear of detection can stop some people—most people—from destroying or damaging others who fail to "worship" them adequately, but that's not enough. A bigger change is needed. The heart has to change. The "object of worship" has to change.'

'Exactly, young Morris—exactly.'

'So how do I do that? How do I change myself? How do I heal what is within me?'

'You don't. You can't.'

'Then the situation's hopeless!' I almost wailed.

'Yes, our condition *is* hopeless. And that is why we must place ourselves in the hands of Another.'

I said nothing, but a quizzical expression must have come across my face because Jack continued, 'When you're physically ill you place yourself in the doctor's hands. You trust yourself to the doctor. And, if all goes well, the doctor does for you what you cannot do for yourself—he heals you.'

Jack paused to light his pipe and gaze at the line of low, rolling hills that formed the horizon.

'Your spiritual condition,' he resumed, 'and mine is identical to that. We need to place ourselves in the hands of Christ. We need to trust ourselves to him, and to his treatment.'

'And what treatment would that be?'

'Think about that expression "spiritual cardiac surgery". Jesus himself calls it being "born again". Christian thinkers over the centuries have called it "regeneration".'

'How does it happen?' I asked quietly. 'What does it *feel* like?'

'The first, faint stirrings come when one becomes aware of the need. One of these days I shall write about my own experience, but for the moment picture it like this: it's like becoming aware of a danger and at the same moment becoming aware of an offer of rescue from that danger. That, I can assure you, is irresistible.'

Jack stared at the distant horizon, and at the pale grey clouds that were slowly rolling in, as if he was gazing into eternity.

'There was a moment,' he said, 'when with great reluctance I was dragged into seeing my true state, and—in the same instant—offered rescue from the state I was in. In that instant I understood what Christianity has been saying down through the ages: forgiveness is powerful. Forgiveness heals the corrupt heart. Forgiveness displaces the idol of Self on the altar of the human heart and puts in its place the rightful occupant: God himself.'

I said nothing, but realised that Jack was speaking from the other side of a border that I had never crossed.

'I also realised,' said Jack, 'that forgiveness is costly. There is always a price to pay. And Christ paid that price. In his death on the cross, Christ fought an almighty battle with my enemies—with condemnation and death—and he won. Because he paid that price and won that battle, I can be forgiven, God can be reinstated as the proper object of my life, and my heart can begin to heal.'

FORTY-SIX

~

As we were talking we had begun retracing our steps back down the gravel road. With such big issues whirling through our heads, we were deep in thought and barely aware of our surroundings.

As a result I was almost the victim of violent bloodshed.

To picture what occurred you need to understand that as Jack and I walked side by side he was on the soft grassy shoulder while I was on the gravel of the road bed itself. This put me directly in the path of the builder's lorry when it rumbled up behind us.

I believe I came close to the Olympic record for the standing high jump when the lorry driver loudly tooted his horn from a distance of approximately two inches behind my left ear. I leaped onto the grassy shoulder of the road, landing with a thump beside Jack as the tip-truck rumbled past.

We watched as it disappeared in a cloud of dust, bouncing over the ruts and bumps in the uneven road. I reassembled my shredded nerves and dusted off my jacket.

'Are you all right?' Jack asked.

'Shaken, not stirred,' I replied with what I hoped was a confident grin. Then I added, 'I should be getting back to the school. I have to take the Fourth for English in second school, which is'—here I glanced at my watch—'only minutes from now.'

'You hurry along then, Morris,' said Jack. 'I shall dawdle. An idea is forming in a remote corner of my brain that may prove useful.'

A few minutes later I was calling the Fourth to order and telling them to get out their poetry books.

'Aw, poetry, sir? Do we have to?' came a voice from the back, joined by a general chorus of moans.

'We're doing Lord Byron this morning,' I said firmly. 'Books out! Now!'

Their surrender was followed by a general shuffling of books.

Once they were settled I said, 'Turn to page 127. There you will find one of the best poems about an ancient battle ever written.'

'A battle!' said an unidentified voice, this time from close to the front of the room. 'Why didn't you say it was about a battle?'

'We like battles, sir,' chirped another voice.

I silenced them and began to read 'The Destruction of Sennacherib'.

'Now, what does it mean, boys,' I asked, 'when it says the Assyrian army came down "like the wolf on the fold"? Anyone?'

'They came down slashing their swords,' said one boy, waving his ruler in the air to demonstrate and almost removing the left ear, one nostril and a collar stud from his neighbour.

'Does anyone remember what a simile is?'

Jones down the front, who always knew the answers, had his hand up, but so did Stanhope. This was an encouraging sign. Had the young blighter actually starting studying then?

'Yes, Stanhope—what is a simile?'

'It's when you say something is like something else, sir.'

'So if the poet says the Assyrians attacked "like the wolf on the fold", what is being compared to what here?'

Blake's hand shot up. 'Sir! Sir! I know, sir!'

'Yes, Blake?'

'To a pack of wolves swooping down on a flock of sheep and tearing their throats out with razor sharp teeth.'

This bloodthirsty image pleased the rest of class, who expressed their approval in a rumble of murmurs that swept across the room.

For as long we focussed on Byron and the image of warfare the class was with me, but when I told them to get out their Bibles to look at the original story the poem was based on, there was a collective moan.

'But we've been to chapel already this morning, sir,' complained Fox.

'This is not chapel, this is English. A great deal of English literature cannot be understood unless you understand the Bible that stands behind it. So no more complaints—open your Bibles at Second Kings chapters eighteen and nineteen.'

There were more grumbles so I added, 'And if you're not quick about it, I shall imitate the Assyrian and come down on you lot like the wolf on the fold.'

By the time the bell rang to mark the end of second school I had the whole class engrossed in the story—both the original and Byron's retelling of it.

From the classroom I made my way to the Senior Common Room, my tongue hanging out for a cup of tea.

McKell was already in his usual chair with a large sheet of paper spread across his knees.

'Ah, Morris,' he said, 'take a look at the end of term exam results. I intend placing these on the noticeboard in just a moment. Tell me what you think.'

I ran my eye down the list. As usual Cardew had topped the list, closely followed by Hamilton, Redway and Clifford. I was also pleased to see that young Stanhope had passed. He was just above the pass-fail line, but just above was enough.

Then a grin of delight spread across my face as I saw that Conway and Wynyard had both failed—and failed miserably.

'I thought you'd like that,' said McKell. 'I've decided the humiliation of such a bad performance in the term exam is punishment enough. Unless you disagree?'

'No, no, not at all. You're the Deputy Head, and you have more experience of these boys than I have. I'm content to let it go at that.'

McKell grunted in agreement and rose to go and post the list on the noticeboard in the archway under the Old School.

I carried my tea across to the pigeonholes where letters for the masters were placed each morning, and I was pleased to see an official looking envelope in mine. I grabbed the letter, tore it open and devoured it eagerly.

'Yes,' I said, speaking to no one in particular.

The top of the page bore the letterhead I'd been hoping to see, and the contents said exactly what I wanted.

'Oh, yes.'

'Are you yapping at me, Morris?' growled Henry Beard unpleasantly from the other side of the tea urn.

'Sorry, Beard,' I said. 'I hadn't intended to speak out loud.'

'Then don't!'

But no sourpuss could take away my sense of elation and my heart was as light as a soufflé whipped up by a *cordon bleu* chef. As far as I was concerned, the bluebird of happiness had definitely come out of early retirement and was buzzing around the place whistling a merry tune like billy-o.

'Good news?' said Geoffrey Douglas from behind the cloud of blue smoke put up by his pipe.

'The best,' I said.

'So I take it you proposed and she said yes?'

'A different kind of news entirely,' I chirped.

'Well, then . . .' Douglas urged. 'Spill the beans, old chap. Let us into the secret.'

I looked around and saw that every eye in the Common Room was on me, and suddenly felt the awkwardness of my position.

'Actually,' I said. 'I think I'd better tell the Head Master before I make a public announcement.'

I edged rapidly out of the Common Room, leaving puzzled faces behind me. But their puzzlement failed to dampen my pleasure. I was still gliding on clouds of happiness as I sailed out to the archway where a crowd of eager students was gathered around the noticeboard.

McKell brushed past me on his way back to the Common Room for his second cup of tea. As he did so, I saw Inspector Gideon Crispin and his stolid, silent Sergeant Merrivale enter the cathedral close.

They spotted me, the only master in sight, and walked rapidly across.

'Have you seen Mr McKell anywhere, Mr Morris?' the inspector asked.

I reported that they had just missed McKell by half a whisker as he had been beside me a moment before.

'He's just returned to the Common Room,' I said.

I got a grunt of acknowledgment from Crispin and a sort of half salute from Merrivale, and they plunged into the building in pursuit of the Deputy Head.

Why were these two policemen, at just this moment, in hot pursuit of McKell?

Thoroughly intrigued, I followed close behind them to see what would transpire.

I stepped in through the Common Room door just in time to hear the Scotland Yard man say, 'Mr McKell, I'm Inspector Crispin—'

Before he could say anything more our Deputy Head interrupted brusquely.

'Not now, inspector. You'll have to come back later. I'm busy.'

'Actually, sir, you're coming with us. Mr McKell, you are under arrest. You do not have to say anything, but anything you do say may be taken down and used in evidence.'

FORTY-SEVEN

~

There was a stunned silence in the Senior Common Room as McKell was led away. What was surprising was that he went quietly without a word of protest. As soon as the party of three—Crispin, Merrivale and McKell—had exited down the corridor, a chorus of voices erupted.

'I'm astonished,' said Henry Beard.

'What was that all about?' asked Geoffrey Douglas.

'It's his sister I feel sorry for,' said Mary Flavell, the school nurse.

'You could have knocked me over with a feather,' said David Evans, the organist, who often joined us when tea was on.

Ryan Carleton just nodded in agreement.

'Do you think . . . is it possible . . . ?' murmured our school secretary, Edith Carter. 'Could Mr McKell really be guilty of the murder of Mr Fowler? Surely not! Not our Mr McKell.'

The mention of Muriel McKell made me hurry to the doorway to see, if I could, in which direction the police officers had marched off with our Deputy Head. I looked both ways and saw they were just disappearing around a corner—not towards the exit from the building, but in the direction of the McKells' flat.

Walking back into the Common Room, I said, 'I think they're going to see Muriel McKell now.'

'Curiouser and curiouser,' muttered Beard into his cup of tea.

'Poor Muriel,' Mary Flavell said.

'I suppose they have to inform the sister,' added Edith Carter.

'Unless,' I suggested, 'they're about to arrest her as well.'

'Muriel?' said our school nurse, a note of outrage in her voice. 'Of course not! Why on earth would they want to do that?'

Geoffrey Douglas loudly sipped on his tea, giving us his impersonation of a dredging machine working on the bottom of a harbour, and then said, 'They're very close—brother and sister are very close indeed. Whatever McKell's involved in, I can well imagine his sister being in it with him—all the way up to her bushy eyebrows.'

'But murder?' protested Mary Flavell. 'No. No, I can't for a minute imagine they would be involved in murder. That's not possible.'

'Perhaps it's not murder,' I suggested.

'Then what?' asked Edith Carver.

I chose not to reply and went back to drinking my tea.

'Aha,' said Douglas. 'Young Morris knows more than he's letting on. You've been hanging around with the police quite a lot, Morris. This has been noted, so there's no point in denying it. You know more about this surprising development than the rest of us. I think it's time for you to open up the secret scroll, old chap, and reveal its contents.'

This made me feel a bit uncomfortable. I wasn't sure where Inspector Crispin was up to in his investigations into the diamond smuggling, and I didn't know what I could reveal. What could I tell my fellow staff members? And what did the police regard as still being confidential?

However, I was rescued from my dilemma by an interruption from the doorway.

'If you will allow me,' said Jack's unmistakable voice—a voice that could be heard clearly at the back of the largest lecture hall at Oxford—'I think I can explain all.'

Jack and Warnie cruised into the Senior Common Room as part of a small flotilla—they were closely followed by the local police contingent of Inspector Locke and Sergeant Drake.

As Warnie played 'mother' and poured cups of tea for these late arrivals, Jack launched into his exposition.

'Your Deputy Head Master, Gareth McKell, and his sister, Muriel, have both been arrested and charged with diamond smuggling. Although in the sister's case I believe the actual charge is "handling property knowing it to have been smuggled" or whatever the legal phrase might be.'

There was a stunned silence, and then Henry Beard exploded with a loud protest. 'But schoolmasters don't smuggle diamonds! That's done by criminals! And it happens in London, not in a little place like Nesfield!'

He had unwittingly echoed almost exactly my own reaction, and Warnie's comments, when we first heard of the case Crispin was investigating and the precise nature of his suspicions.

'It's true,' said Inspector Locke. 'This diamond smuggling business is the case that Detective Inspector Crispin of Scotland Yard has been here investigating, and he now has it wrapped up and his suspects charged and under arrest.'

Silence once more descended on the Common Room. I looked around and saw my fellow staff members of Nesfield Cathedral School looking like a row of stunned mackerel in a fishmonger's window.

Speaking more to himself than to the room, Inspector Locke muttered, 'Now, if only I could tie up the loose ends of my murder case as neatly as Crispin has tied up his smuggling case—well, I'd be a happy man. But until I can explain how a corpse can float in the air, invisibly, for hours . . .' His voice trailed away.

At this point Jack intervened to say, 'Actually, on that subject a thought has occurred to me, inspector, that you might like to check out.'

Jack took the inspector by the elbow and led him to a quiet corner where they fell into a huddle in subdued tones.

Around me a hubbub of shocked conversation broke out, expressing a mixture of consternation and disbelief.

I stood back to watch and listen. Which was why I was the only one who saw Sergeant Drake being summoned to join the colloquy involving Jack and Inspector Locke. Drake was then, it appeared, dispatched to carry out a task, and Jack and the inspector returned to the main group.

Questions were fired at them from every direction, in a jumble of voices.

Jack raised a hand to hush the group and was about to speak when the Common Room door flew open once again and the Head Master burst into the room.

I say 'burst', but everything Dr Rogers did, he did with dignity. Better, perhaps, to say that he steamed into the room like a battleship going at its top rate of knots.

All eyes were fixed on him as he began to speak.

'I take it that you are all now aware of this second, awful tragedy that has befallen our beloved school. First, the death of that wretched man Fowler, and now this!'

Clearly the Head Master was blaming Dave Fowler for getting himself murdered on school property. He was probably thinking that there were perfectly good back alleys in which one could have oneself murdered without allowing it to happen in *his* school.

'The police have not yet revealed all the details to me,' the Head was continuing, 'which they assure me they will do in due course. However, what we do know at this stage is that Mr McKell, aided and abetted by his sister, has been engaged in a criminal activity for some time. Of course, this has no direct bearing on the operation of the school—and Mr McKell has carried out his duties towards the school in a thoroughly efficient manner throughout. His other . . . ah . . . criminal life has not impeded any of his work at this establishment. I will be writing to the parents today to make this abundantly clear.'

'How long has this been going on?' someone asked.

'And how? How did he . . . ?' asked another.

'And why would he do it?' asked a third.

Dr Rogers ran a hand over his distinguished brow and said, 'Sadly I can answer none of those questions at this time. They will have to wait until the police make some sort of announcement, which, oh dear me, will no doubt be published in the popular press.'

'Actually,' said Jack from his inconspicuous position near the tea urn, 'I think I can explain.'

FORTY-EIGHT

~

All eyes in the Common Room immediately swivelled towards Jack, who allowed for a suitably dramatic pause before he continued. He always had a sense of the dramatic, which is part of what made him such a good lecturer.

'This story begins,' he said, 'with the local jewellery shop in the town of Nesfield.'

'You mean Jarrett Brothers' Jewellery?' asked Henry Beard.

'That's the name over the shop,' Jack agreed. 'But I gather from my good friend Inspector Crispin that there hasn't been a Jarrett involved in the business for some time. The shop has passed from hand to hand over the years without the trading name being changed.'

'I didn't know that,' Mary Flavell said.

Ryan Carleton agreed, saying, 'I always thought that nice little man behind the counter was Mr Jarrett. It always says "Jarrett" on the receipts.'

'As it would,' Jack continued, 'since that's the trading name of the business. But the current proprietor is a man named Roland McKell.'

'Ah,' sighed Geoffrey Douglas, 'we begin to see the light. This man is . . .'

'A cousin, as it turns out,' Jack resumed, 'of Gareth and

Muriel McKell. And it was this man, cousin Roland, who first proposed the notion of a diamond smuggling operation based here in Nesfield.'

'Oh, dear me, dear me,' groaned the Head Master as he sank into a vacant armchair.

Jack ignored this punctuation in his narrative and continued, 'Crispin tells me that Roland McKell was once in the jewellery trade in London. And there he became involved in handling smuggled diamonds.'

'In fact,' said Warnie with a chuckle, putting in his sixpeneth worth, 'Roland moved here to Nesfield when things got too "hot" for him in London.' And then he muttered, 'I know about these things, you see. Read a lot of crime novels . . .'

Jack picked up the story. 'Roland realised that Gareth's frequent trips to the continent provided a perfect cover for a diamond smuggling operation, and by working from an out-of-the-way place such as Nesfield, he could operate without the powerful London gangs realising what he was up to. Gareth was carrying a new load of gemstones every time he returned from the continent. Muriel would take the stones to Roland, who would clean them and re-cut them if necessary, and then pass them on to his old contacts in the illicit diamond trade in London.'

'You mean this has been going on for some time?' asked Edith Carter.

'It would appear so,' said Jack.

'It just gets worse and worse,' groaned the Head Master.

'Of course this sort of trade can't continue undetected forever. Crispin tells me it was a major London gang that first became aware of illicit diamonds coming onto the market outside their control. They began asking questions.'

'And this often involved beating people up,' Warnie volunteered. 'You'd know all about this sort of thing if you read crime novels.'

'What was happening in the London underworld alerted Scotland Yard that something unusual was going on in the illicit diamond trade. An informer told Crispin of the arrival of gems in London from Nesfield.'

'He's called a "fence", Warnie explained. 'The man who handles stolen property is called a "fence". And it was one of these fences who alerted Crispin to the source of the diamonds.'

'Working from the London end,' Jack resumed, 'Crispin discovered that Gareth McKell was the only resident of Nesfield who made frequent, and regular, trips to the Continent. With his suspicions aroused, he arranged for McKell's rucksack and belongings to be thoroughly searched by customs each time he made the channel crossing. And, of course, he discovered the connection with Roland McKell at Jarrett Brothers' Jewellery in the town.'

'The only thing left,' said Warnie, 'was to discover how the blighter did it. Customs never found the jewels despite the most careful searching. So how was he getting them in? It was Jack who tumbled to the answer, wasn't it, Jack?'

'But it was Morris who put me onto it,' Jack said modestly.

'Me?' I was surprised. 'How did I do that?'

'By telling me about the unusual way McKell treated his boots.'

'His boots?' asked Henry Beard. 'How do his boots come into this?'

'Morris told me that McKell returned to the school with mud and clay still caked around the spikes of his climbing boots. Keen rock climbers such as McKell would normally take much better care of their equipment than that. Diamonds are small and can be hidden underneath—and covered up by—clay and dried mud. So Morris's report aroused my suspicions.'

'You didn't tell me!' I protested.

'I passed my thoughts on to Detective Inspector Crispin,' resumed Jack calmly, ignoring my outburst, 'who thought there might be something in the idea. Then when Morris told me that McKell had handed his boots over to two of the boys here to be cleaned, I realised that the current load of diamonds must have been removed from the clay and mud they had been embedded in around the spikes—and was most probably already at Roland's shop in the town, being prepared for shipment.'

'Very clever chap, my brother,' said Warnie, rocking back on his heels and looking as pleased as punch.

Jack had begun to pace the room, which he often did when he lectured. The more engrossed in his topic he became, the more he was inclined to pace up and down the lecture platform—or, in this case, the floor of the Senior Common Room.

'When Morris mentioned the boot cleaning to me, I hurried into town and alerted Crispin to the news. He decided it was time to act.'

'They conducted a "raid",' Warnie explained. 'That's what it's called in police circles. They took some uniformed officers and raided the jeweller's shop. They caught Roland red-handed, packaging up the gems for shipment to London. And Roland turned out to be a bit of a weedy, spineless chap—under interrogation he told them the whole story.'

'With the result you saw here today,' Jack concluded.

'And that tough we saw in the pub,' I said. 'The one we thought beat up McKell—was he from one of the London gangs? Was he trying to track down his rival diamond smugglers?'

'So the police believe,' Jack replied.

'And how were the diamonds delivered to McKell when he was travelling in Europe?' asked Douglas.

'That was Roland's dealer in Amsterdam. He would travel to wherever Gareth McKell was headed and meet him there,' Jack explained.

The Senior Common Room was so quiet you could have heard one turtledove coughing politely to attract the attention of another turtledove in a subtle way.

At length it was the Head Master who spoke.

'Well, thank you, Mr Lewis,' he said. 'It's for the best that we understand these things. It's encouraging to know there was no direct involvement by the school community in any of this.'

'There was one boy in the school, a boy named Fox,' Jack said, 'who was used as a messenger to carry notes between the school and the jewellery shop. But that was the extent of the school's involvement.'

The Head Master groaned loudly again. 'Oh, dear me. And to think . . . oh, to think how much I trusted McKell!'

'Why did he do it?' asked David Evans. 'Do we know that?'

Warnie chuckled and said, 'Money. That's what lies behind most crimes.'

Jack nodded and said, '"For the love of money is the root of all evil: which while some coveted after, they have erred from the faith, and pierced themselves through with many sorrows."'

'Paul's first letter to Timothy, chapter six,' said the Dean. He was standing in the doorway. He had arrived quietly while we were all so engrossed in the story we hadn't noticed.

Just then Sergeant Drake returned. He pushed past the Dean, who was leaning against the doorframe, and hurried across to where Inspector Locke was standing.

The two of them had a hushed conversation, but I picked

up a few words—something along the lines of 'I went to the worksite'—but more than that I couldn't hear.

But I did notice that Locke caught Jack's eye and nodded to him.

This must have attracted the attention of the Head Master, because at that point Dr Rogers rose from his armchair to his full impressive height and said, 'Now, Inspector Locke—I wish that you would do as well as your Scotland Yard colleague. If you can clear up this other dreadful business of the death of Mr Fowler, we shall have a great shadow lifted from the school. Can you do that, sir?'

'I wish I could. However, at the moment—' Locke began.

But Jack leaped quickly in and said, 'May I make a suggestion? If you wish to place the killer of Mr Fowler under lock and key, I suggest you arrest Henry Beard.'

FORTY-NINE

~

Beard? Beard? I could hardly believe what I was hearing. Why on earth would Henry Beard want to kill Dave Fowler? And, more to the point, how on earth did he do it?

At that point I looked around the group assembled in the Senior Common Room and found that Henry Beard was missing.

Around me voices exploded. Everyone seemed to be asking questions at once.

Raising his voice above the general melee, Warnie said, 'Of course, Mr Fowler was here as a police spy.'

The silence that followed this announcement was like the echoing silence that follows an explosive thunderclap.

Finally the Head Master said, 'No, no, no, my dear chap. You must be mistaken. I employed him myself. He came warmly recommended by another head master.'

'All carefully contrived, I'm afraid,' Jack explained, 'by the police. They wanted their man on the spot, in the school, to observe McKell and try to discover his method of operation.'

'He was what the police call an "undercover man",' Warnie explained, trotting out more of his light reading. 'But before he could report, he was killed.'

'Then surely,' said Mary Flavell, 'as hard as it is to believe, it must have been Mr McKell who murdered Mr Fowler. He must have discovered that he was really . . . and then he must have . . . So why do you say it was poor Henry Beard?'

I was still wondering the same thing, and as I wondered I looked again around the room. Beard was definitely gone. Everyone else was still eagerly gathering around Jack, seeking answers. But of Henry Beard there was no sign.

This, I thought, was where I could help. While the argument and the questions continued, I slipped out into the corridor to go in search of Beard. As an old, and not very old at that, rugby fullback, I thought I should be able to place my hands on Beard and bring him back down to the Common Room, where the police could slap the cuffs on him. If, indeed, they did use handcuffs during arrests anywhere except in those American pulp magazines.

Where would he be?

Obviously the first place to look was his flat.

I hurried across the cathedral close and up the front steps of the terrace house in which Henry and Samantha Beard had their flat.

Stepping in through the entranceway, I stopped at the front door of the Beards' flat. I could hear voices from within. And one of them, I thought, sounded like an angry voice.

I knocked on the door.

There was no response, but the voices fell silent.

I waited as long as I dared, then I knocked again.

From within I heard a woman's voice—Samantha's, I presumed—but speaking so softly I couldn't make out the words. A man replied—it must have been Henry—and while his voice was too muffled by the thick door to be able to make out the words, he sounded angry, very angry.

I knocked a third time.

'Beard,' I called out. 'It's me—Morris. Open up, please, Beard.'

From within the flat came the sound of footsteps, and then other sounds that weren't so clear. But they might have been the sounds of a scuffle.

Then came a woman's voice—crying out, I thought, crying to me for help. The cry stopped abruptly.

Or, rather, it was stopped—by what sounded like a slap, or possibly even a punch. It was certainly the sound of flesh hitting flesh.

What followed was the sound of a woman sobbing.

I could bear this no longer.

'Come on, Beard, open the door,' I shouted. 'You can't stay in there all day. You'll have to open up sooner or later.'

Complete silence fell. What had Beard done to young Samantha? Or what was he doing to her now?

Then I did what I should have done at the beginning: I tried the door knob. It was unlocked.

I opened the door and walked in.

Samantha was on the far side of the sitting room facing me. Tears were streaming down her face and she was shaking with sobs. There was a red weal down one side of her face, and an ugly red mark on her arm.

I turned and discovered that Henry Beard was standing right beside me. He leaned over and pushed the door shut.

'You're a busybody, Morris—a fool and a busybody,' he snarled, his face contorted with anger. 'Pushing yourself in where you're not wanted. Well, you're in now . . . and I'm not so certain you'll get out again.'

He raised his right hand to show me what he was holding— a large, ugly-looking fishing knife.

'Move,' he commanded. 'Go and stand beside Samantha.'

I did as I was told.

Beard advanced towards us, gripping that dangerous-looking knife very tightly.

'What am I going to do with you?' he asked.

'Don't be so foolish, old chap,' I pleaded. 'If you keep going this way, it can't end well. You can't really get out of the building, you know. There are police officers on the school premises. Why don't you just put that knife down and we can talk about it?'

Beard muttered something under his breath. Then he changed course.

He was no longer edging towards us but towards a cupboard in the corner of the room.

When he reached the cupboard, without taking his eyes off us, he flung open the door and reached inside.

I must admit that my heart missed a beat when he drew out from behind that cupboard door a wicked-looking crossbow.

I mean to say, Tom Morris is as chivalrous as the next man when it comes to rescuing a damsel in distress, and I'd opened the door and stepped in because young Samantha Beard was clearly in distress and needed a knightly rescuer. But just at that moment I would have been quite happy if someone else had stepped into that knight errant role.

Beard had dropped down on one knee, reached into the darkness of the cupboard and pulled out an arrow. Well, it's what I would have called an arrow, but I think strictly speaking the things they fire from crossbows are called 'bolts', not 'arrows'. Anyway, whatever it was, it had a sharpish-looking point, and, still without taking his eyes off us, Beard was loading this thing into his crossbow and pulling back the loading mechanism.

I was hoping he'd have to take his eyes off us, or put down the knife, in order to do this. But this crossbow had some sort of lever mechanism that enabled him to do it one-handed. Then he was on his feet again.

And he was holding the crossbow.

'Hey! Come on, Beard,' I protested. 'Don't point that thing at me! It might go off!'

Some guttural sounds came out of the back of Beard's throat, but they didn't quite amount to being words. This wasn't Henry Beard the schoolmaster I was facing; this was Henry Beard the primitive hunter. And I didn't much like the look of him.

'Look, old chap—violence doesn't really solve anything, does it now? You know that,' I felt like an idiot mouthing such clichés, but somehow I needed to distract Beard from doing anything irreparably violent—especially to me.

'Mr Beard,' came a sharp, commanding voice from the doorway. I looked across and there was Inspector Sexton Locke.

'Just how many eyewitnesses do you want, Mr Beard,' asked Locke, 'to your second murder?'

And then it was all over. Beard's nerve failed, and he sagged like a punctured balloon.

He lowered the crossbow.

Locke was across the room in an instant and took the weapon out of his nerveless hand. Samantha collapsed on the floor, sobbing uncontrollably.

I just stood where I was with a large band of energetic butterflies beating enthusiastically at the walls of my stomach.

That was when I realised that I'd been holding my breath, and I opened my mouth and gasped in fresh oxygen.

I felt like a man slowly coming out of anaesthetic.

Others crowded into the room.

Sergeant Drake had Beard by the arm and was leading him away. Nurse Mary Flavell was sitting next to Samantha with an arm around her.

FIFTY

~

The explanation of what had happened and what it all meant came much later that afternoon. I heard it, oddly enough, in the waiting room of the Nesfield railway station.

I was with Jack and Warnie, who were waiting for their train back to Oxford.

'Morris, stop shaking your head backwards and forwards like that,' said Jack in a warm friendly tone.

I hadn't even realised I'd been doing it. I felt as though my brain was lost somewhere in the Hampton Court Maze and couldn't find its way out again.

'Just lean back on this nice, comfortable wooden bench,' Jack said, 'and I'll explain it all to you.'

So I leaned back, and I think I even closed my eyes, the better to concentrate.

'Henry Beard,' Jack began, 'has confessed to the murder of Dave Fowler.'

'Yes, I understand that much,' I said, a touch irritably. 'But that's the bottom line of the equation. What I don't understand is the algebra that fills the rest of the page and gets us to that result.'

'His motivation,' Jack resumed patiently (years of dealing with students having taught him that logic simply sails over

253

irrational outbursts), 'his motivation was violent jealously upon discovering that his wife, Samantha, had begun an affair—or at least some sort of romantic relationship—with Mr Fowler.'

'How did this come about?'

Jack paused, gathered his thoughts, and then resumed in the steady, carefully-chosen-words style for which he was famous.

'I am told that Beard had what is called "a bad war". He was wounded in the trenches, and diagnosed with shell shock after the war. He became a morose, withdrawn and lonely man. You knew him as a grumpy, surly schoolmaster. And he had very little life outside of schoolmastering. Apart, that is, from regular fishing holidays. He stayed in the same remote village every year, and stayed in the same farm house with the same couple. This couple had a daughter.'

'Samantha?'

'Precisely. In the village there was a shortage of young men of her own age, again because of the devastation of the war. But there was Henry Beard—older, not a happy man, but a man who was offering to marry her.'

'Which is how she turned up here as Mrs Henry Beard?'

'Indeed. But the marriage was not, by all accounts, an altogether happy one. Then along came Dave Fowler—younger, good looking, more ebullient. And he took an interest in her—an interest that flattered her, and to which, against her better judgment, she found herself responding.'

'How far did it go?'

'We'll probably never know. But it certainly went far enough to disturb the balance of Henry Beard's mind. How he made his discovery of the relationship we still don't know, but he did. His first reaction was to send his young wife home to her parents, on the pretence that her mother was ill and needed nursing. Then he carefully planned to murder Dave Fowler.'

'But when we saw Fowler that day on the roof—when you and I were in the organ loft of the cathedral—Beard wasn't on the roof with him. There was no one on the roof with him.'

'No one we could see,' Jack responded, his eyes sparkling. 'Because Beard was using a weapon that could strike at a distance.'

'What weapon?'

'The same weapon with which he threatened you.'

'The crossbow?'

'The very same.'

'But Fowler was stabbed with a knife, not shot with a crossbow bolt. Can you explain that?'

'I can now. Beard had modified a knife, fitting a kind of notch protruding from one side of the handle. This could be inserted into the slot that usually held the bolt, and thus fired from the crossbow.'

'A knife fired from a crossbow?'

'That's how Beard murdered Fowler.'

'But we saw no one on the roof, remember?'

'That's because Beard didn't step onto the roof. He didn't need to. He had a weapon that could strike across a distance. All he had to do was to push up the flap of the trapdoor leading to the roof and then, while standing on the top step below the trapdoor, fire his weapon—his knife-firing crossbow.'

I was once again shaking my head. Not in confusion this time but in amazement, because this was an explanation of everything Jack and I had seen: Fowler, alone on the roof, standing up and expostulating with someone (obviously Beard, his head visible at the trapdoor), then staggering when the knife hit him in the stomach.

'But hang on, hang on,' I said. 'Fowler then fell off the roof, right?'

'Quite right. We saw him fall.'

'But he didn't hit the ground until the next day. Now that's just plain impossible. Can you explain that?'

'I believe I can. The explanation came to me today when you were almost hit by the lorry from the building site—the tip-truck that came up behind us on the gravel road behind the school. What if there was just such a truck passing underneath at the moment Fowler's body fell? So that instead of hitting the ground, it fell into the back of the lorry?'

'But wouldn't the lorry driver feel the thump?'

'Not necessarily, because of the ruts and gullies on that uneven gravel road. When the body fell into the open back of his tip-truck, he probably just thought he'd hit a large bump in the road.'

I stopped to absorb this, and then I asked, 'But then the body came back. How did that come about?'

'Well,' said Jack, 'I passed on my truck idea to Inspector Locke and he sent Sergeant Drake to investigate. The result is that we now know the answer to that puzzle.'

Jack, having reached a crucial point in his narrative, stopped to light his pipe—mainly, I believe, to string out the suspense.

'The story the man eventually, when pushed, told Drake,' said Jack between puffs, 'was that he didn't discover the dead body in the back of his truck until the early hours of the following morning, when he was getting ready to go to work. This driver has a criminal record for minor offences. He panicked when he saw the body. He worked out when it must have fallen into the truck—when he felt a large jolt at the back of the school the afternoon before. So, still in the pre-dawn darkness, he drove back to the same spot, tipped the body out of his truck and drove off.'

Suddenly a light went on, and I said, 'Stanhope heard him!

He told me just as we were leaving the dorms to go across to the cathedral for Speech Night. He told me about a truck he heard moving in the dark. That must have been it.'

'Undoubtedly.'

I sat in silence for a moment taking it all in. It was all explained—every detail.

A distant hooting told us that Jack and Warnie's train was approaching.

Jack picked up his battered suitcase, shook my hand and said, 'Well, I hope you enjoy your second term as a school-master, young Morris.'

'There won't be a second term,' I said with a cheerful smile.

'What do you mean?' asked Warnie.

'I'm not cut out to be a schoolmaster, so I applied for several other jobs, and one came through. I'm joining the staff of the *Bath Chronicle* as a leader writer.'

Jack seized my hand in both of his and shook it warmly.

'That's what you want, isn't it?' he said. 'A start on the road to being a writer?'

'Exactly.'

'Now listen, young fellah,' said Warnie. 'I insist that once you're settled in Bath, and they give you a few days off, you must come and visit us in Oxford. Will you do that?'

'I will.'

'Is that a promise?'

'That's a promise.'

AUTHOR'S NOTE

~

This book, like the others in this series, is by way of being a homage to C. S. Lewis. But this time it is also a nod in the direction of the delightful Frank Richards. Despite the name, Frank was no relation to the author—he couldn't be since 'Frank Richards' was one of the pen names used by the prolific Charles Hamilton. It is the name under which he wrote an astonishing number of school stories, originally published in the *Magnet* story paper for boys, about Greyfriars School, it's 'Famous Five' (Harry Wharton and his friends) and 'the fat owl of the Remove', Billy Bunter. In 1935, when our story is set, Billy Bunter et al. were at the top of their form, so it's appropriate that they are celebrated in this novel.

That said, here are a few things worth noticing:

- 'Yarooooh! Oh crikey! Ow! Wow! Beast! Oh crumbs! Ow! Ooooooooooh!' is a salute to the linguistic inventiveness of the great Frank Richards.
- 'Nesfield' is a fictional cathedral town in the novel *The Weight of the Evidence* by Michael Innes, the pen name of J. I. M. Stewart, a colleague of Lewis and J. R. R. Tolkien in the English School at Oxford.

- 'Quelch' is another salute, Quelch being one of the form masters at Frank Richards' fictional Greyfriars School.
- Hamilton, Clifford, Redway and Cardew—from Charles Hamilton's real name and three of his (many) pen names: Martin Clifford, Ralph Redway and Winston Cardew. In all, Hamilton appears to have employed at least twenty-five different pseudonyms in his prolific career.
- *The Nine Tailors* is the eleventh book in Dorothy L. Sayers' series of murder mysteries featuring her legendary aristocratic sleuth, Lord Peter Wimsey. It was first published in 1934.
- Detective Inspector Sexton Locke has been named in honour of one of the most famous fictional detectives of the 1930s, Sexton Blake. One critic described him as 'the schoolboys' Sherlock Holmes'.
- John Dickson Carr (1906–1977) was an American-born mystery writer who lived in England and set many of his stories there. He specialised in 'locked-room murders' and 'impossible mysteries'.
- Gilbert Keith Chesterton (1874–1936) was a famous British writer and defender of the Christian faith. Lewis always said that Chesterton played a key role in his own conversion to Christianity.
- R. Austin Freeman (1862–1943) was a British writer of detective stories, mostly featuring the medico-legal forensic investigator Dr Thorndyke.
- *The Hotspur* was a British boys' paper published by D. C. Thomson & Co. from 1933 to 1959.
- 'Tollers' was J. R. R. Tolkien (1892–1973), author of *The Lord of the Rings* and a good personal friend of C. S. Lewis.
- Douglas Jardine (1900–1958) was a cricketer who played twenty-two Test matches for England, most famously as

captain of the team during the notorious 'Bodyline' series of 1932–33. He retired with a batting average of 46.83.

- Crichton House, Rodwell Regis shares the name of the fictional school in the famous comic novel *Vice Versa* (1882) by 'F. Anstey' (real name Thomas Anstey Guthrie). Lewis once described this as 'the only honest school story ever written' (reflecting his own unhappy school days, as 'Crichton House' is depicted in the novel as an ill-run horror of a school).

- The Martlets was an undergraduate literary society at Oxford of which C. S. Lewis was an active member in 1919. The story is told in 'To the Martlets' by Walter Hooper (in *C. S. Lewis: Speaker and Teacher*, ed. Carolyn Keefe, Zondervan Publishing House, 1971).

- *The Purple Gang*—A non-existent mystery novel referred to a number of times in the comic novels and short stories of P. G. Wodehouse, and therefore an appropriate bit of melodramatic nonsense to be confiscated from a schoolboy.

- 'Cat-like tread'—The song 'With Cat-Like Tread We Creep upon Our Foe' comes from Gilbert and Sullivan's *Pirates of Penzance*.

- (Alfred) Cecil Harwood (1898–1975) was introduced to Lewis by his friend Owen Barfield when all three were undergraduates at Oxford. Harwood had known Barfield from boyhood. Lewis dedicated *Miracles* to Harwood and his wife Daphne, and was godfather to one of their children.

- Karel Capek (1890–1938), Czech writer. His play *RUR (Rossum's Universal Robots)* put the word 'robot' into our language (from the Czech *robota* meaning 'worker' or 'labourer').